A QUESTION OF IDENTITY

A Rona Parish Mystery

Anthea Fraser

severn House

This first world edition published 2012
in Great Britain and in the USA by
SEVERN HOUSE PUBLISHERS LTD of
9–15 High Street, Sutton, Surrey, England, SM1 1DF.
Trade paperback edition first published
in Great Britain and the USA 2012 by
SEVERN HOUSE PUBLISHERS LTD.

British Library Cataloguing in Publication Data

Fraser, Anthea.
  A question of identity.
  1. Parish, Rona (Fictitious character) – Fiction.
  2. Detective and mystery stories.
  I. Title
  823.9'14-dc23

ISBN-13: 978-0-7278-8168-7 (cased)
ISBN-13: 978-1-84751-426-4 (trade paper)

All Severn House titles are printed on acid-free paper.

Severn House Publishers support The Forest Stewardship Council [FSC],
the leading international forest certification organisation. All our titles that
are printed on Greenpeace-approved FSC-certified paper carry the FSC logo.

MIX
Paper from
responsible sources
FSC
www.fsc.org   FSC® C018575

Typeset by Palimpsest Book Production Ltd.,
Falkirk, Stirlingshire, Scotland.
Printed and bound in Great Britain by
MPG Books Ltd., Bodmin, Cornwall.

ONE

'**A** *hypnotist?*' Rona repeated.

'Yes . . . I thought it would be fun,' Magda added, a little defensively. 'He's very good – I've seen him on TV.'

Rona moved the phone to her other hand and reached for her coffee. 'I'm not sure it's Max's idea of an evening out,' she said doubtfully. Nor hers, if truth be known.

'Oh, come on, Rona! Gavin's prepared to give it a go, and I know he'd welcome Max's company.' She hesitated. 'Actually, I've got tickets for Friday.'

Rona's eyebrows rose. 'Jumping the gun a bit, weren't you?'

'They were selling like hot cakes and I didn't want to miss out, specially as Max can only manage Fridays or Saturdays, and they're the most popular evenings.'

This was true; Max held adult art classes during the week at his studio across town. There was a pause, while each waited for the other to speak.

Then Rona said, 'Well, I'll have a word with him, but you'll have to give me something more to go on. Who is this man?'

'An American, name of Ed Bauer. He's a huge hit in the States, and is now touring the UK – the Darcy Hall did well to get him. It doesn't start till eight, so we could eat at the Bacchus first.'

The wine bar was in the same street as the theatre, and did a good trade in suppers both before and after the show.

'What does he actually do?'

'Oh, you know, asks for volunteers to go up on stage . . .'

'And proceeds to make fools of them?'

'Well, it's all very light-hearted. Look, to be honest, I thought you could do with a bit of cheering up. You've had your nose to the grindstone for months.'

Rona, glancing ruefully at her computer screen, couldn't

deny it. What was more, though usually she was never happier than when immersed in her work, that wasn't the case this time.

'OK, I'll see what I can do,' she said.

'Excellent! If I don't hear from you, I'll book a table for six thirty. A bit early, I know, but we don't want to rush. See you there, I hope!'

Rona sipped her coffee, found it was cold, and discarded it. She could speak to Max when he came home this evening, but better to find out sooner rather than later if he was amenable, and if she phoned now she could catch him before his afternoon class.

'Hi, honeybun!' he greeted her. 'An unsolicited call? What's up?'

'Magda and Gavin have asked us to go to the Darcy Hall with them on Friday.'

'Oh? What's on?'

'A stage hypnotist, apparently.'

'Good God! Why in the name of heaven would they want to see him?'

'Magda thinks it's time I did a bit of socializing.'

'She's right, but there are better ways.'

'Actually, she's quite keen. She's seen him on TV, and he's a big hit in the States.'

'Come on, love, he's a fake – they all are!'

'A sweeping statement, but if he is, it'll be a challenge for you to see how he does it.'

'Hold on a minute: do I take it you *want* to go?'

'I wouldn't mind a night out, to be honest.'

He gave a short laugh. 'You make it sound as though you're housebound!'

'We've not been to the theatre for a while. And Magda suggests supper first, at the Bacchus.'

'I presume she's talked Gavin into this?'

'Yes, but I think he'd appreciate your back-up.'

'I bet he would. Look, I must go; it's nearly time for the class and I've not finished preparing the studio.'

'You're happy to go, then?'

'Wouldn't say happy, but if you want to, fair enough. Gavin and I can be fellow sceptics.'

'Thanks, Max; you might even enjoy it!'

Distraction over, Rona turned back to the screen, a sense of dissatisfaction reclaiming her. She ought to be enjoying this, she told herself. After all, she was primarily a biographer, with three highly acclaimed 'lives' behind her. But two years ago, having embarked on researching the thriller writer, Theo Harvey, she'd uncovered far more than she'd anticipated, about not only his work, but also his life and death.

Ensuing legal problems had forced the abandonment of the project, and, unsettled by the experience, she'd postponed starting another, preferring to spend her time writing for the monthly glossy, *Chiltern Life*. It had been intended as a temporary measure, but as time went on she became less inclined to return to biographies. Her series of articles were well received and called for considerably less commitment, most being completed in a matter of weeks or even, in some cases, days. And despite periodic prompting from her husband and her publisher, this state of affairs might have continued indefinitely, had not the family of the artist Elspeth Wilding, who was said to have disappeared, begged Rona to write her life story.

But she'd barely started on it when, once again, death and scandal had intervened. On this occasion, however, the decision had been taken for the book to go ahead. From her publishers' standpoint, not only would the sensational events increase its saleability, but also Rona was under contract and a sizeable advance had been paid. They were also satisfied that the inevitable time-lapse before publication would lessen the possibility of causing offence to the family.

Who, as it turned out, were in favour of the decision.

'Other writers will be jumping on the bandwagon,' Elspeth's sister, Naomi Harris, had written. 'But we *know* you, Rona, and, despite all that has happened, we think you should carry on. You met Elspeth, and we feel we can trust you to treat her sympathetically, however black the circumstances. Also, ironically, you're now free to consult her letters and diaries, which you couldn't while she was alive. I'm sure they'll fill in some gaps.'

At least, Rona thought thankfully, interviews with parents, brother and sister had already taken place; despite their declared willingness, she'd have balked at soliciting personal memories so soon after Elspeth's death. It was also true that the diaries and letters shed light on major aspects of her life, but none of these factors made the task any more enjoyable. At least part of the reason she'd been working so unremittingly was so that the book and all it entailed could be put behind her as soon as possible.

Which wouldn't happen, she upbraided herself, if she sat staring into space. Sliding a sheet of paper into the printer, she started to transcribe her notes.

'I had an email from Charles today,' Max said that evening. 'Next door's just about finished, and he's asked me to go round and check everything's OK. Like to come along?'

Rona hesitated. For as long as she and Max had lived here, the house next door had been occupied by a succession of tenants while its owners lived abroad. Now, their contract in Hong Kong was coming to an end, and for several months the house had been undergoing substantial alterations and redecoration prior to their return. Yet, for Rona, it still retained horrific memories of finding the bodies of the previous tenants in their kitchen.

Max, who, at Charles's request, had been paying regular visits to the house and liaising with the building manager, put an arm round her shoulders. 'Time to lay the ghosts, sweetheart. They've been well and truly banished, but it'll be easier if you satisfy yourself on that score before Charles and Monica arrive.'

She nodded reluctantly. 'Have they got a date yet?'

'Not to move in; they're flying back on the sixteenth of April, but their furniture won't arrive for another couple of months, so they're renting a flat in Alban Road.' He squeezed her shoulder. 'So – how about it?'

'All right,' she said, 'let's get it over.'

Although she'd braced herself for lurking horrors, the moment Max unlocked the front door and they were met with the smell of paint and new carpet, Rona felt herself relax. Though the house was basically identical to theirs, she and Max had knocked down walls on three of the four floors, to make fewer and larger rooms. This house retained the original ground-floor layout, but the thick carpet stretching ahead of them and up the stairs also covered the floors in the two downstairs rooms, unifying while not joining them. When last seen they'd been cluttered with furniture, but, empty, seemed larger than she recalled.

Down in the basement, however, the Furnesses had followed their example by transforming the area into one large, airy kitchen. This was the room above all that Rona had dreaded revisiting, but in the pale pine units, the green Aga and state-of-the-art machines, there was no hint of its previous incarnation and she breathed a heartfelt sigh of relief.

On the first floor, the master bedroom had acquired an en suite, while at the top of the house – which, in their case, comprised a large room intended, though no longer used, as Max's studio – the two attic bedrooms had been supplemented by a shower room, to accommodate the Furnesses' teenage children.

As they moved through the house, Max had been turning taps on and off, flushing lavatories, opening unit drawers and trying light switches.

'Everything seems in working order,' he commented, joining Rona at a window, where she stood looking down on the back garden. It, too, had been transformed. Small though it was, a built-in barbecue had been installed, along with some decking, and in one corner a pond was dug out, though not yet filled. All that remained of its previous existence was the apple tree, beneath which she had sat with Louise, drinking home-made lemonade.

She gave herself a shake, glancing quickly to her right, where, over the high wall, she had a view of their own garden, paved throughout and dotted with statues and containers of plants.

'OK, duty done,' Max said. 'Let's go home and have some supper.'

Rona nodded agreement, and, going ahead of him down the stairs, she sensed that a cloud had lifted. As Max had said, the ghosts were gone, and need never trouble her again.

Magda Ridgeway was the owner of eight boutiques spread around the county, and spent much of her time visiting fashion houses abroad. Her mailing-list contained an enviable number of famous names, and she'd recently introduced cafés into the larger boutiques, which, like most of her innovations, had proved an immediate success.

Now, she pushed her hair behind her ears with concealed impatience. Much as she loved her voluble, vivacious mother, she couldn't spare the time for a long phone call; a representative was due any minute, and she was only halfway through a final check of her requirements.

'Mama,' she broke in tentatively, 'I really—'

'—colour, so rich and warm. It would sell well, *cara*, I—'

'Mama, I'm sorry to interrupt, but I'm expecting someone. Can I call you back this evening?'

'Oh.' Paola King, interrupted in midstream, paused. 'I have the better idea,' she declared. 'You and Gavin must come to supper – tomorrow. We haven't seen you for weeks.'

'We'd love to, but not tomorrow. We're going to the theatre with Rona and Max.'

'Ah, Rona! Give her my best love! What is it that you will see?'

Magda hesitated, anticipating her mother's disapproval. 'Actually, he's a stage hypnotist. Just a bit of fun, really,' she added hastily.

'A hypnotist?' Magda could hear the frown in her voice. 'Is not good, meddling with people's minds *just for the fun*.'

'Gavin says everyone taking part will be planted, anyway.' Magda's eyes were on the wall clock.

'Planted?'

'Part of the act. Look, Mama, I really must go. I'll phone you this evening.'

And, feeling guilty, she broke the connection.

An hour later, as she unpacked a delivery of dresses, Magda's thoughts returned to Rona, and she let her mind drift back through the years of their friendship. She'd never made friends easily, and had been a difficult, prickly child. No doubt this was due in part to having been transplanted from Italy at the age of ten, constantly aware of being *different* – a fact emphasized by the daily sight of Paola, blazing like a bird of paradise among the soberly clad mothers at the school gates.

But for some reason, ten-year-old Rona had befriended her, and from then on life had become easier. She acknowledged she could still be both caustic and astringent, qualities that had lost her a few friends over the years, though marriage to Gavin, coupled with a successful career, had largely mellowed her. But it was Rona, all those years ago, who had started the process, and Magda was accordingly grateful.

On the Friday morning, Rona's twin sister phoned.

'A client's just cancelled,' she announced, 'so I'm free for lunch. How about it?'

Lindsey was a partner in a firm of solicitors.

'Sorry, no,' Rona said. 'It's lunch at my desk till this chapter's finished.'

'Oh, nonsense! A change of scene will refresh you – get the muse going. Anyway, I've something to show you.'

'What?'

'You'll have to meet me to find out!'

Rona sighed. 'So much for willpower!'

'Good girl! Twelve thirty at the Gallery?'

She glanced at her watch. Ten fifteen, which left her a good two hours to finish the passage she was working on.

'I'll be there,' she said.

To Gus, Rona's golden retriever, the Gallery café was a second home, and he lolloped ahead of her up the wrought-iron staircase leading from the main shopping street to the walkway above.

Lindsey was awaiting her at a window table. 'I'm going for cheese and onion quiche with side salad,' she greeted her, sliding the menu over as Rona, having guided the dog under the table, seated herself. 'And miracle of miracles, the waitress approaches, so choose quickly. She passes this way but once.'

Their meal duly ordered, Rona glanced at her twin. 'OK, so what do you want to show me?'

Lindsey reached for her handbag and extracted a badly creased black-and-white photograph, roughly six by four inches. 'What do you make of this?'

Rona took it from her. 'Well, obviously it's a school photo; professionally taken, I'd say, and judging by the clothes and hairstyles, pretty old.'

She smoothed out the creases, swiftly summarizing the details. The picture showed rows of uniformed girls standing obediently smiling, while in front of them, seated on chairs, was a line of adults, presumably staff. Smaller girls sat cross-legged on the grass at their feet, and in the background was a handsome doorway flanked by stone pillars, with a large window on either side. Rona's eyes returned to the staff, and she frowned.

'Someone seems to have been blacked out,' she observed.

'Exactly!' Lindsey said with satisfaction.

'What do you mean, *exactly*? And why are you showing it to me? Where did you get it, anyway?'

'Someone produced it at our book group last night, and asked if anyone could throw light on it.'

'Presumably no one could, since you're now showing it to me.'

Lindsey looked at her despairingly. 'Aren't you the slightest bit curious to know *who's* been blacked out, and why?'

'Probably a teacher who gave too much homework?' Rona suggested.

Lindsey shook her head. 'It's more than that. For one thing, it's not just the face that's been obliterated, it's the whole figure – you can't even tell if it's male or female. As though the aim was to eliminate every last trace.'

'You're reading too much into it, Linz,' Rona protested.

When her twin didn't reply, she asked, with the first flicker of interest, 'Who did you say it belonged to?'

'The mother-in-law of one of our members. She died recently; his wife's been going through her things and came across it.'

'Hadn't she seen it before, while her mother was alive?'

'Yes, that's just it,' Lindsey said slowly. 'She remembered coming across it years ago, at the bottom of a sewing box, of all places. But when she'd asked about it, her mother nearly passed out, snatched it out of her hand, and steadfastly refused to discuss it. Glenda – that's William's wife – assumed she'd destroyed it. She said finding it again gave her a creepy feeling – as though the photo still held unsettling memories.'

'A little fanciful,' Rona commented. 'And I still don't see why this – William – took it to your book group.'

'He's been showing it to everyone, hoping someone might remember the school. Several in the group are in the right age bracket.'

Rona flipped it over. On the back, written in faded pencil, were the words 'Springfield Lodge. July 1951.'

'Isn't there a house of that name out your way?' she asked.

'That's right; it's still there, but in the guise of a private hotel.'

'*Did* any of the oldies remember it?'

'Only vaguely. Someone thought it had closed down in the

early fifties – rather suddenly, they seemed to remember. Which, in view of the date on the photo, might be significant, wouldn't you say?'

Rona tossed it lightly back to her. 'Who knows? If you want to make a mystery out of it, fair enough, but I can't help you; I've never heard of the place.' She looked up suddenly, fixing her twin with a glare. 'Wait a minute: how come *you've* got hold of it?'

Lindsey's eyes dropped, and she poured two glasses of water with exaggerated care.

'*Linz!*'

'Well,' Lindsey began diffidently, 'you know how good you are at digging things out – your contacts, and so on. I just thought—'

'I hope you're not telling me you volunteered my services?'

'Not exactly, I just—'

'Because if so, you can *un*volunteer them. Pronto.'

'Oh come on, Ro! You don't want your detective skills to wither while you're bio-ing! This would keep them ticking over nicely!'

The waitress reappeared, and they sat in silence while she set down their plates. Then Rona said evenly, 'As you well know, my *detective skills*, as you call them, have been greatly exaggerated. All I've done—'

'Is solve a few murders!'

Rona made a dismissive gesture. 'Quite apart from all that, I'm too tied up to take on anything else, even if I wanted to. Tell your friend to try Google.'

'Oh, he has, but drew a complete blank. Hardly surprising, I suppose, when the school closed so long ago. He also tried Friends Reunited and other sites, but again with no luck. It's as though everyone who'd anything to do with Springfield prefers to forget the fact.'

'Oh, come on! A more likely explanation is they're all getting on a bit. The youngest of those in the photo must be in their seventies.' Rona reached for the print, still lying on the table, and turned it to face her. 'Obviously this isn't of the whole school, and since there's quite an age range, it can't be one class. A house photo, perhaps?'

'You see!' Lindsey exclaimed triumphantly. 'You've already come up with something!'

'I can't see it's much help. How about the hotel owners? Has William contacted them?'

'Yes, but without luck. After the school closed, it became a nursing home, and the present owners bought it from them.'

'Then I'm sorry. He's already done anything I could do.' She raised a hand as Lindsey started to speak. 'Really, Linz, I'm not interested, so can we please change the subject?'

For a moment Lindsey looked mutinous. Then, with a resigned sigh, she slid the photo back into her bag.

'Any news of the parents?' Rona went on. 'I've been so wrapped up working, I haven't spoken to either of them for a while.'

'The big news is that Guy's house has been sold.'

Guy Lacey, who had previously lived in Stokely, had moved in with their mother earlier in the year, and put his own house on the market.

'That's excellent!' Rona exclaimed. 'Did he get the asking price?'

'Very nearly. Mum says they'd been afraid, with the market as it is, that it could have hung on indefinitely.'

'And Pops?' Rona asked after a moment.

'I've not spoken to him recently.'

No surprise there, she thought; Lindsey had always been closer to their mother, particularly during the breakdown of their parents' marriage. Tom Parish was renting a flat in town, and when the divorce came through, intended to marry Catherine Bishop, a woman Lindsey still resented.

'And Dominic?'

Lindsey's mouth tightened. 'Nothing new on that front.'

'Meaning?'

'That he's being as bloody un-tie-downable as ever.'

Rona laughed. 'That's the second word you've invented in as many minutes!'

Lindsey picked half-heartedly at her quiche. 'Damn it, Ro, we've known each other for a year now, and we've never spent more than a couple of days together – and *that* was on the blasted boat, with his daughter.'

Rona said carefully, 'Well, you did know what you were getting into.'

Dominic Frayne was a high-flying entrepreneur, twice divorced and with three grown-up children, whose name had been linked with several society women. Although Rona liked him, she was privately surprised that his relationship with her sister – on and off though it was – had lasted so long.

'And talking of his daughter,' Lindsey went on indignantly, 'when I suggested we might actually go on holiday together, he calmly announced he's taking Olivia and the boys to Cyprus for a month in the summer – a *month*! – and can't spare any more time off. Says it might be the last chance of a family holiday before Olivia gets married.'

'You'll have to fall back on Hugh, then,' Rona said lightly. After an acrimonious divorce some years ago, Lindsey's ex-husband had tried repeatedly to re-establish their relationship, a fact that, during gaps in her love life, Lindsey had shamelessly exploited.

'Not so sure he's available,' she replied. 'According to gossip, he's been seen around town with a woman in tow.'

'Really? Who?'

Lindsey shrugged. 'No idea. Good luck to him.'

Despite her offhand manner, Rona suspected her sister regarded Hugh as her private property, and would resent any intruder in his affections. For whatever reason, she was quick to change the subject.

'Doing anything this weekend?'

'We're going to the Darcy this evening, with the Ridgeways. There's a hypnotist on, whom Magda's keen to see.'

'Good grief! Doesn't sound like Max's scene!'

'Nor mine, but it might be fun. We're eating at the Bacchus first.'

Lindsey helped herself to more salad. 'Do you believe in all that ESP stuff?'

'I don't think hypnotism comes in that category; isn't it accepted medical practice?'

'Still weird, though. I shouldn't like anyone messing about with *my* mind.'

Rona laughed. 'They'd probably find more than they

bargained for! But as far as ESP goes, we've always been telepathic, haven't we?'

'Well, that's only to be expected – we're twins. It would be quite different if a stranger was involved, so don't even *think* about going up on stage!'

'Don't worry, I've no intention of doing so! I'll be interested to see what happens, though.'

'Mind you report back.' Lindsey checked her watch. 'I should be going.'

'Me too, though I'll extend my lunch hour and take Gus for a walk. It'll be late when we get back from the theatre, and he'll have to make do with the garden.'

They joined the small queue at the till, their minds already on the afternoon ahead and the tasks awaiting them, and it wasn't until an hour later, as Rona felt in her bag for her front door key, that her fingers encountered the school photo. She drew it out with an exclamation of annoyance. Lindsey must have slipped it in while they were waiting at the till. Well, she'd ignore it, she decided, and wait for her to raise the subject. And with a passing glance at the blacked-out figure that was causing so much interest, she dropped it back in her bag and opened the front door.

TWO

Rona saw them as soon as she walked into the Bacchus – Hugh and a woman she didn't recognize, deep in conversation in one of the booths. They'd not seen her, but they would, and she'd no option but to speak to them.

As a waiter led her to their reserved table, she paused at their booth.

'Hello, Hugh,' she said lightly.

He looked up, and in his startled expression, she saw that for a heartbeat he'd thought she was Lindsey. Then he came to his feet.

'Rona – hello.' He paused, colour tingeing his pale face. 'I don't believe you've met my work colleague, Mia Campbell? Mia – my ex-sister-in-law, Rona Parish.'

His companion nodded with a faint smile.

'Max not with you?' Hugh asked, and Rona sensed the fear that he might have to ask her to join them.

'He's parking the car,' she said. 'We're meeting the Ridgeways here. Since you're eating early, I presume you're also going to the theatre?'

'We are, yes. It should be . . . very interesting.'

'Different, anyway!' Her smile encompassed them both. 'But don't let me keep you from your meal. Enjoy the show!' And she walked to her own table, where the waiter had already pulled out her chair. Max came in as she was seating herself, and, seeing Hugh, exchanged a word on his way over.

'Well, well, well!' he said softly, as he joined her. 'What have we here?'

'Lindsey did say he had a girlfriend.'

'Woman friend might be more accurate. Who is she? I didn't wait for an introduction.'

'A colleague, he said, so I'd guess she works at Hesketh's. She wasn't particularly forthcoming, but then there's no reason she should have been.'

'Especially when she learned who you were.'

'Oh, I doubt that would worry her; she looked very sure of herself, though she mightn't have enjoyed being introduced as a work colleague.'

'Could be that's all she is,' Max said.

The layout of the wine bar, where the tables were separated by five-foot high partitions, meant that, once seated, they couldn't see Hugh nor he them – possibly a relief all round, and as Magda and Gavin joined them, Rona put the unexpected meeting out of her mind. But not before she'd filed away her impressions of 'Mia' to pass on to Lindsey: red-haired, self-assured, attractive. And Max was right – more woman than girl; she looked in her early forties, the same age as Hugh.

'Before I forget, Mama sent her love,' Magda was saying. 'She rang at the most inopportune moment, bless her, and when I phoned back, it was the answer machine. I meant to try again, but never got round to it.'

'I must call in and see her,' Rona said. Paola King had been an important part of her childhood. With her flamboyant clothes, her rich laugh and obvious joy in life, she'd been a stark contrast to her own mother, and their house – where Rona was always welcome – seemed deliciously foreign, with religious pictures and crucifixes on the walls, and the pervading scent of exotic breads and pastries, rich meat stews and succulent pastas. During Rona's early teens, it had been more of a home to her than her own.

'How is she?' she added. 'And your father?'

'Both fighting fit,' Magda replied. 'Though as always, Papa has trouble getting a word in!'

Rona laughed, remembering the quiet Englishman who was happy to let his beloved wife hold sway. It was from George King – 'Just call me King George!' – that Magda had inherited her height of marginally under six feet, which Gavin topped by a few inches. They made a striking couple, she with her heavy-lidded dark eyes and black hair and he ash-blond and blue-eyed.

They ordered a selection of tapas, and as the meal progressed, Magda and Rona exchanged news on mutual friends, while the men discussed rugby.

'So what's the form this evening?' Max asked, as their coffee was served. 'Does this bloke hypnotize people for a solid two and a half hours?'

Magda gave a quick shake of her head. 'Oh no, he's the star attraction and doesn't appear till the second half. First, we have a conjuror, and someone demonstrating telepathy.'

'In other words,' Gavin remarked, 'we're in for a wacky evening!'

'You and Max can amuse yourselves by trying to see how it's done.'

Rona stirred her coffee. 'Lindsey and I were discussing telepathy over lunch,' she said.

'I suppose it's run-of-the-mill to you two!'

'It happens quite often, yes, but only with each other.'

'That's a relief, I must say!' Gavin commented. 'I shouldn't like anyone to know what *I'm* thinking!'

'Then you'd better keep a low profile,' Magda told him. 'We're in the fourth row!'

Rona looked surprised. 'But the seats aren't numbered, are they?'

'They have been for several months. It's much more civilized now; we don't have to rush in and bag places before ordering interval drinks! Even so, we should probably be going. We want time to get settled and look at the programme.'

The Darcy Hall was a two-minute walk away, just the other side of the car park, and they joined a stream of people making their way there. The billboard outside displayed a head and shoulders photograph of the man they'd come to see – bald, smiling broadly, wearing a bow tie.

'I wouldn't buy a used car from him,' Max muttered in Rona's ear.

The Hall, splendidly decorated in green and gold, offered a less expensive alternative to the Carlton Hotel for wedding receptions and dances, since its tiered seats could be removed as required. It was also the venue for concerts, lectures and, of course, plays, being the home of the Acorn Amateur Dramatic Society.

The fourth row seemed uncomfortably near the front, Rona thought uneasily as they took their aisle seats. She wondered

where Hugh and his companion were seated, but had no intention
of looking for them. The little theatre was filling rapidly, and
there was an undercurrent of excited anticipation.

The telepath, Rona noted from the programme, rejoiced in the
name of Jerome Hilton. She hoped fervently that he wouldn't
divine a kindred spirit in her. Then the lights dimmed, the
orchestra struck up, and the entertainment was under way.

From the start, it was an evening of audience participation.
The conjuror, first to occupy the stage, lost no time in calling
for volunteers, and two giggling girls from the front row were
persuaded to respond. The routine was pretty run-of-the-mill:
watches were removed and reappeared in unexpected places,
chiffon scarves were produced from the girls' pockets, a series
of objects taken from a supposedly empty box.

Then another couple of volunteers – man and wife this time
– took their place, and were suitably amazed when coins appeared
in their ears, a live mouse was retrieved from a shirt pocket, and
a box of matches placed under one of four beakers apparently
kept changing position. The act continued in much the same vein,
with varying sets of volunteers, for about forty minutes, before
the conjuror was applauded off the stage, bowing repeatedly as
he went.

'Old hat, but he's quite good,' Max said grudgingly. 'I'm
damned if I could see how he did it.'

As the last of the applause died away, the stage lights were
lowered, the triumphant notes of the orchestra sank to a low,
rhythmic beat, and a very different personage appeared on stage
– Jerome Hilton, no less, resplendent with goatee beard and a
velvet jacket. Rona was only aware her hands were clenched
when Max patted them reassuringly. She glanced sideways at
him, and they exchanged a smile.

Hilton took his time in establishing his routine, starting in a
manner reminiscent of a spiritualist meeting. 'Is there anyone in
the audience with the initials C. A. B.?'

'Safe bet!' muttered Max, and sure enough a hand was raised.

'Could you stand up, please, sir?'

Rather unwillingly, a bushy-haired young man came to his
feet, blinking as a spotlight picked him out.

'And you are?'

'Colin Andrew Bradshaw.'

'Quite so. And you have a sister, I believe, whose name is Alison Jane?'

Rona, who, with the rest of the row, had turned to see who was speaking, saw what seemed to be genuine surprise on his face.

'Yes,' he stammered, 'that's right.'

'And your father's initials are the same as yours, are they not, in his case standing for Charles Arthur Bradshaw?'

'How . . .?'

Hilton smiled. 'Thank you, sir. You may sit down.' He clasped his hands together and closed his eyes for a moment. 'Now, I believe we have a Mrs Elsie Breen in the audience?'

A woman in the row behind them gave a startled exclamation. 'Jack!' she accused in a stage whisper. 'You never told them we were coming?'

There was laughter from those close enough to hear.

'I assure you, madam,' Hilton said smoothly, 'I've not been in contact with any member of your family. But I can confidently state that you received a letter this morning, from your sister Mary in Australia.'

Another gasp. 'Jack, you *must* . . .'

'Who said she hopes to come over for Christmas. I'm right, am I not?'

'A relic from the Victorian Music Hall!' Gavin whispered. 'Spot on, though.'

'They're plants,' Max said dismissively, 'the lot of them!' And, before Rona realized his intention, he rose to his feet. 'Could you tell me, please, what I have in my pockets?' he challenged.

The spotlight that had illuminated Mrs Breen switched to Max, and there was a surprised hush as everyone awaited the man's reaction. He smiled, placing the tips of his fingers together.

'Certainly, sir. Just give me a moment.' Again, his eyes closed briefly. 'Your inside jacket pocket,' he began, 'contains a wallet.'

'Like, I imagine, that of every man in the audience!'

Hilton ignored him. 'Brown leather, with the initials M. R. A. in gold, which stand for – let me see . . . Mark? – no, *Max* . . . Roland? . . . Allerdyce. Is that correct? The wallet contains Visa

credit and debit cards – I'll refrain from quoting the numbers!
– receipts with today's date from Waterstone's, the Bacchus Wine
Bar and Marsborough Art Supplies, three twenty-pound notes
and two ten – oh, and a library ticket.'

Rona felt Max stiffen incredulously.

'Am I right, sir? Perhaps you would satisfy everyone's curiosity? And while you're doing so, I can tell you that your
trouser pocket contains a mobile phone, a handkerchief, three
pound coins, a fifty-pence piece and several twenties – four, I
believe.'

Max had opened his wallet and was checking the banknotes,
knowing as he did so that the man would be proved correct. The
audience, anticipating the result, broke into applause, and, highly
embarrassed, he resumed his seat.

'That'll teach you!' Rona said under her breath.

More volunteers were called for, and six people made their
way up on stage. An outsize pack of playing cards was produced;
one of the men blindfolded Hilton, who then proceeded to guess
which card was selected by each of the volunteers in turn and
held up to the audience. By this stage, no one was surprised at
his hundred per cent accuracy, though the cards were repeatedly
shuffled and cut by the people taking part.

Next, they were asked to write words or even short sentences
on a whiteboard and display them to the audience, and again
Hilton had no difficulty reciting them.

'There must be some kind of signal,' Gavin murmured.

'Then it's your turn to challenge him!' Max retorted feelingly.

'Not on your life!'

The act came to an end, Hilton was applauded enthusiastically,
the safety curtain descended and the lights came up. Having
escaped involvement, Rona breathed a sigh of relief.

'I'm ready for that drink!' Max commented, as they made
their way to the bar.

'How does telepathy work, Rona?' Magda asked, sipping her
gin and tonic. 'I mean, what do you have to do?'

'Me? I don't do anything!'

'But you admitted you and Lindsey are telepathic.'

'Yes, but nothing as concrete as what he demonstrated; it's more
emotions – thoughts, feelings of fear or intense happiness.'

'And you realize they're coming from her?'

'Of course. It's as though she's inside my head.'

'Weird!' Gavin pronounced. 'We should get you up on stage – make some money out of you!'

'Not in a million years!' Rona said emphatically. 'Anyway, you can't do it to order.'

'Jerome Hilton can.'

'He's a professional, I'm definitely not.'

'You could probably tune in to other people if you wanted to,' Magda mused.

'Well, I most certainly don't! I have enough trouble marshalling my own thoughts, without being bombarded with other people's!'

'It was uncanny, how he knew exactly what was in Max's pockets,' Gavin said reflectively.

'Don't remind me!'

'Perhaps *you're* a plant!' Rona said wickedly.

A bell sounded, warning them that the show was about to restart, and they returned to their seats, interested to know what other surprises were in store.

After the restrained manner of the telepath, Ed Bauer was a complete contrast. It occurred to Rona that he was showman first and hypnotist second, but she allowed that she might be misjudging him. Dressed in a loudly checked jacket, his paunch overhanging his jeans, he looked more like a holiday-camp entertainer than someone practising mind control.

'Hi there, folks,' he began breezily. 'Tonight, I'm gonna demonstrate the amazing power of suggestion, whereby it's possible, by means of inducing a trance, to influence the actions and perceptions of other people.

'The practice was well known in Egypt and India thousands of years ago, but the West only caught on when an Austrian doctor by the name of Mesmer started investigating what he called animal magnetism – or Mesmerism – in the eighteenth century. Today, as you know, it's widely used to root out and treat the causes of trauma and mental illness.'

He smiled, spreading his hands in a gesture of apology. 'But hey! You didn't come here for a history lesson! This evening we're gonna have some fun, and to start us off, I'd ask all you good folk down there to stretch your arms high above your heads and clasp your hands together. Like so.' The seams of his jacket strained as he reached upwards.

Only a scattering of people obeyed him.

'Aw, come on, folks,' he urged, 'you gotta help me out here! On the count of three, arms high above your heads – *all* of you! Now, one – two – *three*!' And this time, a little self-consciously, everyone's arms went up. 'There – that wasn't so difficult, was it? Now clasp your hands tightly together and hold for a count of ten.'

He counted slowly, his own arms still above his head, and, on reaching ten, let them fall. 'Well done! OK, that's fine.'

The audience thankfully lowered their arms, but, aware of murmurings around her, Rona saw to her surprise that a number of people still held theirs up, including Magda.

'You can put them down now!' Gavin hissed.

'I know, but I . . . can't!'

'What are you *talking* about? Put them *down*, for Pete's sake!'

'Gavin, I'm *trying*!'

'Well now,' boomed Bauer from the stage, 'seems some folk are having problems here. Those sitting next to them, why not be neighbourly and give them a hand?'

Gavin tugged sharply at Magda's arms, but they were completely rigid and resisted his efforts.

'For God's sake!' he exclaimed. 'What *is* this?'

'No luck?' Bauer stroked his chin thoughtfully. 'Then we'll have to try something else. Stand up, please, everyone with their arms in the air.'

Reluctant and embarrassed, some three dozen people did so.

'Right, now I'm gonna divide you into groups: the first is the folks in the rows from the front here back as far as row M, second group those in the rows behind that, and the third, those of you up in the balcony, and I'm gonna ask you in turn to join me on stage. First, though, we have to get your arms down, don't we, so I'll count to five, and that'll do the trick.'

Sure enough, on the count of five, Magda's hands dropped to her sides, as, simultaneously, relieved laughter broke out around them.

She sat down hastily, rubbing her arms. 'That was the strangest thing! I *wanted* to put them down, I just couldn't!'

'You weren't concentrating,' Gavin told her.

'Well, obviously I wasn't the only one!'

'Now,' Bauer was continuing, 'will the first group come up and join me, please.'

'Oh, no!' Magda gripped her seat with both hands. 'There's no way I'm letting myself in for this!'

But as people began to come out of their rows and move down the aisle, she felt the pull of Bauer's gaze.

'Come along now, lady, it's your turn,' he said jovially. 'Nothing to be afraid of!'

Magda hesitated a moment longer, but, unwilling to make a scene, she reluctantly stood up and went to join the others, five men and five other women.

'Clever way of rooting out the most susceptible,' Max said, as Rona looked anxiously after her friend.

Bauer beamed and rubbed his hands together. 'Right, now I'll explain what's gonna happen. I'll get the orchestra to play "Lullaby of Broadway", and as soon as you hear it, you folks up here will fall asleep. I'll then ask you to perform a number of actions, and when you hear the tune "Wake Up Little Susie", that's what you'll do. OK?'

The participants nodded doubtfully. 'No need to worry, folks,' Bauer assured them. 'I won't get you to do anything too embarrassing or, of course, dangerous, so just sit down and make yourselves comfortable.'

During the interval, a row of chairs had been brought on stage, and everyone dutifully seated themselves.

'Now, just so we feel real friendly, I'd like you to tell me your names, starting with you, sir, at the end.'

'Frank,' supplied the red-haired man, and the rest of them followed suit.

'Great. Now, all nice and relaxed? Then let's get the show on the road.'

Rona's eyes were fixed on Magda, and, as her friend glanced anxiously down at her, she gave a little nod of encouragement. Then the orchestra struck up with 'Lullaby of Broadway', and immediately all eleven contestants sagged forward, their chins on their chests. The orchestra finished with a crashing of chords, making several in the audience jump, but none of those on stage stirred a muscle.

'Sound asleep, as you see,' Bauer said with satisfaction. 'Well now, Frank; you can start us off. You're taking part in an Elvis look-alike contest. Off you go!'

The red-haired man jumped to his feet and began a spirited rendition of 'Blue Suede Shoes', gyrating in the approved manner while the audience laughed and clapped.

'I don't think I like this,' Rona murmured. 'He's got them completely in his power.'

'That's the object of the exercise, love,' Max told her.

'I hope to God he goes easy on Magda,' Gavin said anxiously. 'I bet she's regretting persuading us to come.'

During the next few minutes, Rona became increasingly uncomfortable as the eleven on stage performed like automatons: jumping on their chairs or running round the stage to avoid snakes; singing and clucking like chickens, curtseying and bowing to the Queen. It ended with disturbingly heated arguments, when the volunteers were told the person next to them had wronged them in some way.

Finally, they were instructed to return to their chairs, the orchestra struck up 'Wake Up Little Susie', and, rubbing their eyes and looking about them in bewilderment, they emerged from their trance.

Prolonged applause accompanied their return to their seats.

'Did I make a complete fool of myself?' Magda asked anxiously. 'I don't remember a thing between sitting down on that chair, and waking up to find myself still there.'

'You were fine,' Rona assured her. 'It was very brave of you to go up.'

'Not sure I had any choice!' Magda said ruefully.

Of course you did! Rona thought, instinctively recoiling from her passive acceptance, but Magda had turned to Gavin, and she kept her reaction to herself.

The other two groups were called on in turn, and underwent much the same treatment, and, with Magda safely back beside her, Rona was more relaxed and able to enjoy the performance along with the rest of the audience.

When the third group had returned to their seats and Bauer had repeatedly bowed his thanks for the enthusiastic applause, the orchestra unexpectedly struck up with 'Lullaby of Broadway'. And to Rona's horror, Magda, who'd been speaking to her, suddenly slumped in her seat, as, judging by exclamations throughout the auditorium, did all the other participants.

Almost immediately, the music segued into 'Wake Up Little Susie', which once again revived them, and, to quiet the excited chatter among the audience, Bauer held up his hand.

'OK, OK, I apologize, folks! Just a little trick of the trade to end with! And if you're wondering why the first group didn't fall asleep when groups two and three went under, well, I guess that's a trade secret! But rest assured, you'll be able to listen to 'Lullaby of Broadway' for the rest of your lives in complete safety!'

There was another burst of applause, but again he raised a hand, suddenly serious, and it died raggedly away.

'One thing I must stress, ladies and gentlemen. My aim this evening has been to entertain you, and I hope we've had some fun. But make no mistake, hypnotism is a serious business and can be dangerous if in the wrong hands; so let me close by saying, as they do on kids' TV, "Don't try this at home!"'

He gave a final bow and, with a wave, made his way off stage. The curtains swung across and the house lights went up. It was the end of the show, and not, to Rona's mind, a minute too soon. Having believed Magda's trance was behind her, to see her succumb again had raised the hairs on the back of her neck.

The four of them walked together to the car park, where they separated with promises to be in touch. Rona and Max were silent as he edged their car into the stream of those leaving the car park.

'Well, what did you think of it?' he asked eventually.

'Creepy!' Rona said. 'I'd been most wary of the telepath, but as it turned out, it was Bauer who gave me goosebumps.'

'But you knew roughly what he was going to do.'

'I wasn't expecting Magda to be one of his guinea pigs. She's such a strong character, always so sure of herself. To see her go under so completely just . . . freaked me out. Silly, I know.'

'All three acts were good of their kind,' Max conceded, as they finally moved out on to Market Street. 'I suppose you can't ask for more, though, as you know, it's not my idea of an evening out.'

'Are you still convinced they were using plants?'

He smiled, patting his jacket pocket. 'I'm in no position to criticize, am I?' he said.

THREE

Lucy Coombes stared unbelievingly at the slammed door. Across the table, her three-year-old son's eyes filled with tears.

'Why did Daddy shout?' he asked tremulously.

Why indeed?

'He didn't mean it, darling,' Lucy said steadily. 'He's been working too hard lately, and he's tired.'

'But he said he'd take us out this morning!' objected five-year-old Ben, as the sound of the departing car reached them.

'Perhaps he won't be long. In the meantime, why don't you finish that picture you were painting? Then later, if Daddy's still not back, we'll go into town and you can spend your pocket money.'

The boys trotted off happily enough, but Lucy sat staring uneasily into her coffee. That burst of temper was so unlike Kevin, who'd always been so patient with the children. It was true things were hectic at his office, but this was the first time it had spilled over into his home life.

She stood up determinedly and started to clear the breakfast table, tipping Kevin's uneaten toast and marmalade into the bin. This evening, she resolved, when the boys were in bed, she'd cook a special meal, open a bottle of wine, and persuade him to talk over what was worrying him. Whatever it was, she was sure they could sort it out.

Guy Lacey stood in the hall of the house that had been his home for nearly thirty years, and looked around him.

'I don't know where to start,' he said helplessly.

Avril Parish slipped an arm round his waist. 'We don't have to do this now,' she said. 'They won't get possession for several weeks, surely?'

Guy shook his head. 'I'm not one for putting things off. Anyway, they'll be wanting to come and measure for curtains and so on, and try to visualize where they'll put their own things. The sooner mine are out of the way, the better.'

'Have you decided what you're leaving?'

'Carpets, of course, which are no use anywhere else, and are all old anyway. And curtains, for the same reason, but I don't doubt they'll come down pretty smartly. They're all past their sell-by.'

He sighed. 'It's always just been "home", with all its imperfections, but looking at it through the new owners' eyes I can see there's the hell of a lot to be done. Not structurally; I've always kept that up to scratch, but the kitchen's hopelessly out of date and the decor leaves a lot to be desired.'

'People usually want to redecorate anyway.' Avril paused. 'So where do we start?'

'God knows.'

'Then I suggest you walk round with a pencil and pad and write down what you want to keep, what's to be sold, what might be of interest to Sarah, and what is to go into storage till we get our own house.'

'You won't want any of this junk, surely?'

'Stop being so disparaging! There are some lovely pieces here, those Queen Anne chairs, for a start. And your dining suite is much nicer than mine. I want our new house to be an amalgam of both our previous homes, not just a replica of the one I have now – quite apart from the fact that Tom and Catherine might well want some things from Maple Drive.'

'OK, let's make a start then. You'd like to keep the dining suite – fine; we'll mark that down for storage. Suppose you tell me what else you fancy, because Lord knows, I haven't a clue.'

Avril laughed. 'Come on, Guy! You're not usually so downbeat!'

'I suppose,' he said slowly, 'it's because disposing of everything feels like breaking the final link with Sally. We bought and furnished this house together.'

Guy's wife had died when their daughter was a baby, and he'd brought Sarah up with the help of a series of nannies and housekeepers. It was through Sarah, now a primary school teacher, that he and Avril had met; moving to a school near Avril's home,

Sarah had been her lodger until last Christmas, when she'd moved into her fiancé's flat.

Avril slid her arm through his. 'I know,' she said softly. 'That's why I want you to think carefully before discarding anything. Sally will always be a part of your life, and it's only right that in a sense she should come with us.'

Guy tilted back her chin and kissed her. 'Bless you,' he said.

'Magda?'

'Hi, Rona.'

'I was just . . . wondering how you are this morning?'

Magda sounded surprised. 'Absolutely fine, why?'

'No ill effects from your experiences last night?'

'I had some pretty lurid dreams, if that's what you mean; no doubt that's what comes of letting someone take over your mind!'

Rona gave a little shiver. 'He gave it back, though,' she said sharply.

'Of course – I wasn't serious.'

There was a pause; they had, after all, exchanged all their news the previous evening. It was Magda who broke it.

'I touched base with Mama this morning, and passed on your message. She'd love to see you, and says she'll be sure to have some *copate* waiting for you!'

Rona laughed. The little wafer cakes had been a childhood favourite on visits to the Kings' home. 'Tell her I'll be in touch,' she said.

Apart from an hour's lunch break – fish and chips from the shop across the road – Guy and Avril had worked solidly, emptying drawers and cupboards, sorting through papers, deciding on the disposal of countless items. And at four o'clock, with aching backs and exhaustion setting in, they called it a day.

Together, they made a final round of the house, surveying their handiwork. Every piece of furniture, every picture and ornament, now bore a coloured label – blue for storage, red for the auction house, etc., while in the hall three large boxes packed with books, photographs and other personal items that Guy had not as yet removed awaited immediate transportation to Maple Drive.

At one point, Avril, on her way across the hall, had seen him

perched on the arm of a sofa leafing through what looked like a
wedding album, and had crept away again. In a sense, she thought,
this was harder for him than vacating her own home would be.
At least Tom was still alive, whereas, even after all these years,
this house reflected Sally's tastes: her choice of pictures hung
on the walls, her dressing-table set was still in place – now
destined for Sarah.

When they reached the hall again, Guy put an arm round
her, drawing her against him. 'I was dreading this,' he said
frankly. 'Thank you for coming with me. I couldn't have faced
it alone, and I didn't want to put Sarah through it, even though
she now has a home of her own. This is where she grew up,
after all.'

Avril nodded, wondering how her own daughters would react
when she came to sell their childhood home. They, too, had their
own homes – in fact, Lindsey had recently refurbished hers – but
she knew they shared a strong affection for the house in Maple
Drive.

Guy drew a deep breath. 'Now, I suggest we go home –' he
smiled over the word –'and relax over a cuppa. Then, later, I'll
take you out for a meal. How does that sound?'

'Perfect,' she said.

Rona was surprised, on the Sunday, to receive a phone call from
her mother, inviting her to lunch the following day.

'And I wonder if you'd be a love and bring me a couple of
things from the delicatessen?' Avril added. 'The local shops are
fine for day-to-day, but Sarah and Clive are coming to supper,
and I've some new recipes I'd like to try. I haven't time to go
into town, and anyway, I thought it would be nice to see you.
It's been a while.'

'Question is, which came first, the chicken or the egg?' Max
enquired cynically, when Rona relayed this.

'Wanting to see me, or needing the groceries?'

'Precisely.'

'Well, it's true I've not seen her for some time, and nor has
Linz.'

'And she wouldn't ask Lindsey to run errands midweek,
because she's at *proper* work.'

Rona gave his hand a reproving slap. 'Don't be a stirrer! I shall be a dutiful daughter, and while I'm over there, I can call on Paola. I'll give her a quick ring, and check if it's OK.'

Belmont, the district where Avril lived, was a twenty-minute drive from the centre of Marsborough, and Rona found herself reflecting on the countless times she'd made this journey – often, when her mother was at her most difficult, from a sense of duty rather than pleasure.

With hindsight, she suspected that Avril had been suffering from a form of depression – low self-esteem and general debility. The result was that for as long as she could remember, her mother was continually finding fault, critical of both her husband and daughters. She had long stopped caring about her appearance – drab hair, drab clothes, no make-up – which was why the young Rona had been so dazzled by the colourful, joyful and altogether delightful Paola King. Nor was it surprising that, all those years later, Tom, coming face-to-face with the intelligent and perfectly groomed Catherine, one of his bank's clients, should have fallen for her.

It had been Lindsey – all credit to her – who had finally confronted Avril, forcing her to face what she had become, and sweeping her off to town to buy the latest make-up and a new wardrobe. Sadly, though, the die had been cast, and the transformation came too late.

But credit was also due to Avril. To her daughters' relieved surprise, the loss of her husband shocked her out of her depression. Far from sinking back into her old ways, she had had her hair attractively styled and highlighted, installed an extra bathroom in her home prior to advertising for a lodger – Sarah, as it happened – and taken on a part-time job at the local library. In the process, her self-confidence grew and, as her interests widened, her peevishness gave way to a tentative new contentment. It was at that point that Guy Lacey had entered her life. Last Christmas, he'd asked her to marry him as soon as her divorce came through, and, as his daughter moved out of Avril's home, he had moved in.

Which, though she was glad for her mother, had resurrected Rona's diffidence when visiting her. Still not quite at ease with

Guy, she was careful to time her visits, unless specifically invited, for when Avril would be alone. Guy was still employed full-time, but since her mother worked four mornings a week at the library, at a charity shop on Wednesdays, and had regular bridge engagements, such times were limited. Which was why she was pleased, groceries or no groceries, to be invited to lunch.

It was odd, Rona mused now, that although her father had met Catherine some time before Avril and Guy came together, it was her prim mother who was cohabiting with her lover. Tom, ever the gentleman, had wanted to protect the reputation of the woman he loved and refused to compromise her, though despite their discretion Rona was sure they were enjoying a full sexual relationship.

Whether she was right or not, she much preferred their living arrangements; it meant she could call to see Tom any time she liked without inevitably running into Catherine, who continued for the most part to lead her own life.

Her reflections had brought her to Maple Drive, and she drove the last few yards to the familiar gateway.

Avril met her at the door, gave her a perfunctory kiss on the cheek, and relieved her of the carrier bag.

'Thanks so much for getting these, dear; you must tell me how much I owe you.'

Rona followed her into the kitchen and watched her unload the quail's eggs and artichokes she had bought that morning from the delicatessen near the Gallery.

'I was saying to Linz that it's some time since I've seen you, but I've been working flat out on the bio for weeks now.' Opening her capacious handbag, she retrieved a packet which she laid on the table beside the eggs. 'Here's something you don't need to reimburse me for!'

'Belgian chocs? You really shouldn't have, but thanks so much, dear. We'll sample them after lunch.'

'So how is Lindsey?' Avril asked, as they ate their meal. 'We've spoken briefly on the phone, but I've not seen her lately either.'

'We had lunch on Friday,' Rona replied. 'She told me Guy's house has been sold. That *is* good news.'

'Yes; we spent the whole of Saturday over there, sorting things out. It was all a bit traumatic for him, poor love, bringing back memories, and so on.'

'What's happening to his stuff?'

'Some of it will go to Sarah, some will be sold, and some will go into store till we're ready for it.'

Rona put down her fork. 'How do you mean?'

Avril looked surprised. 'Didn't I say? His being here is only a temporary measure; after we're married we'll have a new home, with no memories to haunt either of us.'

Rona looked round the familiar room, feeling her stomach lurch. 'You'll be selling this place?'

Avril nodded. 'Of course you and Lindsey can earmark anything you'd like, and we'll be taking quite a bit with us.' She put her hand over Rona's. 'Don't look so tragic, sweetie! It's only bricks and mortar.'

'Not to me, it isn't,' Rona said, 'though of course it makes sense. It's just that I assumed, when Guy moved in, that you'd continue living here.'

'Well, it won't be for a while, so you'll have time to get used to the idea. Now, enough of all that. What's new with that sister of yours? Has she still got Dominic in tow?'

Rona smiled. 'I'm not sure either of them would recognize that description! But he's still around, yes.'

Avril shook her head despairingly. 'That girl never had any sense where men are concerned.'

It was a familiar refrain, and, deploying diversionary tactics in her turn, Rona said brightly, 'She brought an old school photograph to show me, with one of the people on it blacked out. Apparently someone in her book group is keen to learn more about it.'

'And why should you know anything?'

'Good question! She asked me to exercise my "detective skills".'

'Is it a local school?'

'It was, by the name of Springfield Lodge. It's a hotel now.'

'Oh, I've heard of Springfield – it was a private school. The sisters of one of my friends went there.'

'Really?' Rona brightened. This was an unlooked-for bonus; if her mother could fill in the gaps it would let her off Lindsey's hook. 'What do you know about it? There was nothing on the Internet.'

'Well, I wasn't even at primary then, but years later Kitty told me about it. She came from a large family, and her sisters, who were a good ten years older than we were, both went there.'

'*What* did Kitty tell you?'

Avril frowned, casting her mind back. 'She said it closed suddenly, in the middle of the school year. Her mother was most put out, because Maureen was about to take her O-levels.'

Rona leant forward, interested despite herself. 'Any idea why it closed?'

'No, but apparently all kinds of rumours were flying around.'

'What kind of rumours?'

'Oh, heavy drinking, abortions, sex – take your pick. But Maureen, who, as I said, was there at the time, insisted it was because the headmaster had a heart attack, which must have been the official explanation.'

'The wilder version might explain why someone was blacked out, though.'

'True.' Avril smiled reminiscently. 'It was certainly the version Kitty and I preferred, but we'd nothing whatever to go on and by the time we heard about it, it was all years in the past and everyone had forgotten about it. Or said they had.'

'Might Pops know anything?' Rona asked hesitantly.

'Not first-hand, certainly; he only came to Marsborough when the bank transferred him from Tynecastle. What about Max? Can't he throw any light on it?'

'Actually, I haven't asked him.'

'Not seen him lately?' Avril asked pointedly. It was a bone of contention that Max and Rona spent a large portion of the week apart, she at home and he at Farthings, the cottage across town where he had his studio. It was an arrangement that had come about since both worked from home, and while Max's art was inspired by music played at full volume, Rona's writing needed total quiet. It was also practical, following his thrice-weekly evening classes, for him to spend the night at Farthings, so as to be able to start painting early the next morning, his preferred time. The arrangement suited them both perfectly; they spoke on the phone at least twice a day, and enjoyed their time together all the more – none of which Avril could understand.

'It's just that I've no intention of doing anything about it,' Rona answered steadily, ignoring the thrust. 'I've enough on my hands with the bio, and I only mentioned it now because you asked about Lindsey.'

Avril shrugged. 'Well, that's all I can tell you, I'm afraid, and if you're not following it up, it's of no consequence anyway.'

There was an awkward pause, and Rona glanced at her watch. 'I should be making a move; I'm calling at Paola King's on my way home.'

'Paola King – there's a name from the past! I didn't know you were still in touch.'

'Only sporadically, but Magda said last week that Paola would like to see me. This seemed the ideal opportunity.'

'I used to be jealous of that woman,' Avril said reflectively. 'You spent more time in her house than in your own home.'

Startled, Rona could think of nothing to say. She reached for her handbag and stood up.

'Thanks for the lunch, Mum. It was delicious.'

'At least for once you've some decent food inside you.'

As Rona's usual lunch tended to be a sandwich or something on toast, this was a fair comment, added to which, disliking cooking as intensely as she did, on the evenings Max stayed at his studio she tended to dine off salads, takeaways or ready-meals, and occasionally, fancying none of these, visited Dino's, an Italian restaurant six minutes' walk from home. It was indeed fortunate, she acknowledged, that Max was an excellent cook, and enjoyed taking over whenever he was home.

'Love to Lindsey, if you see her,' Avril said, as Rona kissed her goodbye.

'Will do, and remember me to Guy and Sarah. Hope your supper party's a success. I might beg the quail's egg recipe, to pass on to Max!'

In stark contrast to Avril's restrained welcome, Paola King came running down the path to greet her and, as Rona climbed out of the car, flung her arms round her and hugged her enthusiastically.

'Rona! Oh, how good it is to see you, *cara mia*! Come inside and tell me all your news!' And Rona, having been, as always, slightly on edge in her mother's company, happily relaxed.

The house was exactly as she remembered it, warm and welcoming with its brightly coloured rugs, exotic pictures and all-pervading smell of baking. A low table had been drawn up to the fire, ready laid with a tray on which Rona recognized the promised *copate*.

'You're spoiling me!' she said. 'I'm not ten any more!'

'Everyone should be spoiled once in a way!' Paola declared, pouring the tea. 'Now, tell me about the book you are writing. So many books and articles! George and I are so proud!'

'Well, this one has rather a chequered history,' Rona said ruefully.

Paola sobered, her hand going to her mouth. 'How thoughtless of me! Of course – that poor woman. Such a tragedy!'

'Yes. It's coming along now, but I'm not enjoying it as much as usual.'

'And that clever husband of yours? What is he working on at the moment?'

'Well, apart from taking four classes a week and putting in a full day at the art school on Thursdays, he's been commissioned to do a portrait of some local dignitary – I forget his name.'

'Such a talented family!' Paola enthused. 'I boast about you to my friends! "These famous people are friends of my daughter," I say!'

Rona laughed. 'And we boast that Magda's *our* friend! I lose track of how many boutiques she has now.'

'Eight,' Paola supplied. She stirred her tea thoughtfully. 'You went with her on Friday, I think, to see this . . . *ipnotista*?'

'That's right.' Rona hesitated. 'He was . . . very good.'

'I do not like this . . . messing with the minds of people.'

'I admit I had reservations, but it seemed pretty harmless. He didn't make her do anything too way-out.'

'*Her?*' Paola repeated sharply. 'Magdalena was *involved*?'

Oh God! Rona thought. Why hadn't she been warned about this?

'Just as one of several groups,' she said hastily.

Paola brushed that aside. 'What did he do to her, this man?'

'Well, he . . . put them all to sleep, of course, and then they
were told the Queen was there, and that a snake had escaped, and
they reacted accordingly.' Her voice tailed off. 'I'm sorry,' she
ended, 'I thought you knew, but it wasn't any big deal, honestly.'

She looked anxiously at her hostess, who was staring down
at the tea tray. Finally, Paola looked up, her eyes troubled.

'You wonder why I make the fuss like this, but we found when
she was young that Magdalena is . . . *sensibile*—' She shook her
head impatiently, searching for the right word.

'Susceptible?' Rona suggested uneasily, resolving not to
mention her later relapse.

Paola nodded vigorously. 'She has much imagination – it is
that, of course, that makes her good at her job – but when she
was small, there were times she could not separate what was real
and what was not. She had an imaginary friend. Did you know
about that, when you were together at school?'

Rona shook her head, her unease growing.

'Anna Lisa, her name was, and every day a place must be set
for her at table. George and I would hear the child talking to her
in her room at night.'

'Lots of children have imaginary friends,' Rona said. 'I'm sure
it's nothing to worry about.'

'And such nightmares!' Paola was continuing. 'She would
wake screaming, night after night.'

'But she grew out of them,' Rona insisted. *I had some pretty
lurid dreams*, whispered a voice in her head.

Paola sighed. 'I worry too much. George always tells me so.'

Gradually, thanks to Rona's sustained efforts, the conversation
teetered on to a more even keel, but for the first time in her life
she was glad when it was time to go.

Having driven round the corner from the Kings' house, she
drew in to the kerb, turned off the engine, and, reaching for her
mobile, pressed the button for Magda's number.

'Magda Ridgeway.'

'Mags, it's Rona,' she said rapidly. 'I've just left your mother.
Why on earth didn't you warn me not to mention your going on
stage?'

'On . . .? Oh, Friday, you mean. God!' Her voice rose suddenly.
'You didn't tell her?'

'Of course I did! She asked about it, I told her, and she hit the roof.'

Rona heard Magda's indrawn breath. Then she said more calmly, 'Well, don't worry about it. She believes meddling with the mind is against God's will, or something. She probably thinks I'll be stuck in purgatory.'

But Paola's concern had been more immediate. Rona said hesitantly, 'She seemed to link it with the imaginary friend you had as a child.'

Magda gave a snort of laughter. 'She's not still on about that? Dear Anna Lisa – I haven't thought of her in years. Mama probably thinks I actually *saw* her, that I'm psychic or something, whereas the truth is I was simply lonely. As you know, I'd no friends till I met you.'

'Well, I'm very sorry if I upset her. Perhaps . . .?'

'Yes, I'll give her a call and set her mind at rest. And *I'm* sorry, not to have warned you in advance. It just never occurred to me, but with hindsight it should have done.'

Lindsey phoned that evening.

'I've been catching up with last week's *Gazette*. There's a review of the show at the Darcy, so I thought I'd ring and see how you enjoyed it.'

'What was the critic's verdict?'

'Oh, he was quite impressed. Were you?'

'Yes, all the acts were good. Max made a fool of himself by challenging the telepath, and had to sit down with a red face!'

Lindsey laughed. 'Serves him right! Was his telepathy as good as ours?'

'Well, apart from Max and a couple of other links with the audience, it was mostly guessing playing cards.' Rona braced herself. 'And talking of guessing, who do you think we saw at the Bacchus beforehand?'

'Haven't a clue.'

'Hugh and his new lady friend.'

There was a long pause. Then: 'Did you speak to them?'

'Literally en passant. He was a bit embarrassed, I think.'

'No reason why he should be.' Lindsey's voice was brittle. 'What's she like?'

'Sleek, sophisticated, in her forties. All I got was a cool nod.'

'Name?'

'Mia Campbell. Have you heard of her? He introduced her as a work colleague.'

'Means nothing to me, but I've not been near HW&B for years. The entire staff has probably changed.' A pause. 'She's attractive, then?'

'Reasonably. She has vibrant red hair, which makes Hugh's ginger look faded.'

When Lindsey made no comment, she added, 'And my other news is that I had lunch with Mum today.'

'Really? How come?'

Rona said wryly, 'She wanted some things from the deli.'

'Par for the course! How is she?'

'Fine. By the way, did you know she's selling the house when she and Guy get married?'

'*Our* house?'

'Yep. It came as quite a shock, actually.'

'But . . . *why*? There's loads of room for both of them.'

'She said they wanted somewhere new, with no ghosts from the past. And we can choose what we want, after Pops and Catherine have had their say.'

'Too bad I didn't know that earlier!' commented Lindsey, who'd recently spent a large amount on new furniture and fittings.

'It's silly, but it quite upset me. I like to think of it *being* there, more or less as it's always been, and Mum ensconced in it.'

'Where will they live, did she say?'

'I don't think they've started looking yet.'

'It's odd to think the divorce will come through after Christmas. Then there'll be a spate of family weddings!'

'Well, two, anyway – unless you're thinking of making it three?'

'Not a hope!'

'Did you see Dominic over the weekend?'

'No; Nicole and David invited me for a meal on Saturday, and suggested I stay overnight, so I could enjoy a drink. There was another couple there I'd not met before, and we had a jolly good evening. I didn't get home till yesterday afternoon.'

Rona's eyes fell on the school photograph, propped up against the toaster, but she was determined not to mention it till Lindsey did.

'Sorry,' Lindsey said quickly, 'there's someone at the door – I'll have to go. See you.'

'See you,' echoed Rona, and thoughtfully replaced the phone.

FOUR

For the next three days, Rona worked steadily on her book. It had taken her a considerable time to sort out the mass of letters and diaries that Gwen Saunders, Elspeth's personal assistant, had delivered after Elspeth's death, and even longer to brace herself to read them. She had never before written a biography of someone she'd met personally, and couldn't rid herself of the sensation of prying into private papers.

In particular, it was painful to read of Elspeth's long friendship with Chloë Pyne, a fellow artist who lost her life under a tube train, and of Chloë's ill-fated love affair. Had Elspeth lived only days longer, she would at least have learned she wasn't responsible for her friend's death.

On the Thursday afternoon, after a somewhat gruelling two hours, Rona closed the diaries, turning instead to the folder listing Elspeth's paintings, with a note alongside of the galleries or private collectors who owned them. Over the last months she'd visited several galleries in Manchester, Liverpool, Dublin and Edinburgh, as well as a couple of Stately Homes where her work was displayed.

Elspeth was known principally for her obsession with clouds, which she had painted in every imaginable way, and Rona admitted there were times when she never wanted to see another cloudscape. Max, however, had been able to talk her through several pictures, pointing out the different techniques employed to achieve the desired effect, and she humbly accepted that, to him, each painting had an entirely different character.

She was trying to decide where to visit next when she was interrupted by the pealing of the doorbell, followed by hysterical barking from Gus, who, assuming she was deaf, took it upon himself to alert her.

It was rare to have visitors in the afternoon, but, glad of the excuse to leave her desk, Rona ran downstairs and opened the door to find her father on the step.

'Pops!' she exclaimed. 'How lovely! Come in!'

Tom Parish returned her hug and bent to pat the excited dog. 'I hope I'm not being a Person from Porlock,' he said. 'You're not at a crucial stage, are you?'

'No, and glad of the break, to be honest. Come downstairs and I'll make some tea.'

'I hoped you might, so I bought a cake en route.'

'Even better!'

He sat down at the table, fondling Gus's ears and watching as Rona filled the kettle. 'It seems ages since I saw you,' he commented.

'I know, Mum made the same complaint; I had lunch with her on Monday.'

'How is she?'

'Very well.' She turned to him, a thought striking her. 'Did you know she intends to sell Maple Drive?'

'No, though I rather thought she might.'

'But . . . surely you own half of it?'

Tom shook his head. 'I made it over entirely when we separated. It was the least I could do.'

'Well, she's intending to invite you and Catherine to choose what you'd like.'

'That's very generous of her.'

'I suppose they'll be faced with trying to fit the contents of two homes into one.'

'We'll be spared that, at least. All I took at the time were my books and personal papers, and, as you know, I'm renting the flat furnished. Avril did offer me my choice of ornaments and pictures – even furniture – but I felt they belonged where they were. So, my pet –' he took the mug of tea she handed him – 'far from having to squeeze in our belongings, we shall have to look for more. In view of which, if that offer still holds, I might welcome the chance to reconsider.'

'Catherine will be selling her bungalow, then?'

'Yes; like your mother and Guy, we decided we wanted a home new to both of us.'

Rona, opening the cake box, felt a spasm of regret. She loved the tranquil charm of Catherine's home.

'Oh, lovely – lemon drizzle!' she exclaimed, lifting out the cake. 'My favourite!'

'Which is why I bought it.'

'You're a star!' She cut two generous slices, and handed him a plate. 'How's Catherine?' she added, seating herself opposite him.

'A bit down, actually. She's worried about Daniel.'

Catherine's son, a computer programmer, lived with his wife and baby daughter in Cricklehurst.

'Oh? Isn't he well?'

Tom hesitated. 'I'm not sure I should be telling you this.'

'Well, you've started, so you might as well finish!'

He took a sip of tea. 'Between you and me, he and Jenny are going through a difficult patch.'

'Really? I thought they were blissfully happy. They certainly give that impression.'

'I think they have been, up to now. The trouble is, Daniel's incredibly busy and having to travel more than he did, which involves being away overnight. Added to which, Alice is still not sleeping through, Jenny's missing out on her own sleep, and it's been getting on top of her.'

'So how serious is it?'

Tom sighed. 'It looks as though she's seeing someone else.'

'God!' Rona stared at him. 'And Daniel went running to his mother?'

'Lord, no: he was away this week, and Catherine went over on Tuesday to babysit, to give Jenny a break. And while she was at the cinema with a girlfriend, this chap phoned.'

'Oh dear!'

'Without giving her a chance to speak, he launched into plans for their next meeting, before realizing he was speaking to Jenny's mother-in-law.'

'Big mistake! Did Catherine tackle her about it?'

'I'm not sure what happened. She was very upset, as you might imagine, and blurted out the gist of it when she got home; but she didn't go into details, and I suspect she now regrets having mentioned it.'

'So presumably Daniel knows nothing about it?'

'Presumably not.'

Rona finished her cake in contemplative silence. 'Poor Catherine,' she said then. 'She must be wondering whether or not she should tell him.'

'Yep. Don't pass this on, will you?' Tom said anxiously. 'I probably shouldn't have told you.'

'I won't say a word,' Rona promised, 'but I do hope they sort it out; I like them both.'

'What were you dreaming about last night?' Gavin asked curiously, at breakfast the next day. 'You were tossing and turning and muttering most of the night.'

Magda looked up quickly. 'Sorry if I disturbed you.'

'But what was it about, can you remember?'

'And this is the man who says nothing's more boring than other people's dreams!' She reached for the cafetière. 'But since you ask, I *can* remember, because, unusually enough, the dreams I've had this week have stayed with me all day, and frankly I wish they hadn't!'

'Why? What are they about?'

'It wasn't so much the content. They were the usual mishmash – snatches of scenes and people, not making any sense when you analyse them. But it was the way I felt when I woke. Disorientated and – *angry*, somehow.'

'Better not eat any more cheese at supper, then!' Gavin advised, and returned to his newspaper.

Driving to work that Friday morning, Lindsey wondered, with mild irritation, when her sister would refer to the photograph she'd slipped into her bag. Admittedly, there was no hurry – the book group wouldn't meet for another three weeks – but she'd like to have at least some news to pass on to William in the interim.

The group met once a month at the home of Debra Stacey, who had initiated it some six months ago, and who lived in one of the turnings off Alban Road North, a five-minute drive from Lindsey's flat. There were ten of them in all, none of whom had known each other before replying to Debra's advertisement in the local paper. Most were older than Lindsey, several considerably so, but they were a friendly bunch, who all contributed to their literary discussions.

William Stirling, the provider of the photograph, Lindsey judged to be in his mid-fifties, a tall, well-built man with an easy manner and pleasant smile. At their first meeting he'd explained his wife's absence by saying she had no interest in books, preferring to spend her time playing golf or bridge, neither of which appealed to him. From this, Lindsey inferred, rightly or wrongly, that they went their separate ways. In any event, following that early comment he'd not mentioned his wife again until the previous week, when he'd produced the photograph.

For some reason she couldn't fathom, Lindsey found him quite attractive – Rona always maintained she preferred older men – and she suspected her interest was reciprocated, a source of secret satisfaction when Dominic was at his most obtuse. Though she'd not analysed it too closely, part of her reason for volunteering Rona's help had been to establish a contact with William outside the group – which made it all the more frustrating that her twin was studiously ignoring the photograph.

She parked the car and, her mind still on William, was considerably startled when, rounding the corner into Guild Street, she cannoned into him.

'Lindsey, hello!' he exclaimed, putting out a hand to steady her. 'Sorry – I always dash along at a rate of knots! Are you OK?'

'Fine, thanks.'

'On your way to work?'

'Yes, I'm at Chase Mortimer.'

'Better mind my p's and q's, then! I'm just round the corner – Frinton Insurance.' He paused. 'We've been wondering if your sister was able to help with the photo?'

'Not as yet,' Lindsey answered evasively. 'I left it with her; I hope that's OK?'

'Of course. She's agreed to look into it, then?'

'Not exactly, but I'm working on it.'

'Look, I wouldn't want to impose. If she hasn't time, or she's not interested, please don't—'

'Oh, don't worry, she'll get round to it.'

'Well, as long as we're not making a nuisance of ourselves . . .' He paused again. 'Glenda was wondering if she's by any chance the Rona Parish who writes for *Chiltern Life*?'

'She is indeed.'

He smiled. 'No wonder you mentioned her detective skills!

We always enjoy her articles. Look, I mustn't hold you up now, but here's my card. I know she must be busy, and I certainly wouldn't want to press her, but if anything should come up before the next book group, could you give me a call? It's just that this photo has really got to Glenda, and I know she won't be happy till she knows who was blotted out and why.'

'We'll see what we can do,' Lindsey promised, and, with a brief smile, hurried on her way, obscurely disappointed with the outcome of the meeting.

Had she but known it, Rona was at that moment staring with a mixture of resentment and curiosity at the offending photo, which she'd taken up to her study and propped against her pen holder. She'd stopped work the previous day at a sticky patch – never a wise move – and a night's sleep had done little to solve the problem. Open to distraction, she succumbed and, leaning forward, picked it up and studied it closely for the first time.

The print was black-and-white with a gloss finish, and despite being badly creased, the faces of those depicted were still clearly defined, frozen in a long-ago summer's day.

Passing quickly over the pupils – bright, expectant faces, ready for whatever life might throw at them – Rona focused on the eight members of staff: four women, three men, and one, gender unknown, completely obliterated by the ink splodge.

On impulse, she reached for the phone and pressed the button for *Chiltern Life*.

'It's Rona, Polly,' she said. 'Is Barnie free, by any chance?'

'Hi, Rona. Yes, no one's with him as far as I know.'

'Then could you put me through, please?'

'Rona!' The features editor's voice boomed over the phone. 'Great to hear from you! How are things?'

'A bit slow, to be honest, but I'm ploughing on.'

'Not ready to rejoin our ranks?'

'Not at the moment. Actually, I'm hoping to test your memory. Does the name Springfield Lodge ring any bells?'

'The hotel, you mean?'

'I was thinking more of its previous incarnation.'

'It's had several, one of them being a private girls' school.'

'That's the one. Do you know anything about it?'

'Not really; it closed down years ago.'

'Any idea why?'

'Hey, Rona, what is this? Twenty questions?'

'Sorry! I've come across an old school photo dated 1951, and a member of staff has been rather spectacularly obliterated. I was wondering why.'

'If it belonged to one of the girls, it could be any reason, ranging from a sudden fit of pique to long-standing resentment or revenge for favouritism. Why, is it important?'

'It isn't really, but some friends of Lindsey's are curious.'

'So they turned to the Number One Ladies' Detective Agency?'

Rona laughed. 'You know me – I can't resist a challenge. What I was wondering, though, is if it's possible to trace the photographer on the off-chance that he still has the negative. *Chiltern Life*'s full of photos – I thought perhaps you could tell me which firms specialized in school photos.'

'That long ago? Have a heart! And as you'll appreciate, everything's changed since it went digital. Your best bet would be to try the *Gazette*; it could be the original's in their archives, though it's rather a long shot.'

'That's an idea. Thanks, Barnie; if I decide to take it further – which, frankly, I doubt – I'll do that.'

'In the meantime, when are we going to see you? Dinah could do with being cheered up; Mel's baby's not due for a couple of months, but she's already starting to panic.'

The Trents' daughter Melissa lived in the States, and her last pregnancy had been difficult enough to warrant her mother flying out to be with her.

'Heavens, yes – I was forgetting. How is Mel?'

'She says she's fine, but Dinah's convinced that's only to stop her worrying.'

'Surely Mitch would let you know of any problems?'

'Of course he would, but try telling Dinah!'

'Well, you must come over for a meal and we'll take her mind off it. It's some time since we saw you.'

'Now you're embarrassing me! I wasn't fishing for an invite, honest!'

'It's well overdue, what with everything that's been going on. I'll have a word with Max and come back to you.'

Only as she rang off did Rona realize that she, too, had come up against a brick wall in her enquiries about Springfield Lodge.

Jenny Bishop stood at the kitchen sink, staring blindly out of the window. Daniel would be home within the hour, and God knows what she could say to him. Catherine must have told him of Paul's phone call, and when he'd rung midweek she'd been ready with counter-accusations. But he'd failed to mention it, leaving her limp with relief.

Though maybe, she thought now, he preferred to wait till they were face-to-face? The coldness inside her intensified. *How* had this happened? She loved Daniel – of course she did – but these days it seemed she hardly saw him. Even when not away, he was seldom home before seven, and by the time she'd settled Alice and they'd eaten it was time for bed. Where, she thought, her throat tightening, he immediately fell asleep, while she lay tensely awake, listening for Alice's inevitable cry.

Jenny could hear her now through the open door, chuntering away to herself in her playpen. The fierceness of the love she felt for her baby had taken her by surprise, and, looking back, she admitted that since her birth Daniel had been assigned a back seat. Alice needed her, and it seemed Daniel did not, though which had come first she could now not be sure.

Then, when she was at her lowest, Paul had come on the scene – successful, debonair Paul, seemingly without a care in the world and with at least one divorce behind him. He had pressed all the right buttons, showering her with compliments, buying her chocolates, taking her out for lunch, and suddenly there was excitement in her life again. It was wrong – she knew that – and she kept promising herself she'd end it. Just not yet.

But procrastination was dangerous. Though they'd met a month ago, when he'd come into the florist's where she worked, they'd not yet slept together. Their affair – if it could be called that – had consisted of phone calls, lunches out, and increasingly passionate kisses in the car, reviving memories of her teenage years. Then, last week, Paul had suggested coming to the house after work.

'Look,' he'd argued, 'we might as well face facts. I want you, you want me, and your husband considerately goes away. What could be better? We have a warm, comfortable house at our disposal – a distinct improvement on a car seat! – with only a baby as chaperone. And she's not going to tell, is she?'

The idea had excited her, and, like a fool, she'd agreed. Paul had arrived with a bottle of champagne, but throughout the meal the atmosphere between them grew increasingly electric and she began to panic. Then, just as they finished eating, Alice had awoken and refused to be comforted, and, with a mixture of relief and disappointment, she'd insisted that Paul leave. He'd been very tight-lipped about it, and the phone call Catherine intercepted had been to suggest a return visit. And Jenny knew only too well how that visit would end.

The phone interrupted her musings, and as she lifted it she heard traffic noise before her husband's voice.

'Hi, sweetie. I'm on my way, but I have to call at the office to collect some papers, so—'

'But that's miles out of your way! It'll add a good hour to your journey!'

'I know, it's a pain, but I'll need them first thing on Monday.'

She tried to keep her voice level. 'I was expecting you any minute. When *will* you be home?'

'I was late leaving, so not before eight, I'm afraid.'

'Then you'll miss Alice,' Jenny said tautly, 'and you haven't seen her for four days.'

'I know, but tomorrow's the weekend . . . OK?' he prompted, when she didn't speak.

'I suppose it will have to be.'

'Give her a big kiss from me. See you soon.' And he rang off.

Turning quickly, she hurried into the adjoining room and scooped the baby out of her pen.

'Bath time!' she said unsteadily, kissing Alice's curls and wetting them with her sudden tears. Holding the child tightly to her, she carried her upstairs.

Fifty miles away in Marsborough, another homecoming was not going as planned. Kevin Coombes strode into the house just after six, brushing past Lucy in the hall, and without a word made straight for the drinks cupboard and the whisky bottle. She watched from the doorway as he poured himself a generous measure and tossed it straight back.

'Bad day at the office?'

'You could say that.' He refilled the glass, frowning as the two little boys came running into the room.

'Daddy!' They hurled themselves against him, hugging his knees and both talking at once, and Lucy, with sinking heart, saw the flash of irritation on his face. To her relief, though, he ruffled their hair.

'Will you bath us tonight, Daddy?' Archie was pleading, while Ben clamoured for him to come and see his latest drawing.

'Hey, give me a break, boys! I've only just set foot in the house!' Though his tone was jovial, Lucy could see the effort it cost him.

'Daddy's tired,' she said quickly. 'Come up with me and let him relax for a while, then perhaps he'll read you a story.'

Her eyes flashed an appeal, and reluctantly he nodded. 'Off you go, then,' he said, with undisguised relief.

A month ago, she thought numbly, he'd have tossed them over his shoulder, squealing delightedly, and swept them upstairs. The bathroom would have rung with laughs and yells, and when she went in to collect their clothes, she'd have found the floor awash. If only she could turn the clock back.

The promised bedtime story was short and sweet, after which Kevin left Lucy to settle their sons, and when she came down to join him she found him slumped on the sofa with his head in his hands.

'Darling, what is it? What's wrong?' She slipped to her knees in front of him, taking hold of his hands, and he pulled her convulsively against him.

'God, Luce, I wish I knew! What's the *matter* with me? I just can't get my head round anything at the moment.' He paused, and she felt his arms tighten about her. 'I damn nearly got the sack today, and I'd have deserved it.'

She pulled back, staring into his face. 'What happened?'

'Old Netherby was being his usual pompous self, criticizing everything in sight, and I just snapped and . . . lashed out at him.'

'Kevin!'

'Oh, he ducked in time, thank God. It was touch and go for a while, but my abject apologies and excuses finally won through. I'm on borrowed time, though; the slightest cause for complaint, and he'll see that I'm out.'

He hesitated, not meeting her eyes. 'And that's not the only thing. Several times lately I suddenly seem to come to, and – this sounds idiotic – I'm not where I expect to be.'

She stared at him with wide, frightened eyes. 'You mean you have blank spells?'

'I don't know what the hell I mean.'

'But Kevin, you must see a doctor! This could be—'

'No!' He slammed his hand down on the arm of the chair. 'It's strain, that's all it is,' he added more calmly. 'Overwork. I'll look in at the chemist tomorrow and get a tonic of some sort. That should do the trick.' Putting her gently aside, he rose to his feet. 'Anyway, that's enough of my troubles. Let's go and eat.'

And Lucy, whose world seemed suddenly unsure, reluctantly followed him into the kitchen.

'Mum?'

'Lindsey! Talk of the devil! I was just saying to Guy that I've not seen you for a while.'

'I know; sorry about that. The reason I'm phoning is that I have to visit a client in Belmont on Monday, and I'm wondering if I can scrounge a free lunch?'

'Of course! That'll be lovely.'

'I gather Rona's been over?'

'Yes, last week. One of these days, perhaps I'll see you both together! Did you find out any more about the photograph?'

Lindsey stiffened. 'What photograph?' she asked carefully.

'The one of Springfield. I knew a girl who went there. Surely Rona told you?'

'No, actually, she didn't.'

'Oh. Well, she went on to Paola King after leaving me, so perhaps it slipped her mind. What time can I expect you on Monday?'

Lindsey wrenched her mind back to the lunch. 'My appointment's for eleven, so around twelve fifteen, twelve thirty?'

'I'll look forward to it,' Avril said.

'And exactly when,' Lindsey began without preamble, 'were you thinking of telling me what you learned from Mum about Springfield?'

'Ah!' Pulling a face at Max, Rona perched on the kitchen table, the phone to her ear.

'"Ah" indeed! I presume you're paying me back for slipping the photo in your bag?'

'Partly,' Rona admitted, 'but as I told you, I didn't want to get embroiled in this while I'm immersed in Elspeth.'

'Then why ask Mum about it? What gets me, though, is that even though we've spoken since, you never said a word!'

'All right, it was childish, but I was waiting for you to bring it up.'

'Well, I'm bringing it up now. I'm seeing her on Monday, so will you kindly fill me in?'

Rona took a sip of the vodka Max handed her. 'Basically, Mum's friend Kitty Little – the one who was her bridesmaid – had two much older sisters who went to Springfield, and one was still there when it closed. The official explanation was that the headmaster had a heart attack, and presumably no one was prepared to take it over. But it seems rumours were rife.'

'What kind of rumours?'

'The usual – sex, drink, abortions. So any one of those – or none of them – could lie behind the defacing.'

'Anything else?'

'I'd have thought that was enough to be going on with!'

'You're sure you're not still holding something back?'

'Come on, Linz, I'm sorry, all right? But that's all there is, honestly. If Mum's been thinking about it in the interim, she might have remembered more. How come you're going to Belmont on a working day?'

'I've a client to visit, and thought I might take a leaf out of your book.'

'Fair enough. Let me know if you learn anything.'

'I might,' Lindsey said, and hung up.

Daniel had still not mentioned the phone call that had obsessed her since Tuesday evening. Jenny almost wished he would. There'd been no further word from Paul; he must be wondering if there'd been any fallout, and when it would be safe to resume their liaison.

What would she tell him when he contacted her, as he was

certain to do? She was still attracted to him, still obscurely angry with Daniel, but Catherine . . . Oh God, what a hopeless, impossible situation!

Now, as they ate their delayed meal and he talked of the problems he'd experienced with his client, her mind circled uselessly round possible courses of action.

Until suddenly, with a flood of relief, the blindingly obvious solution came to her, and, interrupting him, she blurted out, 'I think I'll go to Mum and Dad for a week or two.'

Daniel put down his knife and fork and stared at her. 'A *week or two?*'

Jenny's visits to her parents in Cheshire usually took the form of a long weekend.

'I . . . need to get away,' she said a little wildly.

'But . . . why? Sweetheart, what is it? Is something wrong?'

'No!' She shook her head violently.

'What about work?'

'It'll be OK, I'll take unpaid leave. Kelly will stand in for me.'

He was looking at her with concern. 'I knew you shouldn't have gone back so soon. But you don't have to go away, surely? I mean, just stay at home and take it easy. Meet the girls for coffee like you did on maternity leave, take Alice swimming . . .' His voice tailed off.

'I need to get away,' she repeated, and flinched when she saw his eyes darken.

'From me?'

'Just – away.'

'I'll miss you,' he said.

'No, you won't. You're hardly ever here.' Her voice was sharper than she'd intended.

'Sweetie, that's not true! I know I've been extra busy these last few weeks, but this particular job won't go on much longer, then I'll be more or less back to nine-to-five.'

She felt herself waver; yet if she stayed, she knew without doubt that she would sleep with Paul, and that really would be the end. Because even if Daniel never found out, she couldn't lie to him for the rest of her life.

Desperate now to end the discussion, she pushed back her chair and stood up. 'Then I'll come back when the job's finished.

I hate being alone night after night, especially when I spend half of it rocking Alice to sleep. The house rustles and creeks and I keep thinking I hear noises downstairs. I know I'm being silly, but it . . . frightens me.'

He was staring at her, a line between his brows. 'You've never mentioned that! Why didn't you tell me?'

'It's not only that – we just don't seem close any more. When you *are* home, you're tired all the time.' Her eyes, full of tears, challenged him. 'Can you even remember when we last made love?'

He looked as though she'd struck him, made an instinctive move towards her, but she backed away.

'Please don't try to stop me, Daniel. I *need* to go.'

'Jenny . . .' He lifted his hands helplessly. 'At least give me a chance to put things right. Why not invite your parents down here for a while? They'd be company for you, and I'm sure they'd love—'

'*No!*' she cried desperately. 'Please!'

Already she was lying to him. Of course she was tired, of course the house was a bit creepy at night, but she could deal with that. What she couldn't admit was that she had to get away in order to save their marriage.

Paul would get the message. She'd never fooled herself either of them was in love; now, with searing insight, she accepted that were she no longer available, he'd move on to someone else. He must have thought he'd fallen on his feet! she thought bitterly: an absent husband, a susceptible, lonely wife and an empty house. He'd even said as much. God, what a fool she'd been!

Daniel was still standing by the table, staring at her with pain in his eyes. *Had* Catherine said anything? Surely she couldn't have, or he'd have accused her by now.

'Only for a week or two,' she pleaded. 'I'm sorry, Daniel, I've just got thoroughly run down and I need some pampering.' She forced a smile. 'And you needn't worry that I'll make a scene next time you have to be away for a night or two. It's just . . . a combination of things at the moment.'

'Well, if you're really sure. And I *shall* miss you. It's knowing you and Alice are at home waiting for me that keeps me going when things get tough at work.'

Her tears spilled over, and this time she didn't stop him putting his arms round her.

'Just for a week or two,' she repeated.

He tilted her chin back, looking searchingly into her eyes. 'And even though I'm a thoughtless brute at times, you do still love me?'

'Of *course* I do!' Of that, at least, she was sure.

'That's all right then,' he said.

FIVE

L indsey didn't report back on her visit to Belmont, leaving Rona to wonder whether she'd not learned anything new, or, in fact, had, but was determined not to pass it on. Not that it mattered, one way or the other; as she'd told her mother, she'd no intention of following up the photograph.

The decision was, however, taken out of her hands in an unexpected way. On the Wednesday morning, having made a note of the galleries she still had to visit, she turned to an appendix listing the names of lesser known paintings in private possession, together, where possible, with the name and address of the owner. And, unbelievably, a small watercolour titled *Samson and Delilah* was shown to be in the possession of a Mrs Beryl Temple of Springfield Lodge Private Hotel, Marsborough.

It was not only the coincidence that piqued Rona's interest; she'd been unaware that Elspeth painted biblical subjects, and was at a loss to understand how she'd missed this. She must get in touch with Gwen Saunders, but first, her curiosity mounting, she reached for the telephone directory, checked the number of the hotel, and promptly dialled it, asking to speak to Mrs Temple.

'Is it in connection with a booking, madam?' an efficient voice enquired.

'No, it's . . . a private matter.' She gave her name, and a moment later an older voice came on the line.

'Ms Parish?'

'Yes; good morning, Mrs Temple. I hope you don't mind my contacting you, but I believe you're the owner of a painting by Elspeth Wilding?'

'I am indeed.'

'I've been asked by the family to write her biography, and I—'

'Of course! I thought I knew the name! You're the writer, aren't you?'

'That's right, and I was wondering—'

'You'd like to see the painting?'

'I should, very much, if that's possible.'

'Of course, you're welcome to come any time. You know where we are?'

'Yes, my sister lives out your way.' Rona hesitated. 'Would this afternoon be convenient?'

'I've a meeting at two, but it shouldn't take long – an hour at most.'

'Shall we say three thirty, then?'

'Fine. I look forward to meeting you.'

And I you, Rona thought, replacing the phone. And not only to view the painting; it would be interesting to see for herself the building which was arousing so much curiosity at the moment.

Frances Drew drove out of her gateway and immediately pulled up outside the house next door, giving the arranged two toots on the horn. Every Wednesday she and Lucy drove into Marsborough, where they separated to do their individual shopping before meeting for lunch and arriving home in time to collect the children from school. Today it was her turn to drive, and she glanced expectantly up the Coombeses' path towards their front door. Which, to her surprise, remained shut.

It was unlike Lucy to be late. She tooted again, again without result. With a sigh she switched off the engine, locked the car and walked up the path, giving three quick rings on the bell – another of their identifying signals. When there was still no response she began to wonder if she'd made a mistake. It *was* Wednesday, wasn't it? Lucy hadn't said last week that she wouldn't be able to make it?

She was on the point of returning to the car for her mobile when the door opened at last and Lucy stood in front of her. Frances gasped. Her face was pale, her eyes red-rimmed, but it was the livid bruise on her temple that most alarmed her friend.

'Lucy – what happened? Are you all right?'

Lucy's eyes filled. 'I'm sorry, Fran, I can't come today. I should have—'

Frances moved swiftly inside and, taking her arm, led her down the hall to the kitchen and sat her down at the table, seating herself opposite and reaching for her hand.

'Tell me what happened.'

Lucy shook her head helplessly. 'I don't know,' she whispered.

'Lucy, that bruise. How did you get it?' Then, with dawning horror, 'It wasn't *Kevin?*'

Tears rolled down her cheek. 'It was an accident. I fell, catching my head on the corner of the table.'

'*Why* did you fall?'

Lucy didn't reply. Frances moistened her lips and steeled herself to ask the impossible question. 'Did Kevin hit you, honey?'

Lucy looked up, her eyes anguished. 'He didn't mean to, Fran!'

'But he must have *thought* he had a reason?'

She shook her head. 'It was all so silly,' she whispered, and, as Frances waited for her to continue, went on reluctantly, 'It was about Roger.'

'Roger Crane?'

Lucy nodded. 'You know he can be a bit of a flirt. Kev has always maintained he fancies me, and admittedly he does make a beeline for me at parties and chats me up, but it's only his way. We've laughed about it in the past, but last night – I can't remember how it came up, but Kev suddenly accused me of egging him on, even rather fancying him myself. It was all so *stupid!*'

'And that's why he hit you?'

'He didn't mean to,' Lucy repeated. 'He's ill, Fran – sometimes he doesn't know what he's doing.'

'Sounds like a good excuse,' Frances said tightly.

'No, really! When he saw the bruise, he . . . cried!'

Didn't violent husbands always show remorse – until they did it again? But *Kevin*, of all people!

'I just don't understand it,' Lucy went on brokenly. 'It started out of the blue a few weeks ago, and it's getting worse. Sometimes he looks at me as though he doesn't know who I am, sometimes he doesn't hear when I speak to him. Then, when I repeat it, he swears at me. He's frightened, Fran, and so am I, but he absolutely refuses to see a doctor. I . . . think he's afraid of what he might be told.'

'Does anyone else know about this?'

'No.'

'Would you mind if I told Greg? He might be able to help.'

Lucy raised a hand from the table and let it fall again, which Frances took to be assent. 'In the meantime,' she went on rallyingly, 'there's no point in sitting at home worrying. Go and wash your face, then we'll hit Marsborough and treat ourselves to lunch at the Bacchus. How does that sound?'

And Lucy, unable to think of an excuse, agreed.

As Rona turned into the gateway of Springfield Lodge, she saw that the grass which had been the setting for the photograph had been replaced by a paved parking area. Two or three cars were drawn up, and she pulled in beside them.

The building itself, however, looked unchanged – a handsome Georgian house with a pillared entrance, and its air of solid, understated elegance was carried through into the tiled entrance hall.

Rona paused, looking about her. On her right, through glass doors, was a comfortable-looking lounge where a couple were enjoying afternoon tea, while on the left she glimpsed a panelled room with tables laid for dinner. Immediately ahead, to one side of the imposing staircase, a young woman was surveying her from behind the reception desk.

'Good afternoon, madam. Can I help you?'

'I have an appointment with Mrs Temple,' Rona said.

'Ms Parish?'

'Yes.'

'One moment, please.' She picked up an internal phone, spoke quietly into it, then, replacing it, came round the desk.

'If you'd like to follow me . . .'

She led the way down a short passage to the door at the end, knocked briefly, then opened it and announced, 'Ms Parish, Mrs Temple.'

The room into which Rona stepped appeared part-sitting room, part-office, since in addition to easy chairs and a low table bearing a tea tray, a large desk was positioned against one wall, with a bookcase stuffed with files alongside.

Beryl Temple came quickly to greet her, hand outstretched. 'So pleased to meet you, Ms Parish,' she said with a smile. 'Since we have a subscription to *Chiltern Life*, I almost feel I know you!'

She was a small woman in her early sixties, with short, smartly styled hair and horn-rimmed spectacles. Her cashmere jumper was in a soft lavender shade, her skirt grey flannel, and her shoes Cuban-heeled. Every inch the business woman, Rona thought.

'It's good of you to see me,' she said.

'Not at all. And I expect, without further ado, you'd like to see the painting.'

She gestured down the room to a small framed picture on the wall, and Rona went eagerly to look at it, stopping short with an amused exclamation. She turned apologetically to her hostess.

'I'm sorry: it's absolutely charming, of course, but, from the title, not at all what I was expecting.'

Samson and Delilah proved to be a regal-looking bloodhound and a svelte Burmese cat.

Beryl Temple laughed. 'Of course – it could be misleading.'

Rona leant closer, studying the painting. It bore all the trade-marks of Elspeth's later work – attention to detail, sympathetic treatment of her subjects, fur lifelike enough to be stroked.

'She didn't paint many animals,' Rona remarked. 'In fact, I've only come across one other – of her art teacher's black spaniel.'

A knock on the door heralded the arrival of a young woman bearing a silver teapot and hot water jug, which she set down on the tray and silently withdrew.

'You must have met Elspeth, then?' Rona enquired, as they seated themselves by the fire.

'Sadly, no; my husband's parents knew hers, and I suspect that even though it was before she was well known, a few strings must have been pulled. In any event, it was arranged that she should paint our pets as an anniversary present. My husband supplied several photos, and I believe on a couple of occasions, when he knew I'd be out, she actually came to the house to see them in the flesh and make sketches.'

She glanced fondly down the room. 'I've always loved the painting; she captured the animals perfectly, and it brings them back to life. And, of course, more hard-headedly, it must now be something of an heirloom. My husband refers to it as our pension!'

They talked for several minutes about Elspeth and the tragedy that overtook her, then Rona tentatively brought up the subject of the hotel's past.

'Have you always been in the hotel business?' she began.

'For over twenty years,' Beryl Temple answered, 'the last eight of them here.'

'It's a lovely house. I believe it was once a girls' school?'

Mrs Temple passed her a plate of scones. 'You know, you're the third person in a matter of weeks to refer to that.'

'Oh?'

'First, a gentleman phoned, wanting to know if we knew anything about the school, particularly why it had closed, which it apparently did rather suddenly. I told him I couldn't help, since the house was a nursing home when we took it over, and I knew nothing of any school.'

That would have been Lindsey's friend William, Rona thought. But Mrs Temple was continuing.

'Which was true enough at the time; but by a strange coincidence the wife of a couple staying with us last week used to be a pupil here.'

'Really?' Rona's interest quickened.

'It was quite fascinating; she took us all over the house, telling us what each room had been when she knew it – classrooms, art studios, science labs, and so on.'

'Did *she* know why it had closed?'

'Not really; she heard some of the senior girls had been caught drinking, but that would hardly warrant closing the entire school.'

'No.' Rona thought for a moment. 'Did the man who phoned by any chance mention a photograph?

Mrs Temple looked surprised. 'Of the school you mean?'

'Some pupils and staff, taken out at the front.'

'No, he never mentioned a photo. Why? Was it special in some way?'

'A member of staff had been scratched out, and various people are wondering why.'

'How extraordinary! But why should it have any significance?'

'I really don't know,' Rona said. She'd no intention of launching into the story of William's wife's mother nearly fainting when she saw it.

But having had her curiosity aroused, Beryl Temple was reluctant to let the subject drop.

'Taken out at the front, did you say?'

'Yes, with the house in the background.'

'I'd be most interested to see it. My husband and I have a scrapbook showing the progress of the work we've done on the house – a kind of "before and after". How it was when we took it over, with plywood partitions and hideous washbasins in the bedrooms, then the gradual transformation. It would be fascinating if we could find pictures of when it was a school.'

'This one wouldn't help,' Rona assured her. 'It looks the same as it does now, except there was grass where you have the car park.'

'Ah well, perhaps some others might come to light. Our guest promised to look up old albums when she got home, though I dare say she's forgotten.'

Rona left soon after, having, with Mrs Temple's permission, taken a photograph of the painting for possible inclusion in the bio. At least that part of her visit had been successful, she reflected as she drove home, but she'd learned little of the hotel's previous incarnation.

'I've an odd question for you,' Magda said, as they sat over coffee in the Gallery café.

Rona raised an eyebrow. 'As you know, odd answers are my speciality. Fire away!'

Magda smiled absently, staring down into the cup she was holding with both hands. 'Do you ever dream about people you don't know?'

'All the time. Everyone does.'

'But the *same* people, night after night?'

Rona hesitated. 'Well, I'm not sure about that.'

Magda leant forward. 'They're so *real*, so clearly defined, I feel I *know* them, even though, when I'm awake, I know I don't! It's as though I'm having someone else's dreams. I just wish I knew whose, because I'd like them to stop.'

'Why, what do they do, these people, "night after night"?' Rona asked, her curiosity aroused.

'Nothing much really; things switch around as they usually do in dreams. I'm having a meal with them, or I see them across the road.' She came to an abrupt halt and lowered her voice.

'And that's the crux of it, Rona. Yesterday I *did* see one of them – *really* saw, during the day. It gave me quite a turn.'

'Then obviously you'd seen him or her before, without realizing it, and—'

Magda was shaking her head. 'No, I'm sure not. It's most unnerving. I never used to remember my dreams, but now they linger all day and leave me with an unpleasant kind of feeling.'

'I've always remembered mine,' Rona said. 'If I wrote fiction, they'd be an endless source of material.'

'You don't think . . . there's anything the matter with me?'

'Of course not! No one really understands dreams, Mags. Some people claim they foretell the future—'

'Don't!' Magda shuddered.

'I'm not saying *yours* do, but in any case you don't seem to have dreamt of anything significant.'

'Not yet,' Magda said in a low voice, 'but there's something just below the surface, I'm sure. I'm almost afraid to go to sleep now, in case they . . . progress in some way.'

'That's nonsense!' Rona said roundly. 'Have you spoken to Gavin about it?'

'Yes, but he already knew, because I keep waking him. What makes it worse is that I suffered from nightmares for years as a child, and I'm terrified of slipping back into them.'

'Then take a short course of sedatives, just to break the routine. They'll ensure you both get a good night's sleep.'

'It's an idea, certainly.' Magda looked at her watch. 'I must go; I've a meeting at eleven. Thanks for coming at short notice, Rona. I just . . . needed to talk about it.'

'Any time,' Rona said. 'But I'm sure there's nothing to worry about.'

Back in her study, Rona transferred the picture of Samson and Delilah from her BlackBerry to her computer, and sat staring at it. Odd, in the circumstances, that it should have surfaced at Springfield Lodge. Her eyes slid to the black–and–white photograph, still propped against her pen holder.

On impulse, she caught up the phone and rang the mobile number of Tess Chadwick, a reporter for the *Stokely Gazette*.

'Hi, Rona!' came Tess's throaty tones. 'Stumbled over any dead bodies lately?'

'Thankfully not,' Rona replied. 'I have a more mundane question for you: do you have any school photos in your archives?'

'Probably. What date are you thinking?'

'1951.'

'Blimey – the dark ages!'

'Well, that's what archives are for, isn't it? To shed some light on them?'

'We've nothing here that goes that far back, but you could try the county archives in Buckford. Or, of course, take the easy way and surf the Net.' She paused. 'Why the sudden interest in school photos?'

'Just that someone's trying to identify the people in one.'

'Well, sorry, that's the best I can offer.'

'Thanks, Tess. I'll look on line.'

But she wouldn't, Rona decided, ending the call. She'd wasted enough time on that photograph, which wasn't really of interest anyway, and most probably just the work of a disgruntled schoolgirl.

She picked it up, looked at it one last time, then slid it into her desk drawer. She'd give it back to Lindsey next time she saw her. With a sense of relief, she turned instead to her computer screen, meeting the soulful eyes of 'Samson'. She'd write up this painting, while it was still fresh in her mind.

Clicking on the file in question, she settled down to work.

'Daniel?'

'Ma – hello! How are you?'

'I'm well, thank you. Are you at home, by any chance? I've been trying to reach Jenny, but I keep getting the answerphone.'

'No, actually I'm in Birmingham.' He hesitated. 'And Jenny isn't home, either. She's staying with her parents for a week or two.'

Catherine's hands tightened on the phone. 'A *week* or two?'

An echo of his own reaction, Daniel thought wryly. 'Yes; things were getting her down a bit, and we thought it would be good for her to have a break.'

Catherine said carefully, 'She is . . . all right, isn't she?'

'Yes, just, as I say, a bit run-down.'

'What about the shop?'

'She's taken leave. They were quite amenable; Mothers' Day's over and there's a lull until Easter.'

'So you're on your own for the moment?'

'When I'm home.' He gave a short laugh. 'Which, as Jenny pointed out, isn't all that often at the moment.'

There was a brief pause. Had Daniel found out about Paul? Catherine wondered anxiously. Had he and Jenny had a row of some kind? It must be serious, for her to flee to her parents.

She cleared her throat. 'The reason I was phoning was to invite you all for the weekend. I hope you at least can come?'

'Oh Ma, I'm sorry. I'll be going up to Cheshire.'

'Of course.' That, at least, was a relief; communications must still be open. 'When shall I see you, then?'

'Well, I'm meeting someone in Marsborough next week, so—'

'You can stay the night? Better than either a hotel or an empty house!'

'Indeed it is! Thanks, that'd be great. I'm not sure which day yet, but I can let you know after the weekend, if that's all right?'

'Quite all right. I'll look forward to seeing you.'

Catherine put down the phone. When she saw him she'd be able to tell much better how things stood, but she must be careful not to give the impression of suspecting something was wrong. And at least he'd be seeing Jenny over the weekend. Perhaps, she thought on a sudden surge of hope, her daughter-in-law had come to her senses and decided to put some distance not between herself and Daniel, but herself and Paul. Which could only be a good thing.

Feeling determinedly more cheerful, Catherine switched on the television and settled down to watch the news.

'I was speaking to Barnie the other day,' Rona commented to Max on Friday evening. 'Dinah's getting uptight about Mel's baby, which is due in a couple of months. I said we'd invite them for a meal, to take her mind off it.'

'Fine,' said Max from behind his newspaper.

'So, when shall we make it? Have you any preference? A Friday or a weekend?'

Resignedly he put the paper down. 'Depends if you're thinking of lunch or an evening meal. But I hope the occasion won't be dominated by baby talk!'

'I'll try to get it over quickly. According to Barnie, Mel insists she's fine, but Dinah's ready to pack her bags and fly out at a moment's notice.'

'Go for Friday, then, and leave the weekend free. We've nothing on next week, have we?'

'Not so far. OK, I'll suggest a week today.'

'Barnie's not trying to wheedle you back to *Chiltern Life*, is he?' Max asked idly. 'That's not why he phoned you?'

'No, actually I phoned him. About the school photo.'

'What school photo?'

'The one Lindsey gave me, of course. The one she rang up about last week. You were there at the time.'

'I make a point of not listening when you talk to Lindsey. Anyway, I was cooking dinner. Come to think of it, though, I did hear something about a school where your mother's friends went.'

'Yes, Springfield Lodge, which is now a hotel. I told you I went there myself on Wednesday.'

'To see one of Elspeth's paintings, yes. But you never mentioned a photo.'

'Well, it's no big deal. Someone at Lindsey's book group gave it to her to see if she could identify anyone – or rather, if I could.' She pulled a face. 'My reputation going before me.'

'An old photo?'

'Yes, 1951. Why I should be expected to do any better than anyone else, I can't imagine. Still, I'm not going to bother any more.'

'So what was so special about it?'

'One of the staff had been rather viciously inked out, and the woman who owned it, and who has since died, nearly had a heart attack when she saw it again. Her daughter, whose husband is in Lindsey's book group, is curious to know why.'

'And Barnie couldn't help?'

'No, and nor could Tess. She suggested I try the Internet.'

'Surely, in this day and age, the family concerned have already done that?'

'They looked up the school, yes, but couldn't find any trace of it. I don't know if they looked for photographers; I'll suggest it to Lindsey, but I'm not going to waste any more time on it. I'm trying to concentrate on Elspeth, and at the moment I'm being distracted on all sides, what with Lindsey and the photo, and Magda and her dreams.'

'Magda's dreams? You're talking in riddles this evening!'

'We met for coffee, as I told you. She's been dreaming of people she doesn't know, as we all do, but now she's freaked out because she saw someone in the street whom she'd dreamt about and didn't think she knew. I told her to take sleeping pills.'

'Good advice,' said Max, and retired again behind his paper.

SIX

Dominic Frayne stood at his penthouse window, staring over the sloping green of the park to the roofs and steeples of Marsborough beyond.

In the bed behind him, Carla Deighton, his personal assistant, stretched her arms above her head. 'What kind of day is it?'

'Glorious,' he replied without turning. 'Not a cloud in the sky.'

'And it's Saturday. Are you seeing Lindsey?'

'Yes, I'm flying her over to France.'

'Just as well she can't see us now!'

'I'm not married to her,' Dominic said shortly.

Carla had worked for him for almost eight years, making herself indispensable in both his business and private life; it was she who bought cards for his ex-wives and reminded him of his offspring's birthdays. Occasionally they spent the night together, usually when he was fraught over a business deal, often while they were abroad. And, crucially, when she left him the following morning, their relationship instantly reverted to employer and employee and the incident was never mentioned. He had come to value what he regarded as these therapeutic sessions; they enjoyed each other's bodies, and there were no emotional complications.

The arrangement suited Carla equally well. She liked and admired her employer, finding him stimulating both mentally and physically, and these infrequent comings together augmented her own sporadic and discreet affairs. In the past, she'd booked many a romantic weekend for Dominic and his current mistress, but she was aware that, although he was not one to commit himself, his relationship with Lindsey Parish was of a different order. Consequently she'd been surprised when, the previous evening, he'd phoned down to her flat on the floor below and invited her upstairs. She'd wondered if things between him and Lindsey weren't working out, but his plans for the weekend seemed to discount that.

Hers not to speculate, she thought philosophically, and, sliding her feet to the floor, reached for her clothes. Her shower would, as always, be taken in her own flat.

At the bedroom door she paused, looking back. Dominic was still at the window, his mood hard to gauge.

'Have a good weekend,' she said.

'What's this – an example of modern art?'

Clive Gregory, about to open the fridge, had paused to survey the picture held to its door by magnets. It depicted a square house with a slightly off-centre roof, in front of which stood four stick figures, laboriously and unevenly labelled 'Mummy, Daddy, Me, Archie'.

Sarah Lacey, coming up behind him, laughed. 'Pretty traditional, isn't it? It's amazing how kids of all generations produce identical artwork at the age of five or six. In this case, the artist is Ben Coombes. Do you know him? His mother, Lucy, is on the PTA, and they live just round the corner. I know I'm not allowed favourites, but if I were, Ben would definitely be top of the list.'

'Yes, I know Ben – an engaging kid.' Clive was a sports master at the same school. He opened the fridge door and took out a bottle of milk. 'So, what's on the cards today?'

Sarah sobered. 'I promised Dad we'd go over to Stokely and see what furniture and stuff he's earmarked for me. I've been putting it off, because I don't want to see the old place stripped of everything that made it home, but he's anxious now to empty it.'

'We haven't room for any more furniture,' Clive said doubtfully.

'Not here, no, but we won't be here for ever, and there are things I definitely want to keep. We can put what we choose in storage, separate from Dad and Avril's.'

'Will they be there too?' Clive asked, pouring out his cereal.

'No, they can't do any more till we've been. It's better by ourselves, anyway; it'll give us time to think up a tactful excuse, if we don't want everything he's put aside.'

'OK' said Clive equably, 'you're the boss.'

It had been a wonderful weekend, Lindsey thought contentedly, as Dominic's chauffeur-driven Daimler drew up outside Richmond

House, where he had his flat. Having left her car there the previous day, she would spend the night with him and go straight on to work the next morning.

'So,' he said, a little later, handing her a drink and settling beside her on the sofa, 'what did you enjoy the most?'

'Hard to say,' she replied, 'it was all perfect.'

A hired car had met their early flight, and having arranged to meet the pilot at five the next evening, they'd driven to Honfleur to find the Saturday market in full swing – glowing piles of fruit and vegetables, fish, chickens, eggs, and all the dairy produce for which Normandy was famous. To Dominic's amusement, Lindsey had insisted on buying a selection of cheeses and some butter for good measure.

She had been charmed by the picturesque port, the ships with their coloured sails, and the tall, slate-fronted houses, familiar from paintings by Monet and Boudin. They had visited old churches, wandered round the Musée Boudin, dined regally on superlative seafood, and made love in a hotel that looked like a chateau.

'It was all perfect,' she repeated, adding, 'That's the second time we've been to Normandy; is it your favourite part of France?'

'Not necessarily, but being a mere hop across the Channel it's ideal for a day out or a weekend visit.'

'Romantic or otherwise?' she asked teasingly.

'As you say.'

'I bet I'm not the first you've taken there!'

He smiled and sipped his drink, piquing her curiosity.

'Am I?' she persisted.

'What do you want me to say?'

'The truth!'

'Then no, I have to say you're not.' *And won't be the last* seemed to hang in the air between them.

Lindsey bit her lip. 'No doubt,' she said tightly, 'all efficiently arranged by the inestimable Carla?'

Dominic shrugged. It was true this was normal practice, and though on this occasion he'd made the bookings himself, he was damned if he was going to tell her.

Lindsey stared mutinously into her wine glass. She'd always

been jealous of Carla – cool, blonde, unflappable, and – even more unforgivably – close to Dominic. From a remark he'd made in the early days, she'd gathered they'd occasionally slept together, and though she'd assumed this intimacy to be in the past, it seemed suddenly imperative to confirm it.

'Have you ever taken her?' she demanded abruptly.

There was a pause. Then: 'To France? Many times, on business. And to Italy, Germany—'

'On a romantic weekend?'

He raised an eyebrow. 'Is it any of your business?'

Ignoring the warning note in his voice, Lindsey persisted. 'Yes, I think it is.'

'Don't do this, Lindsey,' he said quietly.

'But I'm interested to know. After all, you told me yourself you've slept with her.' She turned to him, incipient jealousy, combined with tiredness and too much wine, sweeping caution aside. 'So tell me: when was the last time?'

For a long moment their eyes held, while Lindsey's blood rushed in her ears and she wished, frantically, uselessly, that she could retract the question. Too late.

'Friday night,' he said flatly.

For a wild moment, she thought she had misheard. '*What* did you say?'

'I said Friday night.'

'*Last* Friday?' Her voice rose. 'You're telling me you slept with Carla the night before you made love to me?'

'You did ask,' he said stonily, and watched the emotions cross her face in quick succession: disbelief, incredulity, hurt, anger.

'But . . . what about us?' she stammered.

'What *about* us?'

'Don't you love me?' she cried.

A spasm crossed his face. 'I'm very fond of you,' he said more gently, 'as you must know. But we haven't an exclusivity agreement, have we?'

For a moment longer she stared at him. Then she stood up and laid her glass carefully on the coffee table.

He frowned. 'Where are you going?'

'Home,' she said.

'Lindsey, let's get this in proportion. As you said, you knew—'

'That you'd slept with her, yes. Not that you were still doing so.'

She turned to the door, and he rose quickly. 'For God's sake, sit down again. Things will look different in the morning. Anyway, you're in no state to drive.'

'I've had less than half a glass.' She was mildly surprised at the calmness of her voice. Her suitcase was still in the hall and she bent to pick it up.

'Now, yes, but at lunch—'

'Will you ask for my car to be brought round?'

He hesitated, but she waited, unmoving, and he picked up the internal phone and rang the basement garage. 'This is Dominic Frayne. Would you please bring round Miss Parish's car?'

'I'll make my own way down,' she said, pressing the lift button.

'You'll do no such thing. And if you insist on leaving, I think I should drive you.'

She gave a twisted smile. 'You've had more to drink than I have.'

He couldn't deny it. 'Lindsey—'

But the lift arrived, its doors glided open, and, taking the case out of her hand, he followed her inside. They rode down in silence. As they reached the foyer, Lindsey's red sports car drew up to the front entrance. Dominic went out with her and handed her case to the attendant, who placed it in the boot.

'Are you sure you want to go?'

'Positive.' She looked up at him, her eyes brilliant. 'Thanks for the weekend. I hope I wasn't an anticlimax.'

And before he could reply, she gunned the engine and the car shot forward in a spray of gravel. Dominic stood watching until her tail lights turned the corner, then, with a sigh, went back into the building.

Rona and Max had just sat down to watch a DVD when there was a prolonged ring on the front doorbell, followed immediately by impatient knocking. Gus, who'd been asleep on the rug, shot up and started barking.

Max paused the DVD, frowning. 'Who the devil is that, at nine o'clock on a Sunday evening?'

'In a hurry, whoever it is,' Rona commented, as he went to answer it. A minute later, to her surprise, Lindsey appeared in the doorway, her face flushed.

'Linz! I thought you were in France?'

'Just back,' said Lindsey briefly. 'Sorry to drop in on you like this. Is it OK if I stay for a bit?'

Behind her, Max raised his shoulders in puzzlement.

'Of course,' Rona said quickly. 'Can we get you a drink? Tea? Coffee?'

'Gin,' said Lindsey succinctly.

Max went to pour it, and she seated herself next to Rona on the sofa, glancing at the frozen figures on the screen.

'I'm interrupting,' she said. 'Please go on watching.'

'It'll keep,' Rona replied, reaching for the remote, but her sister interrupted her.

'Really. I'm perfectly happy just to sit here and . . . watch.' She took the glass Max handed her with an absent-minded smile.

Max said smoothly, 'In that case, since it's only just started, I'll rewind it so you can see it from the beginning.'

Lindsey nodded and took a gulp of her drink. 'Cheers!' she said belatedly.

For the next hour and a half, unable to concentrate on the film, Rona kept stealing anxious glances at her twin. Lindsey's eyes were fixed on the screen. She laughed and exclaimed in the right places, but Rona doubted that she was following the plot any more than she was.

As the credits began to roll, Max stood up. 'I'll take Gus for his walk,' he said, and left the room, the dog dancing at his heels.

There was a moment's silence, then Lindsey said fervently, 'God, I wish I smoked!'

'Are you going to tell me what's wrong?' Rona asked quietly.

Lindsey looked down at her tightly clasped hands. 'He's sleeping with bloody Carla,' she said.

'Oh, Linz!' Rona reached out impulsively, but, as Lindsey backed away, let her hand drop, accepting that physical contact might breach her twin's fragile defences. 'How do you know?' she asked tentatively.

'Because he told me.'

Rona stared at her. 'He just . . . came out with it?'

'No, he told me because I asked him.'

Rona looked bewildered. 'But you did go to France?'

'Oh yes. We had a lovely time. But when we got home, I found out that he'd slept with Carla on Friday night, before taking me to France on Saturday and sleeping with *me*.' Her voice cracked. 'You can imagine how . . . how . . . *special* that made me feel.'

'Linz—'

Lindsey cut her off with a gesture. 'I was going to drive home, but once in the car I found I wasn't quite . . . up to it. So I came here.'

'Would you like Max to take you back?'

'I'd rather stay the night, if that's OK? I've got my work clothes with me, because I was going straight there from Dominic's in the morning.'

It was the first time she'd said his name, and there was a tremor in her voice.

Rona said doubtfully, 'Well, you're welcome, of course, but as you know, we haven't a spare room.'

'If you could just put up the camp bed in Max's studio, like you did before?'

Lindsey had stayed with them a few months earlier while her flat was being redecorated. 'I don't need all the mod cons,' she added quickly, 'the lamp and the dress rack and stuff. It'll only be for tonight.'

'Well, if you're sure . . .'

'I couldn't even make a dramatic gesture and ask him to choose between us,' Lindsey continued, 'because I know damn well who he'd pick. She's so much a part of his business life, he'd never let her go. And if by any wild chance we *did* get back together – which is unlikely in the extreme – I'd always be wondering. Even if we were *married*,' she added savagely, 'and had what he terms an *exclusivity agreement*, I could never be completely sure.' She looked up, meeting her sister's sympathetic eyes. 'So you do see how hopeless it is, Ro? We're finished. There's no going back after this.'

'Did you tell him so?' Rona enquired.

'Not in so many words, but I think he got the message.'
'He'll probably phone, or call round, or something.'
'He probably won't,' said Lindsey.

Eight thirty on Monday morning. Max had left for his studio and Lindsey for her office, still shying away from the hug her twin was aching to give her.

Rona stood in the large empty space that, before they bought Farthings, had been Max's studio. Old canvases were still stacked against one wall, suitcases, a picnic hamper and rolls of carpet against another. And in the centre, as though marooned on some desert island, the hastily erected camp bed, whose crumpled sheets and dented pillow spoke of a restless night.

Rona felt a surge of pity for her sister, albeit tinged with impatience. *Why* was Lindsey's love life always so fraught? Was she simply unlucky, or did she bring these regular heartaches on herself? What was it her mother had said? *That girl never had any sense where men are concerned.* Rona conceded that she was right.

She sighed, shook herself out of her retrospection, and, pulling the sheets off the bed, dismantled it and stood it back in its corner. Order restored, she thought ironically, looking about her. Then, scooping up the bedlinen, she started down the stairs; but had gained only the first floor landing when the telephone rang. Dropping the sheets, she went into her study to answer it. 'Hello?'

'Rona.' To her surprise, it was Gavin's voice and she felt a shaft of alarm. 'Look,' he hurried on, before she could reply, 'I know this is an ungodly hour, but I'm on my way to work and I need a quick word with you.'

'Yes?'

'Not over the phone. OK if I pop in for a minute? I'm just turning into Fullers Walk.'

'Of course,' Rona said quickly. 'Gavin, is Magda—?'

'Be there in two minutes,' he said, and rang off.

Obscurely anxious, Rona retrieved the bedlinen and ran down the two remaining flights to the basement kitchen, where, having dumped it beside the washing machine, she switched on the percolator. He'd seemed in a hurry, but he might have time for coffee. Her unease at his imminent arrival was, she knew, not wholly on Magda's account; before she'd met Max, she and Gavin had been on the point of becoming engaged, and though both were now happily married, there was still a faint, unacknowledged link between them that sometimes caused awkwardness in each other's company.

She poured coffee into two mugs and carried them up to the sitting room, setting them on the coffee table as the bell rang. She went to answer it, accompanied, as always, by Gus, barking hysterically.

'Gavin, hello. Come in.' She accepted his kiss on the cheek, and gestured him into the sitting room. 'You've time for a coffee?'

'If it's ready, I'd love some.' He bent to pat the dog. 'Hello, old fellow.'

He looked tired, Rona thought, surveying him critically. There were lines round his eyes and smudges beneath them. He took the mug she handed him, nodding his thanks.

'Sit down,' she invited.

He did so, and she seated herself opposite him. 'Now, tell me what's wrong.'

'Have you seen Magda recently?' he asked abruptly.

'Yes, last week.'

He looked up, meeting her eyes. 'How did she seem?'

'Fine; why?'

'Did she mention these dreams she's been having?'

Rona's unease spread. 'Yes,' she admitted slowly. 'Always about the same people, whom she doesn't know.' She hesitated. 'She thought she saw one of them locally the other day; I . . . told her she must have seen him before without realizing it.'

Gavin nodded and took a sip of the hot coffee. 'I said much the same. But Rona, it's not only the dreams.'

'How do you mean?'

'Well, for one thing she seems different in herself, more . . . unpredictable. As you know, she could always be pretty cutting when she wanted and she's never suffered fools gladly. But lately . . . I don't know . . . she seems to fly off the handle for no reason at all.' He paused, then added almost reluctantly, 'And though I tell myself there can't be a connection, she told me she wakes up from these dreams feeling angry. It's almost as though they're spilling over into everyday life.'

'Has she extra worries at work, do you know?'

'I don't think so. In fact, considering the economic climate the boutiques are doing exceptionally well. But there's another thing: she's started . . . remembering things that haven't happened. Only a couple of times, but it scared the hell out of me.'

Rona moistened her lips, her own coffee untouched. 'What kind of things?'

'The first one was pretty innocuous; she started talking about a film she insisted we'd seen together. I'd certainly never seen it, but I couldn't convince her, and when I suggested she must have been with someone else, she became quite upset.'

There was a brief silence. Rona said, not entirely truthfully, 'I'm always accusing Max of doing or saying something he swears he hasn't.'

Gavin nodded absently and gulped down some more coffee. 'But last night it was much worse. We were watching a documentary on TV about Hong Kong's floating market, and she suddenly said, "It doesn't look as good as the one in Thailand, does it? Remember the houses on stilts and that fabulous wood-carving workshop, where they made elephants and buffalo out of rotten wood?"

'I said I'd not seen that programme, and she said, quite sharply, "What do you mean, programme? I'm talking about when we were *there*, in Thailand."' He looked up, his eyes haunted. 'Rona, neither of us has been to Thailand in our lives.'

'It must have been another documentary, as you—'

Gavin was shaking his head. 'She went on and on about it, about the wonderful furniture they'd made – dining suites with elephants' heads carved in the backs of the chairs, and how we'd joked about the difficulty of getting them home on the plane. I was getting more and more worried, and she finally stopped arguing and said accusingly, "You think I'm making this up, don't you? But you're the one who can't remember!" Then – God help me – I said, "Perhaps you dreamt it?"

'I could have bitten my tongue out, because she immediately went still, her eyes wide and staring. Then she jumped up and ran out of the room, and the next minute I heard the front door slam and the car start up. I ran after her, but she'd shot out of the gate and away. I rang her mobile continuously for fifteen minutes before she picked up.'

'What did she say?' Rona demanded fearfully.

'Oh, she was perfectly calm. Said she'd just felt like a drive before bed, and she'd be back in half an hour. And she was.'

'And the subject wasn't referred to?'

'Not on your life! She acted as though nothing had happened, and I certainly wasn't going to risk bringing it up again. But Rona, she ought to see a doctor. How the hell can I convince her of that?'

'God, Gavin, I don't know. Have you spoken to anyone else?'

'No; I didn't want to alarm her parents, and I know the two of you are close. I was hoping she might have said something that could explain it.'

'Afraid not.'

He made a helpless gesture. 'I'm sorry to spring this on you, but I lay awake all last night, wondering what the hell I could do. I'm just . . . terrified she's . . . losing her mind or something.'

'Oh Gavin, I'm so sorry. I don't know what to say.'

He brushed a hand across his eyes. 'Could you arrange to meet her? See if she'll talk to you, when she won't – or can't – to me? I keep wondering what she'll "remember" next, and what it might lead to.'

'She mustn't know we've discussed her,' Rona warned.

'Perish the thought!' He smiled bleakly. 'Could you suddenly decide you need a new outfit? Suggest meeting at one of the boutiques and having lunch after? That way you'd see her in two different environments, which might help you to form a judgement.'

'I still think you should have a word with her father.'

'I will, but see how she strikes you first. Please.' He glanced at his watch and came quickly to his feet. 'I must go.'

'Of course I'll see her,' Rona said. 'Try not to worry; there must be some logical explanation.'

'You're an angel. Thank you.' He gave her a quick, hard hug.

'Do you know where she's working today?' Rona asked, as she walked with him to the door.

'Here in Marsborough, I think.'

'That makes life easier! I'll call in, then.'

'Bless you, Rona. I really am grateful.'

'I'll report back as soon as I've seen her.'

He nodded, then hurried down the path and, with a quick wave at the gate, turned in the direction of his car. So now she had Magda as well as Lindsey to worry about, Rona thought resignedly, as she closed the door.

'How was France?' Carla asked casually, as she laid the morning's post on Dominic's desk.

'French,' he replied briefly. 'Could you get me Donaldson on the phone? I want to chase him about the Sanderson business.'

'Of course.' It would seem, she thought to herself as she left the room, that everything in the *jardin* was no longer *belle*. And she couldn't help wondering if Lindsey had somehow got wind of Friday's frolics. If so, Dominic had only himself to blame; she'd warned him often enough. It would be interesting, though, to see how long it would take him before he mentioned Lindsey Parish again. If, indeed, he ever did.

Stretford Row was Marsborough's answer to Bond Street, a road leading off Guild Street full of designer boutiques, expensive shoe shops and top-of-the-range leather goods, frequented by its more well-heeled residents.

Rona had judged her arrival to fit in with the suggestion of lunch afterwards. The problem was that, as in her other boutiques, Magda had introduced a small café at the back of the premises that offered coffee, light lunches or afternoon tea. She'd be unlikely, Rona felt, to open up when surrounded by her staff and customers.

Having tied Gus's lead to the post outside, she entered the shop with mentally crossed fingers, hoping Gavin was right and this was indeed where Magda was based today. Thankfully, she caught sight of her immediately and for a brief moment was able to study her unobserved. To the casual onlooker she must seem her usual efficient self, but knowing her as she did, Rona could detect underlying tension.

Then Magda looked up, saw her, and came hurrying over.

'Rona! This is an unexpected pleasure! How can I help?'

'I've decided to treat myself,' Rona said. 'I've been looking at my spring and summer clothes and decided I'm tired of the lot of them!'

'That's very welcome news!'

'For the moment, though, I'm limiting myself to one new item, and what I need most is a light, summer-weight jacket. Can you help?'

'I'm quite sure we can,' Magda declared, and led her over to a rail crammed with jackets of every description.

The next half-hour was taken up with trying on a selection and eventually choosing a loose-fitting jacket in pale green linen. The time, Rona noted surreptitiously, was just after twelve thirty.

While it was being wrapped in layers of tissue paper, she said artlessly, 'Can you spare the time for a spot of lunch?' And as Magda automatically glanced towards the back of the shop, she added quickly, 'For some reason, I really fancy a pizza!' Which, she knew, was not on *Magdalena*'s menu.

Magda hesitated. 'Can't I tempt you to a quiche instead? We have—'

'Humour me, Magda! After all, I've just added considerably to your coffers!'

Magda smiled in capitulation. 'Far be it from me to deny you your pizza! I think I can manage a quick trip to the Gallery.'

The Gallery café was almost directly opposite Stretford Row, a fact Rona had relied on, and having retrieved Gus, they walked together down the road and across Guild Street in the warm spring sunshine. During the past forty minutes or so there'd been little in Magda's manner to give cause for concern, and Rona had begun to hope that Gavin might be overreacting.

But as they settled at their table and Gus curled up beneath it, it was Magda herself who raised the subject.

'Actually,' she began, knotting her hands together, 'I'm glad to have the chance of a talk.'

'Oh?'

'Remember, last time we were here, I told you about my dreams?'

'Yes?'

'Well, they've been getting worse.'

'The sleeping pills didn't help?'

Magda shook her head. 'And it's odd, Rona, I seem to have a very short fuse these days. I'm always letting fly for no real reason, and usually with Gavin, bless him. I don't seem able to help myself.'

'Is anything else worrying you?'

She didn't answer, and in the pause, the waitress came to take their order and went away again.

'Magda?' Rona prompted.

She said in a low voice, 'I don't seem able to distinguish any more between dreams and reality. Sometimes I'm *sure* something's happened, or we've been somewhere, and Gavin says not.' She bit her lip.

Rona said gently, 'Might it help if you went to see someone?'

Magda's head reared up. 'A psychiatrist, you mean? You think I'm going mad?'

'Mags, seeing a psychiatrist doesn't mean you're mad! Americans do it all the time!'

'Well, I'm not American.'

'But you realize you need help, don't you? That's why you're telling me about it.'

'I'm telling you,' Magda said bitterly, 'because I was hoping you'd say it was nothing to worry about, like you did last time.'

'Well, I'm sorry. That's what I thought last week, but if things are . . . escalating, then it's only sensible to do something about it. Go to your GP and see what he suggests. He could put you in touch with someone.'

'Oh *God*!' Magda said. 'I can't spare the time to be ill – there's too much to do!'

'But if you go on worrying about it, it will only get worse. Much better to get it sorted out now.'

'You think it *can* be sorted out?'

'Of course it can!' Rona said staunchly. 'It'll probably turn out to be a well-known condition.'

Their pizzas arrived, and she drew a cautious breath of relief. She had done what was required of her, and hopefully Magda would follow her advice. Now she was free to change the subject and enjoy her meal.

In Belmont, Avril and Guy were sitting over a leisurely supper. Sarah and Clive had been to Stokely at the weekend and earmarked the items she would like to keep from her old home. Everything that needed to be sorted out had now been attended to, and tomorrow the removal men would complete the process.

'Are you sure you don't want me to come with you?' Avril asked.

'No, love, there's nothing you can do. It's just a question of supervising the removal, making sure everything goes where it's supposed to go, then locking up and depositing the key with the estate agents. But I don't mind telling you I'll be glad when it's over.'

'I know I'll feel sad when the time comes to leave here,' she said quietly. 'There are so many memories.'

Before Guy could comment, his mobile started ringing.

'Who on earth can it be at this hour?' he asked rhetorically, rising from the table and retrieving it from his jacket pocket. He glanced at the display panel. 'It's Sarah,' he said in surprise. 'Hello, sweetie, what—'

'Dad!' Her voice was shaking, and he instinctively stiffened. 'Can you come round to the flat? Now?'

'Sweetheart, what is it? Are you all right? What's happened?'

There was an agonizing pause. Then her voice, almost unrecognizable, reached him. 'Someone I know has just been murdered!'

SEVEN

Sarah and Clive lived the other side of Belmont, a seven-minute drive from Avril's home. During the journey, Guy's imagination had covered and discounted every possible murder candidate, and his alarm escalated as, just short of their flat, he passed a couple of parked police cars.

Screeching to a halt in front of their building, he saw Sarah waiting for him, silhouetted against the open door of the flat. She started down the path and they met halfway, Guy catching her as she half-fell against him.

'You're all right, darling? And Clive?'

She nodded against his chest. 'Yes – oh, Daddy it was *awful*!'

'Suppose we go inside, and you can tell me?'

He led her gently up the path, to where Clive was waiting.

'Sorry to drag you out at this time,' he said.

'The police cars up the road . . .?'

Clive nodded.

'Who . . .?'

'It's Lucy Coombes,' Sarah said, and burst into tears.

'Lucy?' Guy repeated, bewildered, as they all moved into the living room. 'Should I know her?'

Clive shook his head. 'She's one of the parents from school,' he explained. 'Her little boy's in Sarah's class.'

'Perhaps you'd better start at the beginning.'

Sarah sat down and dried her eyes. 'Ben didn't come to school today,' she began. 'I was surprised, because Lucy always phones if he's ill, and he was fine yesterday.' She choked to a halt, steadied herself, and continued.

'As I said, I was surprised, but certainly not worried. He'd come top in a test we did on Monday and won a star, and as I pass their house on the way home, I decided to take it round for him, and see how he was.'

She drew a deep breath. 'There was a staff meeting after school so I was later than usual, but it was only about five o'clock, and when I reached their house the first thing I noticed was that the curtains were all drawn, upstairs as well as down. Then I saw bottles of milk on the step. They were from the same dairy as ours, so I knew they'd have been delivered at about six this morning. That was when I really started to worry. I phoned Clive at home, and he came round to join me. We rang the bell and knocked, but there was no answer, and since the curtains were drawn, we couldn't see inside.

'We were wondering what to do when a car pulled into the drive next door. The neighbour, who we later learned was Frances Drew, looked surprised to see us there, so I explained we were from the school and that Ben hadn't been in today, and asked if she knew if anything was wrong.

'When she saw the milk and the curtains, she was worried too. It turned out she had their key, so she collected it from her own house and we waited while she opened the Coombeses' front door and called Lucy. When there was no reply, she asked us if we'd go in with her – for moral support, I suppose.'

Sarah's fingers tightened on the handkerchief she was holding, and it was Clive who continued.

'The sitting room looked as though they'd just left it to go up to bed. The cushions on the sofa were still dented, and a copy of yesterday's paper lay on the floor. There were mugs on the table, with coffee dregs in them.

'In the kitchen, pans were piled in the sink, presumably from last night, waiting to be washed. It was . . . like the *Mary Celeste.*'

He sat down next to Sarah, taking her hand. 'So . . . we went upstairs, still calling her name.' He cleared his throat. 'She was lying on the bedroom floor, and it was . . . obvious that she was dead. There was no sign of anyone else, but the boys' beds had been slept in. The covers were thrown back, and there was . . . a teddy bear on the floor.'

'God!' Guy said under his breath.

Sarah had started to tremble. 'I don't understand it!' she said on a high note. 'They were a devoted family – everyone said so. It *couldn't* have been Kevin, but then where *is* he, and where are the boys? God, Dad, they're only five and three! You don't think whoever killed Lucy would kill them too?'

'I'm sure they'll turn up safe and well,' Guy said firmly,

though he was sure of no such thing. 'Go on; what did you do next?'

'Frances just . . . went to pieces,' Sarah said shakily. 'She was screaming and crying and trying to get to Lucy, but Clive insisted she didn't touch anything. We took her back next door, and he phoned the police while she rang her husband.

'Then the police arrived, and because we'd been first on the scene, we had to wait till we could be interviewed separately, in case one of us remembered something different. A policewoman sat with us, so we weren't able to discuss it. Frances's husband arrived home, but they wouldn't let him see her. We could hear him shouting in the hall, and Frances started crying again. It was . . . like a nightmare, when you try to wake up, and can't.'

Guy leant forward. 'You say you knew at once Lucy was dead. *How*, when you didn't feel for a pulse? Was there . . . any blood?'

Sarah shook her head. 'Not that we could see, but it was her face . . . her eyes. They were *open*.' She shuddered to a halt, covering her own face.

'I'm sorry, darling,' Guy said contritely. 'I was just wondering if there was any clue as to how she might have died.'

There was a brief silence, then Clive said awkwardly, 'I appreciate there's nothing you can do, but Sarah just . . . wanted to see you.'

'Of course. I'm glad you phoned. What happens now, do you know?'

'We have to go to the police station in the morning and sign our statements. We might also have our fingerprints taken for elimination, though actually we didn't touch anything in the house, and Frances only touched the front door.' He hesitated. 'It's a bit late, I suppose, but I really feel I should let the Head know, and preferably before the news gets out.'

Guy looked at his watch. It was just after eleven o'clock. 'I think you should phone now,' he said. 'Who is the Head?'

'Miss Rawlings.'

'You have her number?'

'I can find it quickly enough.'

'Then you go and do that. I'll wait with Sarah.' Guy glanced at his daughter, who was winding the crumpled handkerchief back and forth between her fingers. 'Have you any sleeping pills?' he asked her.

She shook her head.

'Then I suggest a glass of brandy. You need something to knock you out for the night.'

'I keep seeing her face, Dad,' Sarah said sombrely, 'and then remembering her at school, laughing and full of fun. It just doesn't seem . . . *fair!*'

'Murder seldom is,' Guy said, and immediately thought how trite it sounded.

She put a hand over his. 'Thanks for coming. Clive was wonderful, but I needed you.'

'That's good to know.'

Clive came back into the room. 'Poor woman, she's very shaken,' he said, 'and, of course, desperately worried about Ben and his little brother.'

'Do they both go to the school?' Guy asked.

'No,' Sarah said, 'Archie's still at play school. He comes with Lucy, though, when she collects Ben.' It seemed too soon to use the past tense.

Guy looked up at Clive, still standing uncertainly by the door. 'Have you any brandy?'

He shook his head. 'There's some whisky, which Dad drinks when he visits us.'

'Then I suggest you both have some, to help you sleep. If there's nothing I can do, I should be going; Avril will be worrying. I have to go to Stokely tomorrow to meet the removal men, but I'll phone when I get back. You might have some news by then.'

He stood up, and Sarah with him. 'Try not to worry about the children,' he said quietly. 'If it *was* her husband, and he meant to kill them too, he'd have done it at the same time. He's most unlikely to hurt them now.'

But, he reflected grimly as he got into his car, wasn't that just the unhinged, desperate thing fathers did in these circumstances? He sent up a quick prayer for the safety of the little boys and also for their father, wherever he was, that he'd contact the police the next day.

*   *   *

'Just along the road from Sarah!' Avril was saying on the phone. 'It's . . . unbelievable, isn't it? And it was she and Clive who found the body!'

'That's awful, Mum!' Rona exclaimed, genuinely shocked.

'Sarah phoned Guy as soon as the police let them go, and he went straight round. He said there were still police cars outside the murder house.'

'And there's no sign of the husband or children?'

'Not so far. He must have snatched them out of their beds, bundled them in the car, and sped off with them.' She paused. 'It was on the local news this morning; didn't you hear it?'

'No.'

'Well, all I can say is, thank God you're not involved this time. I must say, it makes a change!'

Rona had intended to spend the day working on the biography, but her mother's news had shaken her and she couldn't settle. It was Max's day at the art school and Lindsey would be at work, so neither was available for a chat. In fact, she'd not spoken to Lindsey since she left the house on Monday morning, and her two messages had remained unanswered.

Reaching a decision, she rang her father's number, and was relieved when he picked up at once.

'Hello, poppet, this is a nice surprise! How are things?'

'Mixed, I'd say. I've just had Mum on the phone about a murder in Belmont, which Sarah and her fiancé stumbled on.'

'Good God!'

'I'm in need of company, and I was wondering if I could pop round and join you for a sandwich or something?'

'Of course; I'd be delighted to see you. A good excuse for a pub lunch!'

'See you in about an hour, then.' Putting down the phone, Rona logged on to the BBC and clicked 'News'. The murder featured prominently, with more details than Avril had been able to furnish. The husband of the murdered woman, she read, had spent Tuesday evening at the local rugby club, not leaving until eleven o'clock. Friends he'd been with expressed horror and disbelief at the subsequent turn of events, claiming that he had been in good spirits when he left for home.

So what, Rona asked herself, had happened when he got there?

The Swan was an unassuming little pub, ten minutes' walk from Tom's flat.

'Catherine and I sometimes come here when neither of us can be bothered to cook!' he said, as they settled at a corner table. 'It's quiet and no frills, but the food is good.'

'Will this be her birthday treat tomorrow?' Rona teased.

Tom smiled. 'I think we can rise to something a bit grander for that!'

'Which reminds me.' She took a gift-wrapped package from her bag and handed it across. 'Could you pass this on, with love from Max and me?'

'Thanks, darling. It will be on the breakfast table.'

'I was remembering last year,' she went on, 'when we were all at lunch in Cricklehurst and Jenny went into labour.'

'Yes, indeed. We're hoping for less drama this year!'

Rona hesitated. 'How is Jenny? And Daniel?'

'They seem OK. She's staying with her parents at the moment, but he went up to see her last week and is going again tomorrow, for Alice's birthday. As it happened, work brought him in this direction on Tuesday, so he spent the night with Catherine. She said he seemed fine, and gave no sign of anything being wrong.'

'Then perhaps nothing is,' Rona said.

'Let's hope you're right. Now, tell me how Sarah got mixed up in this murder.'

Rona relayed what she had learned. 'From all the signs, it looks as though it must have been the husband,' she finished, 'though according to Sarah they were regarded as the ideal couple and adored their children. The main worry at the moment, of course, is to find them.'

'Poor little blighters; whatever happens now, their lives will never be the same.'

'Sarah's particularly upset because the five-year-old is in her class, and one of her favourites.'

'A bad business all round.'

Their food was laid before them – shepherd's pie for Tom, cod and chips for Rona.

'On a more cheerful note,' he continued, reaching for the salt and pepper, 'how's that twin of yours? I've not spoken to her in weeks.'

'Things aren't going too well on the love front, I'm afraid.'

'Oh no, not again! I was hoping this chap would be the one.'

'I think she was, too,' Rona said sadly. 'I know they had a row at the weekend; with luck it'll blow over, but at the moment she's a bit fragile.'

'Poor love! I must give her a call.'

'Don't say I mentioned Dominic,' Rona warned.

'I'll be discretion itself! She'll probably be in touch, anyway, with a present for Catherine.'

Rona hoped he was right, and the fact that Lindsey was distracted about Dominic and not overfond of Catherine in the first place had not erased all thoughts of the forthcoming birthday. Perhaps she should give her a reminder.

As it happened, Lindsey forestalled her by phoning that evening, immediately after Max's routine call.

'I presume you still have the photograph?' she began without preamble.

Her head full of other matters, it was a moment before Rona's mind clicked into gear. 'Oh – yes, yes I have.'

'I've just had William on the phone, and there's been a development. He's invited me – and you, if you'd like to come – to go round for coffee and hear about it.'

'Linz, I really—'

'And you could return the photo at the same time.'

Rona sighed. 'When would this be?'

'Unfortunately not until Monday, because I'm away for the weekend.'

'Oh Linz, that's great! Did Dominic—?'

'Nina and Steve have invited me down to their cottage in Hampshire. Double N have just redone it.'

Nina and her friend Nicole, trading as Double N, had been responsible for the make-over of Lindsey's flat.

Rona said tentatively, 'Has Dominic—?'

'Dominic,' said Lindsey, 'is history. I told you that.' And before Rona could comment, she hurried on, 'No doubt Mum's been in touch about this murder? There was a garbled message on my answerphone when I got in. I suppose I'll have to ring her back.'

'Yes, it's all rather horrific,' Rona said, accepting, since she'd no choice, the switch in subject. 'It's a woman who was on the PTA at Belmont Primary, and her little boy's in Sarah's class. There was no sign of a forced entry, Mum said, so it looks as though the husband's the culprit.'

'It usually is,' Lindsey agreed. 'Now, are you going to come and hear what William's found, or not? After the time you've hung on to the photo, I think it's the least you can do.'

'All right, I'll come. Oh, and Lindsey, before you go: you haven't forgotten tomorrow's Catherine's birthday, have you?'

The ensuing silence informed Rona that indeed she had. 'God!' Lindsey said then. 'One thing after another! OK, thanks for the reminder; I'll send some flowers. The coffee invitation's not till eight o'clock, by the way, so I suggest we have something to eat first. Meet me at Dino's about six?'

'I'll be there,' Rona said.

The murder made the ten o'clock news, and Rona watched, mesmerized, as white-coated figures moved up and down the path of the house in Belmont. It reminded her shudderingly of when she had watched the same performance at the house next door.

'Police have issued a photograph of the victim's husband, Kevin Coombes,' the newscaster intoned solemnly. 'They're appealing to him to get in touch with them, and to take his young sons to the nearest police station, where they'll be cared for until relatives can collect them.'

A photograph came on the screen of a dark-haired man in his forties, whose only distinguishing feature was a deep vertical line between his eyes. Rona stared at it, trying to reconcile it with the devoted family man Sarah had known, picturing him playing cricket on the back lawn with the boys, carving the Sunday roast, watching television with his wife. Could this really be a killer's face? In the last year or two she'd been unlucky enough to come in contact with several murderers, but there'd been no common factor to set them apart, mark them out for

what they were. Of more immediate urgency, was it the face of
a man who would harm his children? She could only pray it was
not.

Barnie Trent was a large and jovial man, though the staff at
Chiltern Life spoke darkly of a formidable temper if deadlines
were missed. He had a high, domed forehead and astute grey
eyes that missed nothing. At six foot two he towered over his
wife, a mere five foot. However, what Dinah lacked in height
she more than made up for in personality; she'd a mass of wiry
black hair, a singularly deep voice and the most infectious laugh
Rona had ever heard. She was extremely fond of both of them,
and in the past had felt far more comfortable in their home than
she did in her parents'.

By the time they arrived for supper the next evening there'd
been no further news on the Belmont murder. Avril, who seemed
to have taken it on herself to issue a daily bulletin, had reported
that they were saying prayers for Ben at school assembly, though
thankfully his classmates were too young to appreciate his danger.
Sarah and Clive had been to the police station during their lunch
break, and, having signed their statements, hoped that ended their
official involvement. Though Avril didn't say so, Rona knew that
on a personal level it would last at least until Ben and his brother
were safely restored to what was left of their family.

As features editor of a glossy monthly, the case didn't fall
within Barnie's remit, though he was concerned to learn of the
connection, albeit tenuous, with Rona's family.

'Mum says Sarah's terribly upset,' she ended. 'She had to take
her class as usual, and Ben's empty place was hard to ignore.
She only just managed to get through it before breaking down.'

'You read of these cases every day in the press,' Dinah
remarked, 'but you never expect it to happen so close to home.'

'Still,' Rona said rallyingly, 'we have more cheerful things to
discuss! How long is it now till Mel's baby's due?'

'About seven weeks,' Dinah replied.

'And Barnie says she's having a much easier pregnancy than
last time?'

'So far, thank God, but I worry about her having her children
so close together; Sam's just four, and the next one might well

be born on Martha's third birthday. Just think – three children
under five!'

'She's a healthy young woman,' Barnie put in, 'and she thrives
on motherhood.'

'I suppose you'll fly over to see the baby?'

Dinah smiled. 'Try and stop me!' She reached into her bag.
'And I wouldn't be doing my grandmotherly duty if I didn't
produce photographs. These are the latest.'

She passed Rona half a dozen prints, all showing the two
children in the garden of their home. Sam hadn't changed much
since Rona had seen him on their visit a couple of years ago – a
taller, sturdier version of the toddler she remembered. Martha
though, who'd been a baby at the time, was unrecognizable – a
solemn little girl with large eyes, darker than her blond brother.

'They're lovely,' Rona said dutifully.

Max, who had been busy in the kitchen, reappeared. 'Dinner
is served, ladies and gentleman, if you'd care to come down.'

With no dining room, the kitchen was of necessity called on
for entertaining. The table, laid with the best silver and crystal,
was positioned alongside the patio doors leading to the garden,
and in the darkness beyond them, reflections of the candles danced
like fireflies.

True to form, Max had produced a gourmet meal of blinis
with smoked salmon and sour cream, followed by roast duckling
and ending with lemon parfait served in scooped-out lemon
skins.

'Found out any more about that photograph you were asking
about?' Barnie enquired, as coffee was served.

'To be honest, I've not given it much thought. But believe it
or not, the owner of Springfield Lodge has a painting by Elspeth
Wilding. I went to have a look at it last week, and while I was
there I asked about the school, but she couldn't help.'

'Did you get in touch with the *Gazette*?'

'About photographers? I asked Tess Chadwick, but she said
much the same as you and referred me either to the archives in
Buckford or the Internet. I did go on line, but there was no easy
route, and I gave up.'

'I've thought about it a couple of times since you phoned,'
Barnie remarked, helping himself to cream, 'particularly the

person who was inked out. There's a faint chance there could be a story behind it, and if there is, and you run it to earth, you might write an article on it.'

Dinah laughed. 'Any excuse to tempt you back!'

'Well actually, the man who owns the photo has come across something and he's invited Lindsey and me round to hear about it.'

'There you are then!' Barnie said triumphantly. 'I wouldn't suggest a series while you're engaged on the book, but it might even be beneficial to take time out to do the odd article. It would give you a break, and you could then return to the bio with "renewed vigour", as the dog-food ads used to say.'

Rona smiled. 'Let's see what turns up next week,' she prevaricated.

But after the guests had left, Barnie's suggestion lingered in her mind. It might, after all, be interesting to follow it up a bit, and a possible article was an added incentive.

On the way to bed, she made a detour to the study and picked up the photograph, looking at it thoughtfully. Then, on the spur of the moment, she slipped it into the scanner. If she had to hand it back on Monday, at least she'd still have a copy of it.

On Saturday there was welcome news, and as before, Rona heard it from Avril.

'Have you been watching the lunchtime news?' she began excitedly.

'No?'

'The little Coombes boys are safe and well! They were delivered to their grandparents' house in Buckford at five thirty this morning!'

'That *is* a relief. No sign of their father?'

'No, but police found his car round the corner. It seems he walked the boys to the house, rang the bell, and then, I imagine, waited out of sight till someone opened the door.'

'Pity he didn't hand himself in at the same time,' Rona commented.

'It seems he's no intention of doing so, and now he's ditched the car they were looking for and freed himself from the children, he'll be even harder to track down.'

'Did the boys say where they'd been for the last three days?'

'Oh, I shouldn't think they've been questioned yet, and when they are, they'll have specially trained people.'

'Well, I'm very thankful they're safe, and I'm quite sure Sarah is. Thanks for letting me know.'

Eleven o'clock on Sunday morning. Rona was in the back garden, deadheading the blooms in the various pots and urns. She loved this paved Italianate garden, surrounded as it was by brick walls and dotted with statues and containers of every shape and size. No grass to cut, virtually no weeds to root out, just an endless succession of flowers that she changed with the season, so there was always something interesting to look out on.

Gus came bounding through the patio doors, ears flapping, tail wagging, barking excitedly.

Rona straightened. 'What is it, boy? The doorbell? If so, Max can answer it.'

But as she returned to her task, she heard her name called.

'What is it?' she called back, dusting the soil off her hands, but there was no reply. 'We'll have to go and see then, won't we?' she said to the dog, who accompanied her, still barking, back into the house. She could hear voices, and paused to wash her hands at the sink before going up the basement stairs to investigate.

A group of people were standing chatting in the hall, and Rona saw with pleased surprise that it was the Furness family, newly returned from Hong Kong.

'Rona!' Monica came forward to hug her. 'I hope you don't mind our barging in like this! We've just been looking round the house, and felt we had to knock on your door.'

'Of course! I didn't realize you were back!'

'We only arrived yesterday, but we couldn't wait to inspect our new-look home.'

'Are you pleased with it?'

'Oh, it's fabulous! That's really why we came round; Charles wanted to thank Max for overseeing everything.'

'I was glad to do it,' Max replied. 'There really was no need for this very generous present.' He indicated the box of wine at his feet.

'The least we could do,' Charles said, adding as he kissed Rona, 'Lovely to see you again.'

Behind him, she caught sight of the children standing shyly in the background, and noticing her smile at them, he beckoned them over. 'You remember Rona, kids? Come and say hello.'

Harriet, aged fifteen, was tall and fair like her mother, her hair hanging in a single plait down her back. Giles, at thirteen, was wiry and small for his age, taking after his father.

'You were at the cinema when we met your parents in October,' Rona reminded them, 'so it must be four years since we saw you. Welcome back to the UK!'

Harriet said shyly, 'I've read one of your books, the one about Conan Doyle. I was interested because I love Sherlock Holmes. I'm not sure about the fairies, though!'

Rona laughed. 'Who knows, they might be at the bottom of *your* garden!'

'Have you time for a coffee?' Max asked. 'It will only take a minute.'

'No, really, thanks, we must get back to the flat. We've not even unpacked yet.'

'Is it OK, the flat?'

'It's comfortable and convenient, which is all we ask of it. It'll suit us nicely for the next couple of months.'

'Have you got a date when you can expect your furniture?' Rona asked.

'Not an exact one till we know when the ship's sailing,' Monica replied, 'but the estimate's mid-June. In the meantime we must measure up the windows and choose new curtains, so we've plenty to keep us busy.'

'How about schools?'

'We were lucky enough to get them both into the High School; they start straight after Easter, so one of our first tasks will be to buy uniforms. Fortunately, since they were at a British school in Hong Kong, it'll be the same syllabus, which is useful with GCSEs looming.'

They moved in a group to the front door. 'You must come for a meal,' Max said. 'Have we got your phone number? And your address, come to that?'

'I had cards printed.' Charles handed one across. 'Give us a week or two to settle in, then you must come to us – a flat-warming! See you soon, and thanks again, Max, for keeping an eye on things.'

As she watched them pile into their car outside number seventeen, Rona reflected that ever since she and Max had lived here the house next door had been occupied by tenants, some of whom they'd come to know, others they hadn't. It had added an unsettling quality to their lives, and it was good to know that the Furness family would now become their permanent neighbours.

EIGHT

As Daniel drove out of his parents-in-law's drive with a final wave, Marion Chalmers put an arm round her daughter's shoulders. 'All right, darling?'

Jenny nodded. She hated seeing Daniel leave, but this would be the last time. The job that had kept him travelling was coming to an end, and next weekend, after Easter, she and Alice would go home with him. As she'd hoped, the break had restored her and she was ready to take up her life again. Paul would already have forgotten her, and if by any chance they met – in the florist's, for example – she knew she was strong enough to deal with it. Now, she intended to make up to Daniel for her lapse, even though he was unaware of it.

'I think you're being very brave,' Marion went on quietly, as they went back into the house. 'This can't be easy for you.'

Jenny looked at her questioningly. 'I'm . . . not sure what you mean?'

'Oh come, darling! We've known from the start that Daniel's been having an affair.'

Jenny gasped. 'No – no he hasn't, Mum! You've got it all wrong.'

Marion smiled and patted her shoulder. 'If you say so, dear, though you don't have to pretend with us.'

'Really he hasn't – I promise! Things have been a bit difficult, yes, but only because he's had to be away so much, and I let myself get run down.'

'And what was he doing, may I ask, while he was "away so much"? Are you sure it was all to do with work?'

Jenny stared at her mother in frustration. 'Why won't you believe me?' She took a deep breath. 'All right, if you must know, *I* was the one who was playing around!'

Marion gave a light laugh. 'Really, darling, you'll have to do better than that!'

'It didn't come to anything,' Jenny hurried on, 'but it would have done, if I'd not come away. Daniel doesn't know about it, and if he ever finds out, it has to come from me. You do understand that?'

'Oh, I assure you I shan't mention it.'

'You still don't believe me, do you?'

'Let's just say I admire your loyalty, and since you refuse to discuss the matter, all I'll add is there's really no need for you to go back next weekend. You know you and Alice will be welcome here indefinitely.'

As Jenny started to reply, Marion raised a hand. 'Now, go and collect her from your father and we can take her up for her bath.'

'Can't sleep?'

Sarah looked up to see Clive in the doorway. 'Sorry, did I wake you?'

He joined her at the kitchen table. Huddled in her dressing gown, both hands round a mug of hot chocolate, she looked like a refugee in some transit camp and his heart ached for her. 'I was only dozing myself.'

'I can't get the picture of her out of my head,' she said in a low voice. 'Lying crumpled like a . . . like a doll that's been tossed aside. And her *eyes* – wide open, and staring at nothing.'

She shuddered and Clive put a quick hand on her arm. 'At least the little boys are safe.'

'Yes, thank God. But what will happen to them, Clive? How can they have a normal childhood after this? Especially if it really was Kevin who killed her.'

'He always seemed such a pleasant chap,' Clive said reflectively.

'He *was*! And they were all so happy together, he and Lucy and the boys. I can't *believe* he'd hurt her!' She looked up, sudden hope in her eyes. 'There was that neighbour across the road, wasn't there, who said a man came hurrying down their path as she was drawing her bedroom curtains. Why hasn't he come forward? Suppose *he* killed her, and Kevin, who'd been out all evening, came back and found her dead? Perhaps in a panic he just wanted to get the boys out of the house, away from her body?'

'Hardly a normal reaction,' Clive pointed out. 'Surely he'd have phoned for an ambulance or the police or something?'

'But it is just possible, surely? God, Clive, I don't *want* it to be Kevin!'

'I know, sweetie, I know.'

'Did you hear the late news?'

'No further developments. The police still want him to "help with their enquiries".'

'Perhaps we'll know more in the morning,' she said.

Six o'clock was early for Dino's clientele, and when Rona arrived on Monday evening, only a couple of tables were occupied, both by families with young children. Dino greeted her with his usual effusiveness and ushered her to a corner table.

'It is some time since we saw you, *signora*. All is well, I trust?'

'Fine, Dino, thank you. My sister will be joining me; we have an appointment at eight, so if you don't mind we'd like to take our time over the meal.'

'Stay as long as you wish, *signora*. Now, a glass of something while you study the menu?'

'Sounds like a good idea!' said Lindsey, coming up behind him. 'Good evening, Dino.'

'*Buona sera, signora.*' He pulled out her chair and with a flourish spread a napkin on her lap. 'I bring you the wine list.'

'Have a good weekend?' Rona asked. Lindsey was pale, she noted; withdrawal from Dominic?

'Excellent, thank you,' she answered briskly. 'The cottage is in a wonderful position, and they've done it up beautifully. We went for long walks and ate in country pubs. I might think of buying a rural retreat myself.'

Rona smiled, shaking her head. 'Sister dear, a country girl you are not! You'd soon miss the bright lights!'

'I don't mean *live* there,' Lindsey said irritably, 'just for week-ends and holidays.'

'And since when has your idea of a holiday been to bury yourself in the country?'

Lindsey smiled reluctantly. 'Oh, all *right*. I suppose as long as friends invite me down occasionally, that will suffice.'

'Precisely.'

They chose their food and wine, and gradually the tables around them began to fill up.

'You're lucky to have this place right on your doorstep,' Lindsey remarked. 'I have to get in the car to go anywhere.' She glanced under the table. 'Where's Gus?'

'Max took him this morning, since we'll be out quite a while. I'll collect him tomorrow. By the way, the Furnesses are back.'

'Who?'

'The owners of the house next door. They've finished their stint abroad and are moving back permanently.'

'Good, that rules out any more weirdos,' Lindsey said, and didn't notice her sister's shiver.

'They looked in yesterday,' Rona continued after a moment, 'having inspected all the alterations and redecorations. Max has been keeping an eye on the work, and Charles brought a case of wine as a thank you.'

'Now that's the kind of neighbours to have!'

Their *antipasti* were laid in front of them.

'So – what do you think we're in for this evening?' Rona asked.

'No idea, William didn't go into details. All he said was that Glenda had been going through more of her mother's things. You have got the photo, haven't you?'

'I've got it,' Rona confirmed. 'Have you met his wife?'

'No; he says she never reads anything except magazines, and spends her time playing golf and bridge. Which is why he escapes to the book group once a month.'

Rona reached for the Parmesan. 'If this *does* turn out to be something, Barnie asked me to write an article about it.'

'Ah! So that's why you're interested, all of a sudden!'

'Except that I don't suppose it will. Odds are it'll end in anticlimax.'

'Then why did Mrs Thing nearly pass out when she saw the photo?'

'Linz, she was an old lady. Perhaps it was just the shock of suddenly seeing something from the past.'

'Well, I'm sticking to the illicit sex till we learn otherwise,' Lindsey said firmly, and turned her attention to her *crespelli*.

Dino was as good as his word; service was leisurely and they lingered over each course. By the time they were drinking their espressos, it was after seven thirty.

'Where do these people live?' Rona asked, as, at last, she signalled for their bill.

'Barrington Road. We'll be there in under ten minutes.'

'Near Magda and Gavin, then,' Rona remarked, and wondered, with a shaft of unease, how her friend was, realizing guiltily that it was a week since she'd lunched with Magda and learned of her latest fears. She should have been in touch, but the murder, followed by dinner with the Trents and the return of the Furness family, had temporarily driven her out of mind. She'd phone tomorrow, she resolved.

As Lindsey had said, it was a short drive from the restaurant and entailed passing Farthings in Deans Crescent North. Rona glanced up at the lighted studio window, and wondered what Max had set his students this evening. Then they had turned into Barrington Road, and were drawing up outside a substantial-looking house.

'Here we go, then!' Lindsey commented, locking the car. 'Let's hope she's come up with something interesting.'

William Stirling opened the door to them. He was a tall, broad-shouldered man with a shock of greying brown hair and a ruddy complexion, whom Rona guessed to be in his fifties.

'Come in, come in!' he said heartily, standing to one side. 'Good of you to come. And you must be Rona – delighted to meet you. God, you're alike, aren't you?'

He took their jackets and led them into the sitting room. 'Glenda won't be a moment; she's just getting the coffee. Please make yourselves comfortable.'

The spring evening had turned chill, and Rona was glad to see a live fire in the grate. On a rug in front of it, a red setter raised its head to survey them, sleepily thumped its tail, and went back to sleep. Glancing round the room, Rona's eyes came to rest on a framed photograph showing their host with, presumably, his wife and mother-in-law, standing in front of a church. Since the women wore fashionable hats, Rona guessed they were attending a wedding. The older woman was smiling at the camera, one arm linked with her daughter's, the other leaning on a stick. She of the fainting fit, Rona thought.

She looked away quickly as Glenda Stirling came in wheeling a trolley with a coffee pot, cups and saucers, and what looked like a carrot cake on a silver stand. Probably much the same age as her husband, her hair was a soft grey, but her skin, devoid of make-up, still had a youthful bloom.

'I do hope we're not being a nuisance,' she said, after warmly greeting them. 'I'm afraid this has all rather escalated; William had only intended showing the photo to his book group, in the hope that someone might remember the school.' She glanced apologetically at Rona. 'But your sister kindly volunteered your services, and since you're known for solving mysteries, it was an offer we couldn't refuse!'

'I'm not at all sure I can help,' Rona demurred.

'But you've already found someone who was there, haven't you?' Lindsey prompted, and as Rona looked blank, added, 'Kitty Little's sister.'

Glenda looked at her expectantly.

'I've not exactly found her,' Rona said reluctantly, 'but our mother knew her when she was young. She was actually at the school when it closed.'

'That's wonderful!' Glenda exclaimed, adding quickly, 'But I'm forgetting my duties! Do please sit down and let me give you some coffee. Then, when we're all settled, I can fill in a few details.'

When this had been accomplished and they were balancing plates of carrot cake on their laps, she continued, 'The first thing I should explain is that my mother was a teacher all her working life. We used to tease her about it sometimes, because she was always recounting stories of pupils and teachers she'd come across in her long career. We knew – or thought we knew – every school she'd taught in. But she never even mentioned Springfield Lodge.'

'She *taught* there?' Lindsey interrupted. 'I thought she must have been a pupil?'

'So did I, briefly, when I first found the photo. She grew up during the war and had been to lots of different schools; my grandfather was in the army, and while he was stationed in England the family kept moving to be near him. But when I saw the date I realized it didn't fit; in 1951, which was scrawled on the back, she'd have been twenty-two.'

'Is she *in* the photo?' Rona asked, the thought occurring for the first time.

Glenda shook her head. 'That's what has puzzled us ever since I found it: that she should have kept a photo all these years that didn't, on the face of it, have any connection with her.' She paused. 'I presume William told you of her reaction, when I came across it a couple of years ago?'

Rona and Lindsey nodded.

'It was . . . frightening, really. She snatched it out of my hand and started shaking violently. I thought she was having a stroke. Later, when she was calmer, I tried to ask her about it, but she refused point-blank to discuss the matter. I was sure she'd have destroyed it at the first opportunity, and couldn't believe my eyes when I found it among her things.' She looked round at them all, lifting her shoulders in bewilderment. 'Why ever would she keep something that upset her so much?'

Rona said hesitantly, 'I don't suppose . . .'

'Go on,' Glenda invited, when she did not continue.

'Well, I'm probably way off-beam, but you say she was a member of staff but isn't in the photograph?'

'Yes?'

'I just . . . wondered if she might be the one who's blacked out?'

She bit her lip, conscious that the rest of them were staring at her.

Glenda had paled. 'Oh God,' she said softly. 'I must say that never occurred to me.'

'I'm sure she isn't,' Rona said quickly. 'For one thing, if she *had* been, she certainly wouldn't have kept it, would she? All the same, her being on the staff does rather alter things, because if she's *not* the one blacked out, presumably she's the one who did it. I'd thought it might have been a disgruntled girl who'd been given detention or something, but for an adult it would surely have had to be something more serious.'

There was a brief silence. 'Did you try to remove the ink?' Lindsey asked then. 'By sponging it, for example?'

'I started to,' Glenda replied, 'which is why it's a bit smudged, but the ink has seeped into the paper, and I didn't want to risk damaging it.' She drew a deep breath. 'Anyway,' she continued, 'seeing it again reawakened my curiosity, and I went through her papers more carefully. And lo and behold, underneath a pile of exam questions and reports I discovered some diaries – only three, but the latest was for 1951.'

She picked up a volume from the table beside her. 'It's a page-a-day format, and as you can see, big enough to write quite detailed accounts of one's doings.'

'Does it help at all?' Rona asked, anxious to expunge her previous suggestion.

'Actually, it raises a lot more questions. In the first few pages it records returning to Springfield Lodge for her "second term", which was the first indication we had that she'd been there herself. It was January, of course, and since we now know the school closed in December '51, she could only have been there just over a year in total. She'd already formed a close friendship with a fellow teacher called Susie Baines, and there are references to her almost every day. They seem to have spent all their spare time together, most of it discussing Susie's boyfriend, Andrew. A vicarious romance, as far as Mum was concerned.

'Well, that continued throughout the term, and they met once or twice in the Easter holidays. But during the summer there's a distinct change of tone. Mum seems to have turned against Andrew for some reason, and several entries report having "long talks" with Susie, with no detail as to what they were about. They also started to have quarrels, but again no details.'

Glenda leafed through the diary. 'No mention of meeting during the summer holidays. Mum seems to have spent her time with various friends at the Festival of Britain, going to exhibitions and shows and visiting the Festival Gardens in Battersea Park. But in September, back at school, we have: "Long and difficult talk with Susie. I HAVE to make her see sense." And a few weeks later, "Susie refuses to discuss it any more. I'm at my wits' end to know what to do."' She looked up. 'And that's the last mention of her. The diary continues for another couple of weeks, and comes to an abrupt end the second week in October.' She snapped the book shut, as if in confirmation, and looked round at them. 'So what do you make of that?'

'There's nothing that gives any hint that the school's about to close?' Lindsey asked.

'Not a word. We only know about that because someone in the book group remembered it.'

Rona said slowly, 'Then if it's not your mother who's scratched out, and it's her photo, it must surely be Susie.'

'That's what I thought,' Glenda admitted, 'but *why*? All right, they'd been great friends and then for some reason fallen out. But it's rather an extreme reaction, isn't it, and Mum wasn't a vindictive person. Why not simply throw it away?'

She paused. 'The more I think about it, the more certain I am that something traumatic happened that last term – which might explain something else we could never understand. When Mum's arthritis got really bad and she was having mobility problems we wanted her to come and live with us, but she wouldn't hear of it. In fact, since we came to Marsborough six years ago she's never even been to visit – coming up with a variety of excuses for us to go and see her instead. It's almost as though she couldn't bear to come near the place.'

She looked down at the diary, as though the explanation might after all lie in its pages.

'It would be interesting to know what those long and difficult talks were about,' mused William after a moment.

'Exactly; if she'd been as frank about them as she was with earlier discussions about Andrew, we'd be a whole lot wiser.' Glenda looked at Rona. 'I was wondering . . . if you could spare the time . . . if you could possibly take the diary and . . . study it, or something? As a biographer, you must have a trained eye for this kind of thing and you might pick up something I've missed.' She gave an embarrassed little laugh. 'Or have I a nerve even asking you?'

'I'd be very interested to read it,' Rona replied honestly. 'I've been ploughing through Elspeth Wilding's diaries for the last few months, but this sounds much more intriguing.'

She reached for her bag, took out the photograph under discussion, and laid it on the arm of her chair. 'I've been trying to work out what this group represents. It's not a class, because the girls are of different ages, and there's no sports gear or anything that might give a pointer. One of the Houses seems the best guess, but it would be a start if we could confirm that.'

'Perhaps your mother's friend could help?' Glenda suggested hopefully.

'If I can trace her, I'll certainly ask.' Rona hesitated. 'Actually, I was at Springfield Lodge about ten days ago on a different

matter, and took the chance to ask about the school.' She looked
at William. 'As I believe you were told, the present owner knows
nothing about it. However, she did say she'd recently had a guest
who'd attended the school.'

'She didn't tell me that!' William exclaimed.

'It was after you'd phoned, but you'd aroused her curiosity
and she asked the woman if she knew why it had closed. The
guest thought alcohol was involved.'

William shook his head impatiently. 'That won't wash. It could
only have been among the senior girls, and surely wouldn't have
necessitated closing the entire school.'

'That's what Mrs Temple said. The guest was going to look up
old photo albums, but hadn't got back to her.' She turned to
Glenda. 'Had your mother any other photos that might help?'

'None that covered that period. She seems to have . . . obliterated all traces of it.' She hesitated. 'Might it be possible to
speak to this hotel guest?'

'I was wondering that. Mrs Temple's unlikely to hand out
addresses or phone numbers, but she might agree to ask her to
phone me. It's worth a try. She might also remember your mother.
What was her maiden name?'

'Cowley,' Glenda supplied. 'Patricia Cowley, known as Trish.'

'Have you a photo of her at about that time? It might help to
jog people's memories.'

'There's one of her graduation; she wouldn't have changed
much between then and '51. I'll look it out for you.'

Talk continued for another half-hour or so, but nothing
constructive emerged. As they were leaving, Rona handed back
the photograph, apologizing for having kept it so long.

'But won't you need it, to show people?' Glenda asked.

'I made a copy,' Rona told her. 'I hope you don't mind; I
didn't want anything to happen to the original.'

'That's fine, and here's the diary in exchange. Let me know
how you get on with it.'

'Are you going to book group on Thursday?' Lindsey asked
William, as he helped her on with her jacket. 'It's the day before
Good Friday.'

'Yes, I'll be there. We're not going away for Easter – the boys
are coming to us.'

'Your sons?' Rona asked Glenda.

'Yes; they're both at university now. It will be lovely to have them home, though we probably shan't see much of them!'

Moving towards the front door, either William or Lindsey said something in a low voice that Rona didn't catch, and they both laughed. Then the door was open, they were saying goodbye and walking back down the path.

'Marks out of ten?' Lindsey asked casually, as she started the car.

'What?'

'William. Marks out of ten?'

'The thought never crossed my mind.'

'Oh, don't be stuffy! He's rather sexy, isn't he? We keep catching each other's eye at book group, which adds a bit of zing.'

A discomfiting suspicion crossed Rona's mind. 'Is that by any chance why you dragged me into this? To give you an excuse to meet more often?'

Lindsey's only reply was a low laugh.

'Linz, he's a married man with a charming wife and two grown-up sons!'

'I always did like older men,' Lindsey remarked, doing a three-point turn and negotiating the corner into Deans Crescent North.

'Even if they belong to someone else?

'I have to have a man in my life,' Lindsey said defensively. 'You know that.'

'You're hardly on the shelf! Until last week you had Dominic!'

'I told you, he's finito. Still, William's not my only option; Hugh would come running if I snapped my fingers and probably Jonathan too.' (Jonathan Hurst was a fellow partner at Chase Mortimer, with whom Lindsay had had a brief relationship.) 'That would show Dominic, wouldn't it?'

'At what price?' Rona asked heatedly. 'You'd drop either of them if something better came up and you know it. Don't you care who you hurt?'

'All's fair in love and war,' Lindsey declared smugly.

Rona, defeated, took refuge in silence. Sometimes, she thought, talking to her twin was almost like talking to herself. And at other times it wasn't.

*   *   *

The next morning Rona was impatient to speak to both her mother
and Magda, but was forced to contain herself. Avril would be
working at the library till lunchtime and Magda, out at one of
her boutiques, would be virtually incommunicado all day. She
did, however, phone Springfield Lodge and extracted a promise
from Mrs Temple to contact the lady in question, a Mrs Grayson.

'She hasn't come back to me,' Beryl Temple said ruefully.
'She's probably forgotten all about it, but if she *does* find any
photos of when the Lodge was a school I'd be most grateful for
a copy for our records. Perhaps you'd remind her of that.'

Rona promised to do so, hopeful that Mrs Grayson might be
more reliable in phoning her back than she'd been in contacting
Mrs Temple. To her considerable surprise, she did so within the
hour.

'Ms Parish? This is Heather Grayson. I hear from Springfield
Lodge that you'd like to speak to me about my time there?'

'Oh, Mrs Grayson, thank you so much for phoning. Yes, indeed
I should, if you wouldn't mind.'

'I gather from the manageress that you're a writer?'

Bypassing Beryl Temple's demotion, Rona replied, 'I am, yes,
but I'm wearing another hat at the moment.'

'Something about a photograph, I believe?'

'That's right. There's someone I'm quite anxious to identify,
and wonder if you could help. Have you any photos yourself of
your time there?'

'Oh yes, quite a few. I meant to look them out when I got
back from Marsborough but never got round to it. You're most
welcome to see them, if you'd care to?'

'I should indeed.' Rona was curious to know the dates Mrs
Grayson was at the school, but as it would equate to asking her
age, she decided against it. 'I don't know where you live?'

'Lincoln,' Heather Grayson replied. 'Quite a drive, just to look
at a few photographs. And it takes much the same time by train –
between two and three hours, with the added disadvantage that you'd
have to get to King's Cross first, making the journey even longer.'

'I've never been to Lincoln,' Rona said thoughtfully. 'Perhaps
I could persuade my husband to come with me and make a
weekend of it.'

'That would be an excellent solution. I could be available on Saturday afternoon, if that would help? Oh, but it's Easter, isn't it? You probably have family commitments.'

'Actually no, but perhaps you have?'

'No, we've nothing planned. Well then, if you're prepared to face the holiday traffic let's go ahead. If you've got satnav, I'll give you our post code.'

Rona made a note of it, and after fixing the appointment for two thirty on Saturday she rang off and clicked on Max's number. 'How would you like to spend Easter weekend in Lincoln?' she asked.

'Lincoln? What brought that on?'

'There's a lady who's going to look out some photos of Springfield Lodge,' Rona said. 'I'm also hoping she might have some answers to the puzzles I mentioned last night.'

'So you're on the trail of the blacked-out photograph? What about your resolve to keep your head down on the bio?'

'I think I've earned a break. You heard Barnie's views on the subject.'

Max gave a short laugh. 'He's trying to inveigle an article out of you, that's all.'

'Well, whether or not there's one in it, I'm hooked now. As you know I can't resist a mystery. So: how about Lincoln? You've never been, have you?'

'No, and I admit I'd like to see it, but you'll have a job finding anywhere to stay on a holiday weekend.'

'Oh, I'll manage. Speak to you later.'

In fact, she had to try six hotels before she was successful, and then only because they'd had a cancellation. It wasn't as central as she'd hoped, but by that stage, she would have settled for anything within a five-mile radius.

Right, she thought with satisfaction; the first steps on the 'trail', as Max termed it, had been taken.

At one o'clock, Rona phoned her mother. 'Mum, are you still in touch with Kitty Little?' she began at once.

There was a surprised pause, then: 'Good heavens, where did that question spring from? Ah, wait a minute: you're still on about that school.'

'That's right. We've got a bit further, and we now have a possible name for the person blotted out on the photo, but I need to speak to someone who can confirm it.'

'Well, Kitty certainly couldn't. She was barely five when the school closed.'

'But perhaps her sisters could. You *are* still in touch, aren't you?'

'Only by Christmas card, but I have her address. Hold on, I'll get it for you.'

Moments later she was back. 'Here we are. And she's not Kitty Little any more; her married name's Mason. Do you want her address or just the phone number?'

'The number would be fine.' Rona wrote it down. 'You're a star, Mum. Thanks.'

'Let me know how you get on.'

'I will. How's Sarah, by the way? Is the little boy back at school?'

'No, the grandparents thought it would be too traumatic for him. Sarah disagrees; she thinks he needs a familiar routine surrounded by people he knows, but there you go.'

'And they still haven't found the father?'

'No, the hunt's widened to the Continent apparently. I hope to goodness it won't be one of those cases that are never solved.'

'But surely the police must suspect him?'

'No doubt, but they still have to find and charge him.'

Which, Rona reflected glumly, they didn't seem any closer to achieving.

Kitty Mason was not answering her phone, and Rona resigned herself to spending the afternoon making notes on what had been discussed the previous evening. Though she was impatient to start on Trish Cowley's diary, she wanted to read it all in one session and had set the next day aside for doing so, intending to be as well informed as possible by the time she met Heather Grayson at the weekend.

Then at last it was six o'clock, and though Kitty was still not picking up, it was time to phone Magda.

'Hi, it's me!' she said breezily when her friend answered. 'Sorry not to have been in touch.'

'Why? We didn't arrange anything, did we?' Magda's tone was dismissive and Rona was taken aback.

'No, but I was . . . wondering how you are?'

'Fine. Why wouldn't I be?'

Rona frowned, made herself ask calmly, 'What about those dreams? Are you still having them?'

There was a slight pause, then Magda laughed lightly. 'Oh, the dreams. No, that was just a phase. As Gavin said, I must have been eating too much cheese!'

Rebuffed but still concerned, Rona persisted. 'And the "memories" you spoke of?'

'Imagination run riot! Sorry to have troubled you with them, but they're over now. Look, Rona, you'll have to excuse me; I've some things to get through before Gavin comes home.'

'Right.'

'Thanks for phoning,' Magda said briskly, and rang off.

Slowly, Rona put down the phone. She'd been made to feel intrusive, when it was Magda who had come to her with her troubles. And though she now declared they were in the past, Rona was far from convinced. Something was still very definitely not right. She just wished she could pinpoint what it was.

NINE

Trish Cowley's diary wasn't particularly illuminating. As Glenda had said, a lot of space was taken up by recounting talks between herself and Susie about 'Andrew', Susie's boyfriend, and what they'd done when she visited him in London at the weekends. At one point Trish had written, 'Was horrified when Susie admitted she'd actually slept with him!!!'

Rona smiled to herself. How times had changed!

Trish had met the famous Andrew during the Easter holidays and did not appear impressed: 'He's quite good-looking, I suppose, but older than I expected and seems rather arrogant. It didn't help that Susie was absolutely fawning on him. I tried to suggest afterwards that she tone it down a bit, but she nearly bit my head off.'

Hardly surprising, Rona felt, though as more talks about Andrew were detailed, she found herself sharing Trish's dislike. Whether or not the arguments began because of her criticism, they seemed to grow in intensity, particularly by the end of the summer term, and as Glenda had said, they'd not met at all during the long summer holidays.

By the following term, the tone of Trish's diary had changed and was no longer light-hearted; long talks (unspecified) frequently ended with Susie storming out of the room. Trish repeatedly wrote of her worry about her friend, about her refusing to listen, about her getting out of her depth, but frustratingly never said in what context. And the abrupt cessation of writing, midweek and mid-term, remained unexplained.

In all, having gone through the diary, Rona was none the wiser as to why it came to such a sudden end, or why the school had closed at the end of that term. She could only hope Heather Grayson would throw some light on it when they met at the weekend.

As she entered Debra Stacey's sitting room for the book group meeting, Lindsey was wondering if, after their time together on

Monday evening, there'd be any change in William's attitude. Though she'd told Rona they kept catching each other's eye – a confidence she almost immediately regretted – she knew that in truth he also flirted – if that was the word – with other ladies in the group, and, she suspected, with any woman he came in contact with. It was all a part of his easy charm and not meant to be taken seriously. Having met his wife and seen them together, she was pretty sure he'd run a mile if she attempted to take their acquaintance any further. A pity, but it looked as though she'd have to eliminate him from her list of possibilities. Which left Hugh and Jonathan.

William did, however, come straight over on his arrival, holding out an envelope. 'Glenda asked me to give you this,' he said. 'It's Trish's graduation photo; I believe Rona asked for it. Would you mind passing it on to her?'

'Of course. Thank you.'

He smiled. 'We couldn't get over how alike you are,' he added. 'I bet it causes confusion sometimes!'

'It has been known to,' Lindsey answered lightly, 'but it can also be very useful!'

He laughed. 'I'm sure! We're so grateful Rona's willing to pursue this for us. For the first time, we feel we might have a hope of solving the mystery.'

'She'll enjoy it,' Lindsey said shortly, piqued that his interest seemed to have switched from herself to her sister, and, as Debra approached with a tray of coffee cups, she turned away.

Lindsey phoned Rona as soon as she reached home, just before ten.

'I have Trish Cowley's graduation photo,' she told her. 'William gave it to me at book group.'

'Perfect timing! Max and I are driving up to Lincoln tomorrow, to see the woman from the hotel.'

'Quite a way to go, isn't it? Couldn't you have spoken on the phone?'

'We did, but she has photos of her time there that might give us a clue, and there's a chance she could recognize Trish. Will it be all right if we call in for it on our way?'

'As long as you're not setting off at the crack of dawn.'

'It'll be around nine thirty, I should think. We won't mind if you come down in your dressing gown!'

'OK, see you then,' Lindsey said, and rang off. She stood for a minute, deliberating, then speed-dialled Hugh's mobile.

'Hi,' she said brightly as he answered, 'this is your ex-wife!'

There was a startled pause, then, cautiously, 'Hello, Lindsey. To what do I owe this pleasure?'

'Are you doing anything over Easter?'

Still cautious: 'I have a few plans.'

'Could they stretch to taking me out for a meal?'

A longer pause. 'What about Dominic?'

'What about him?'

'Well, I rather gathered—'

'Then you can stop gathering. Are you free for a meal, or not?'

'Lindsey, I'm really not sure this is wise. Actually, I'm seeing—'

'I'm not propositioning you, Hugh, I simply want a dinner companion.'

The fact that she'd gone back to his flat after a previous meal together hung, unspoken, between them.

'I've a date for Saturday,' he said finally.

Date? Had he used the word deliberately? 'Which leaves Friday, Sunday and Monday.'

'I suppose you can take your pick of the others.'

'Sunday, then. With Monday being a holiday, I can have a lie-in.'

'Lindsey—'

'And it'll give you time to back out, if you get cold feet.'

'I'll collect you at eight,' he said, and broke the connection.

'Well, well,' Mia said softly.

Hugh flushed. 'Sorry about that. Completely out of the blue, as you'll have gathered. I . . . tried to get out of it, but once Lindsey has decided on something . . .'

'You don't have to apologize, Hugh. We're not joined at the hip.'

They were in her sitting room, an ultra-modern space composed of glass and chrome and with what Hugh considered a totally impractical white carpet. On his first visit two weeks ago, he'd been startled to see one of Max's paintings on her wall.

'You do know he's my ex-brother-in-law?' he'd asked, standing in front of it and surveying it critically.

'I do now. I've always admired his work, and my father's legacy gave me the means to indulge in it. I knew he came from Buckfordshire, but not that he lived in Marsborough till I met you.'

Now, Hugh put away his phone and sat down opposite her. Not joined at the hip, she'd said. Trouble was, he *did* still feel joined to Lindsey, body and soul – though probably, he thought with wry humour, mostly body. God, he'd never be free of her if she continued to play cat and mouse with him whenever the mood took her. He should, of course, have turned her down flat when she suggested meeting. He knew quite well no good would come of it, for him at least.

He looked across at Mia, at her oval face, her large, dark-lashed grey eyes and the expertly cut red hair curving in to her cheek. Attractive and self-possessed, she seemed for some reason to enjoy his company. Most men would envy the hell out him, so why was he holding back? He was pretty sure she'd be willing to go to bed with him – might even be hoping for it. But if she did, he'd the feeling that she'd remain just as independent and self-sufficient as she was now. The thought was oddly restful, and he suddenly made up his mind. To hell with Lindsey and her wheeler-dealing!

'Would you mind if I stayed the night?' he asked.

As Max drove out of Marsborough, Rona studied the print Lindsey had handed her. So this was Glenda's mother, who, in a few years, would become the owner of the mysterious photograph. Here, though, she wasn't anyone's mother – just a girl with a round face, sparkling eyes and a tumble of curls that had been crammed under her mortar board and were in danger of escaping. She was holding a rolled-up parchment, and her smile conveyed satisfaction in work completed and anticipation for what lay ahead. Trying to reconcile this portrait with the elderly woman she'd seen in the photo frame, Rona wondered if her life had been as fulfilling as she'd expected.

'Heard from Magda lately?' Max asked suddenly.

'Yes, didn't I tell you? I spoke to her on Tuesday.'

'How was she?'

Rona hesitated. 'Well, she said the dreams had stopped.'

Max glanced at her. 'That's good, surely?'

'Yes of course, but she sounded odd. A bit off-key, somehow.'

'Off-key how?'

'Making light of the whole thing. Dismissive, really.'

'Well, I suppose she's a bit embarrassed, looking back on it. It *was* rather over the top.'

Rona shook her head. 'It was more than that. As though she was reining herself in somehow.'

'Oh, for heaven's sake, love! You worried about her when she was having those dreams, and now she's stopped you're *still* worried! Let it go. She says it's all over – believe her. And if she seemed dismissive, well, Magda can be a bit prickly at times.'

'I suppose you're right,' Rona said.

The traffic was predictably heavy, and it was lunchtime when they reached their hotel. After unpacking the few things they'd brought, they collected some brochures from the reception desk and went into the bar for lunch.

They had most of the four-day holiday ahead of them, with Rona's appointment the only fixed point, and they determined to make the most of it, exploring both the historic city and the surrounding countryside.

Having placed their order, Max opened one of the brochures and began reading snippets aloud: 'The Romans were here from AD 60 to 446, and the city was invaded by the Vikings in 839 . . . The "new" castle ordered by William I dates from 1068, and was one of the first to be built after the Norman Conquest . . . The cathedral library has a copy of Magna Carta and a book containing the first recorded rhyme about Robin Hood.'

'I thought he came from Nottingham,' Rona remarked.

'You don't have to live there to write about him,' Max pointed out. 'Now, since it's already one thirty and we've not eaten yet, I suggest this afternoon we confine ourselves to the sites near at hand. Tomorrow morning we can explore a bit further afield, and on Sunday drive out somewhere. Agreed?'

'Fine by me,' Rona said.

For the next twenty-four hours they kept to their plan, wandering round the ruins of the Bishop's Palace, marvelling at the cathedral architecture, and panting their way up and down Steep Hill, an almost perpendicular street linking the modern shopping area of downtown Lincoln with the historic buildings at the top of the hill. By Saturday afternoon, Rona was quite ready to take time off from sightseeing to keep her appointment with Heather Grayson.

Max dropped her at the gate, it having been agreed she would phone when she was ready to be collected. Then, with a sense of anticipation, she walked up the path and rang the bell.

Heather Grayson was one of those women whose school contemporaries would have no difficulty recognizing years later. Her face was plump and virtually unlined, and though her figure was now ample and her hair grey, she had a healthy glow about her that suggested she'd just left the hockey pitch.

'So good of you to come all this way,' she said, leading the way to her sitting room. 'Do please take a seat. My husband's playing golf so we won't be disturbed. Would you care for some tea now, or prefer to wait a little? Bertie, get down!' This last to a tabby cat that had installed itself in one of the armchairs.

Bertie blinked indolently, but as his mistress made a move towards him he leapt nimbly to the floor, waited till Rona was seated and then jumped on to her lap.

'Oh, I'm so sorry!' Heather Grayson exclaimed.

'Don't worry,' Rona assured her, stroking his velvet ears to an accompanying purr. 'I'm fond of cats.'

'Well, if you're sure . . . Now, what did we decide about tea?'

'Whichever's easiest,' Rona said diplomatically.

'Then we'll wait half an hour, shall we, and get down to business.' She leant forward eagerly with clasped hands. 'So tell me, why are you so interested in Springfield Lodge?'

'For various reasons actually, but principally because I've been asked to try to identify someone.'

'How exciting! Fire away, then!'

Mentally, Rona crossed her fingers. 'Do you by any chance remember a teacher called Susie Baines?'

'Miss Baines? Certainly I remember her, if only because she left suddenly in the middle of the last term. It caused quite a stir.'

Bingo! 'Really? What happened?'

'Well, one minute she was there, setting us prep, and the next she was gone. The last words she said to us were, "Mind you hand this in before the end of the week, because I want to go through it with you in the next lesson." And then, to all intents and purposes, she disappeared. Rumours were rife, as you can imagine.'

'I'm sure. What was the official explanation?'

'That she'd had to leave for family reasons. Of course, we all assumed she was pregnant.'

'What about Trish Cowley? Do you remember her?'

'Yes – my goodness, you *are* stirring old memories! I've not thought of these people in years!'

Rona extracted the graduation photo from her bag and handed it across.

Heather studied it. 'Yes, that's Miss Cowley – a slightly younger version than the one I knew. Wherever did you get it?'

'From her daughter. Did she also leave suddenly?' Rona was thinking of the incomplete diary, but Heather Grayson looked puzzled.

'No, why?'

'She stayed till the end of that term?'

'Yes, I distinctly remember her at final assembly, because she looked so upset. It was all pretty traumatic, you know, what with the Head at death's door and the school closing down.'

'Why *did* it close?' Rona asked curiously. 'I've heard several theories.'

Heather smiled. 'All kinds of weird stories were flying around, but the simple truth was that Mr Lytton had a heart attack and couldn't carry on.'

What her mother had called 'the official explanation'.

'There was no one who could have taken it over?'

Heather shrugged. 'Apparently not.'

Abandoning what seemed a fruitless line of enquiry, Rona passed her the school print. 'Does this ring any bells?'

Heather took it with an exclamation. 'Goodness, that looks familiar! I have one almost the same of my own House. There's Lizzie Barclay in the back row! She was in my maths stream. And – heavens! – Maureen Little next to her! I had a crush on her at the time.'

'You knew Maureen Little?' Rona leant forward, looking with interest at the girl indicated. If Maureen was actually on the photo she might well have a copy herself – without the concealing ink blob.

'Not "knew",' Heather was saying, 'just worshipped from afar. She was older than me, in Exam Year.'

'Can you remember which House they were in?'

'Brontë – it was for day girls. The other three were, predictably, Austen, Eliot and Gaskell, which I was in.'

'It was a boarding school, then?' The possibility hadn't occurred to her.

'Chiefly, yes.'

'So was the day girls' "House" a metaphorical one, for sport and so on?'

'Oh no, it was real enough. It was actually where the staff lived, but the day girls went there for lunch and to do their prep after school. But since they didn't actually *live* there, their House photos were taken outside school.' She picked up the print again, studying it more closely and tilting it towards the light. 'It looks as though someone's spilt ink on it; I can't make out who's underneath it.'

'Actually, that's the person we're trying to identify.' Rona paused. 'Presumably the ones seated are staff; can you name any of them?' The more people she could identify, the easier her task might be.

'One or two, I think; Miss Kendal took me for History and Mr Crichton for RE. The two next to him I don't know – they're probably House staff.' She handed back the photo, shaking her head. 'That's the best I can do, I'm afraid; the last three look faintly familiar, but I can't put a name to them.'

'Is there a member of staff you'd expect to see who isn't there, and might be under the blob?' Rona asked hopefully.

'No, because I don't know who was affiliated to which House, except my own, and I've forgotten most of *them*.'

'I thought you said the staff lived at Brontë?'

'They did, but they were all "honorary members" of one of the other Houses, supporting them at sport, fund-raising for charity and things like that.' She rose, went to a desk, and came back with a somewhat battered photograph album. 'Let's see if any of these help.'

She opened it on the coffee table and Rona, gently removing the cat, moved closer to look over her shoulder. It seemed Heather had been an enthusiastic photographer; there were several pages of sports teams, some of which featured herself, looking very young but instantly recognizable, and some informal snaps of girls lying on the grass, chatting or reading. Then she turned a page, and they were looking at almost the replica of Trish's photo. A different House formed the background – Gaskell, presumably – and there was, of course, a different set of faces, Heather's among them, but the format was identical, with the rows of girls and seated staff.

'Were photos taken at the end of each year?' Rona asked, noting that this was dated 1950.

'Yes; there must be a later one somewhere. There's Miss Cowley, look; she was affiliated to us.' And Rona, searching along the row of seated staff, recognized the now-familiar face.

As another page was turned, several snaps that either hadn't been stuck in or had come unstuck slid out, among them some taken of the interior of the Lodge, identified on their backs as 'Lower Hall', 'Cassie in the Art Studio', 'Class 3b', and so on.

'Mrs Temple would love some of these, if you could spare any,' Rona said, remembering her promise. 'She's building up a pictorial record, and though she has several ghastly pictures of how the Lodge looked as a nursing home, she hasn't any of its school period.'

'Feel free to take them,' Heather said, 'I have masses more. It was an odd sensation,' she added reflectively, 'going back there last month. My husband had a bowls tournament in Marsborough and I decided to go with him, to look round old haunts. I'd no idea Springfield was now a hotel, but when we searched on line for somewhere to stay, there it was!'

Apart from the prints, which Rona gratefully gathered up, the album had yielded little new information, and Heather left her turning the last few pages and went to make the tea. Gradually, things were falling into place, and although there were still a lot of unanswered questions, Rona suspected that her hostess had now supplied as many answers as she was able.

'A worthwhile visit?' Max enquired, as, having collected her, he drove back towards the town.

'Oh, definitely.'

'She identified the blob?'

'Sadly not. Next stop Maureen Little, if I can run her to earth. Believe it or not, she's actually on Trish's photo, so I'm hoping she has an unblemished copy.'

'And hasn't thrown it away years ago,' Max said.

TEN

Lindsey was preparing for her evening with Hugh when her mother phoned.

'Have you heard?' she demanded excitedly. 'The police have arrested someone for the Coombes murder!'

Lindsey tucked the phone between ear and shoulder and continued with her mascara. 'The husband, you mean?'

'No, that's what's so surprising! They're not identifying him at this stage, but word has it he's a "friend of the family", who called at the house that evening while Kevin was out. Sarah feels quite vindicated – she was always sure it wasn't him.'

'Then why did he run off with the children?' Lindsey asked.

'I don't know – he must have had his reasons. Perhaps to protect them?' She paused. 'Do you know where Rona is? I rang to tell her but got the answerphone and her mobile's switched off.'

'She and Max are in Lincoln for the weekend.' Lindsey leant towards the mirror to apply lipstick.

'Lincoln? What on earth for?'

'Something to do with this photograph. Look, Mum, I'd love to chat, but I'm due out in twenty minutes. Can I ring you back later?'

'Going somewhere nice?' Avril enquired.

'For a meal, I'm not sure where.'

'Ah! Dominic?'

'No, Mum, not Dominic.' Having no intention of revealing the identity of her companion, she repeated quickly, 'I really must go. Have a good evening, and I'll phone tomorrow.' And she broke the connection.

She was aware of anticipation as she ran down to open the door to Hugh. She'd taken extra care with her appearance, discarding several outfits before settling on a designer dress and jacket in soft gold wool that clung in all the right places and kindled gold flecks in her eyes.

'Hi!' she greeted him gaily.

'Lindsey.' He kissed her cheek but his eyes were guarded, and, unusually, he did not comment on her appearance.

'Long time no see,' she added, keeping her tone light.

'You've been otherwise occupied,' he said.

It seemed wise to let that pass, and since both his responses had been on the curt side she determined to leave it to him to speak first. However, when, on emerging from the cul-de-sac where she lived, he turned to the right rather than left towards the town, curiosity overcame her resolve and she asked where they were going.

'A new place has opened in Nettleton,' he replied, his eyes on the road. 'I'm interested to try it out.'

'Competition for the Deer Park?'

'Quite possibly.'

Still monosyllabic. Lindsey lapsed into silence, content to let things take their course. They hadn't, after all, seen each other since October, when she'd invited him to take any items he'd like from her flat before she disposed of them. Afterwards they'd gone for a pub meal, and though the atmosphere between them was, as always, charged with sexual tension, they'd been as relaxed with each other as it was possible to be. This time, with Dominic no longer on the scene, she was hoping for more.

Conversation remained sparse throughout the journey, and by the time they reached Nettleton it was starting to get dark. Hugh slowed down, uncertain as to the exact location of the restaurant, but its brightly lit frontage provided a beacon, and as they went inside, Lindsey saw that most of the tables were already occupied.

'Seems popular,' she remarked.

'It's one of the few places open on a Sunday. I took the precaution of booking a table.'

Had he, she wondered, specified a corner one, secluded from the main area? Apparently not; the table they were led to was in the centre of the room, past which waiters continually hurried on their way to and from the kitchen. The noise level was also fairly high, making it difficult to hear what the other was saying. All in all, it hardly seemed destined to be a romantic evening.

On the plus side, the menu was imaginative and the food good, and Lindsey decided to make the best of it, consoling herself with the thought of the twenty-minute drive home and her waiting flat. Meanwhile, across the table, she surreptitiously studied her ex-husband. He still seemed somewhat reserved, as though holding himself in check, and she wished futilely that the surrounding ambience was more conducive to a tête-à-tête.

'I hear they've arrested someone for the Belmont murder,' she said, aware, for the first time between them, of having to make conversation.

'Oh? I hadn't heard. They've found him, then?'

'Not the husband, a friend of the family.'

'Ah. Well, it's good to know the husband isn't always the black sheep.'

She glanced quickly at him, but his face gave no hint of hidden meaning.

'Is Rona involved?' he asked after a minute.

'No, but Sarah, my soon-to-be-stepsister, is, so she's keeping up the family tradition. It was she and her boyfriend who found the body.'

'*Plus ça change*,' Hugh said, and, finally submerged in the surrounding noise, the conversation withered and died.

'Well?' Lindsey challenged, as their dessert was served. 'Has it come up to your expectations?'

'I'm not sure I had any. You wanted a meal out, this was somewhere new, I decided to give it a try.'

Feeling he was putting the onus for any shortcomings on her, Lindsey said tartly, 'And it has the advantage of being far enough away for no one to recognize us.'

He raised an eyebrow. 'Would that have been a problem?'

'Not for me, but your new girlfriend might not be too happy.'

'Oh, she knows about this evening,' Hugh said calmly. 'She was with me when you phoned.'

Lindsey stared at him. *He was here with that woman's permission!* Damn, damn, damn! She pushed her plate away, belatedly aware that the gesture was petulant. 'That's all right, then,' she said tightly.

Then they were in the car driving home, and Lindsey's frustration was building. She'd been so sure the evening would end with them making love; now, this seemed highly unlikely. Though perfectly polite, Hugh had kept her at arm's length and such talk as they'd been able to conduct above the general hubbub had been depressingly impersonal.

He had switched on the car radio, possibly to lessen the need for conversation, and the romantic late-night music seemed a mockery. Damn it, she wanted him, and she was perfectly sure he wanted her too, though he seemed determined to deny it. Was this all down to the redhead Rona had seen him with? Could it possibly be that their relationship was serious? Lindsey had always been confident that, divorce or not, Hugh was there for her whenever she needed him – a fact of which she'd made use more than once over the last year or two. Why, she wondered miserably, had he agreed to this evening, if he hadn't meant to take advantage of it?

He turned into the wide gravel space outside the flats, switched off the engine, and, ever the gentleman, came round to open her door.

'Will you come in for a coffee?' she asked. 'You've not seen the flat since it was redecorated.'

'It's rather late; I'd better be getting back. Another time, perhaps.'

'Tomorrow's a holiday,' she reminded him, trying to keep the pleading out of her voice, but he shook his head.

'Then all I can say is, thank you for the meal.'

'A pleasure,' he said neutrally.

She hesitated briefly, then reached up and kissed him on the mouth. He didn't respond, though she felt a tremor go through him.

'Good night, Hugh,' she said, and letting herself into the flat, ran up the stairs and flung herself on the bed in a storm of tears.

Those tears might have been less bitter had she known that as she shut the door, Hugh rested both hands on the roof of the car and bent his head, drawing in several laboured breaths. It was some minutes before he slowly straightened, walked round to the driver's side, and drove away.

It was Tuesday morning before Rona was able at last to reach Kitty Mason, who, it transpired, had been away, and then it took some time to explain who she was.

'Oh!' Kitty exclaimed finally. 'Avril Beecham's daughter! The writer! How nice to hear from you, dear.' Then, anxiety creeping into her voice, 'Avril's quite well, I hope?'

'Oh yes,' Rona hastened to reassure her, 'never better!' And realized, with slight resentment on her father's behalf, that she spoke no less than the truth. 'She sends her regards, by the way.'

'We used to be in regular contact,' Kitty said regretfully, 'but over the last few years it's become more sporadic – down to Christmas cards, in fact. It would be good to meet again. Now, how can I help you?'

'It's all rather involved, but I've been asked to find out about Springfield Lodge School for Girls, and Mum says your sisters went there.'

'Heavens, you're going back a bit, aren't you? Yes, they did.'

'Were they both there when it closed down?'

'Bridget had left the previous year, but Mo was – about to take her O-levels, in fact.'

'I believe it caused a lot of talk?'

'Oh, there was plenty of gossip at the time, but with hindsight it was probably the proverbial molehill.'

Rona hesitated. 'Do you think Maureen would mind speaking to me about it?'

'I doubt if it would do much good; she won't have anything new to say, and she never believed the rumours in the first place. Why the sudden interest, if I may ask?'

'A friend of my sister's found a photograph belonging to her mother, who'd been on the staff, and someone in it had been vigorously blacked out. She – the friend – is anxious to know who and why.'

'Does it matter, after all this time?'

'Her mother was very upset when she saw it again, years later.' Rona paused. 'And I've just discovered your sister's on the same photo, so with luck she can tell us who it was.'

'Ah! Well, there she might be able to help. Hold on while I look up the number.' There was a thump as the phone was put down, and the sound of a drawer being opened. Then Kitty came back on the line. 'Her husband died last year,' she said, 'and she moved to Somerset to live with Bridget, who's also widowed.

Personally, I can't see it working; they've fought like cat and dog ever since they were girls. Still, it was their decision. Have you a pen handy?'

Rona took down the number. 'Thanks so much. If you could tell me her married name, I'll give her a ring?'

'O'Connell,' Kitty supplied. 'Let me know what happens; it sounds quite intriguing!'

The call ended with Kitty sending best wishes to Avril and promising to contact her. 'We were each other's bridesmaids,' she said.

'Mrs O'Connell?'

'Speaking.'

Rona went through the routine of introducing herself and explaining what she wanted. 'It would be wonderful if you could identify who it was,' she ended.

'A photo dated 1951? My goodness, I should certainly have to wrack my brains!'

Rona crossed her fingers. 'I was wondering if you might have a copy yourself?'

'Oh, I very much doubt it, my dear! We moved a lot during our married life, and my husband was always getting rid of what he called clutter. I know I threw out a lot of old albums when we downsized, as they say.'

Probably too much to have hoped for, Rona thought philosophically. 'Well, even if you haven't a copy, if you saw mine you might be able to tell who was missing.'

'I might,' Maureen O'Connell conceded doubtfully, 'but it's a very long time ago.'

Rona considered asking if she remembered Trish Cowley or Susie Baines, but decided to wait till they met. 'Would it be all right if I came down to see you? Quite apart from the photo, I'd be interested to hear what you remember about the school.'

'You'd be welcome, of course, but it's a long way to come on the off-chance.'

'It shouldn't take much more than a couple of hours, and I'd really like to meet you.'

'Very well, if you feel it's worth it. We can at least give you lunch. I'm living with my sister now, as Kitty might have told you. She was at Springfield, too.'

'Oh, please don't go to any trouble. I—'

'Nonsense; you have to eat, and so do we. Now, I can't manage tomorrow, but Thursday would be all right, if that suits you?'

Arrangements were made, the address given, and at last Rona, putting down the phone, felt she was getting somewhere. Whether or not her optimism was misplaced, she would shortly find out.

Having done her shopping the next morning, Rona paused on the corner of Guild Street and Fullers Walk, her carrier bag heavy in her hand. Gus, surprised at the unexpected halt, looked up enquiringly, and when she made no move sat down on the pavement.

The truth was, she was in no hurry to go home. Earlier that morning her editor, Prue Granger, had phoned.

'No pressure!' she'd said cheerfully, instantly creating it. 'Just wondered how the magnum opus is progressing?'

Almost, Rona thought guiltily, as though she knew it had been temporarily shelved.

'A bit in the doldrums,' she confessed. 'It's pretty routine at the moment, reading through diaries, checking lists and so on.'

'Boring?' enquired Prue astutely.

'A little,' Rona admitted. 'Actually, I thought I might have a week or two's break, so that when I come back to it, I can look at it with fresh eyes.'

'Fine, as long as it really is only a week or two. Any longer, and you might lose the will to continue!'

So – decision time. She could either go home, have a snack lunch, and incarcerate herself in her study, or she could give in to temptation and go to the Gallery for one of their deliciously fluffy omelettes, with garlic bread on the side. And to be logical, it wasn't worth spending time trying to break the work block, when tomorrow would be spent visiting Maureen O'Connell. No contest, really.

She turned, tugging gently at the lead, and walked back along Guild Street to the wrought-iron steps leading up to the Gallery.

As usual, the café was fairly busy, and she was hesitating in the doorway when she heard her name called, and turned to see

Gavin waving to her. He rose as she made her way over to join him. 'I've just arrived myself, and was lucky enough to nab this table as someone was leaving.' He pulled out her chair. 'How are you?'

'Fine, thanks.' Rona sat down and Gus, used to the routine, made his way under the table, nudging their feet as he settled down. 'Actually, I'm playing hooky. I should be slaving over a hot computer.'

'And I should be eating sandwiches at my desk, but I rebelled. I needed a change of scene, and this is as good a scene as any.'

The waitress stopped at their table and they gave their orders.

As she moved away, Rona said carefully, 'You know that after you said you were worried about Magda, I had lunch with her, and she admitted to having worries herself?'

Gavin nodded, his eyes intent on hers.

'Well, I phoned the other day to see how things were and she insisted everything had been exaggerated, she'd stopped having the dreams and all was well.'

Gavin toyed with his knife, not meeting her eyes.

'So is there nothing to worry about after all?' Rona prompted.

'I wouldn't exactly say that.' He paused. 'Did she tell you *how* the dreams stopped?'

Rona looked puzzled. 'No?'

'It happened soon after I saw you and it was pretty terrifying, I can tell you. She'd gone to bed early with a headache, and I'd just come into the bedroom when she suddenly sat up and let out a piercing shriek. Honestly Rona, it was . . . primeval, raising the hairs on the back of my neck. I rushed over and tried to catch hold of her, but she threw me off, twisting first one way, then the other and shouting, "No! No! No!"'

Rona stared at him, wide-eyed, and after drawing a deep breath he continued.

'When I finally shook her awake, she looked at me blankly, as though she'd no idea who I was. Then she said in a whisper, "Oh God! Oh my God!" and started to cry as though her heart would break. I held her, rocking her backwards and forwards and stroking her back, but she went on and on sobbing till I began to wonder if she'd ever stop. Eventually she fell asleep in my arms from sheer exhaustion. I laid her back on the pillow, crept in beside her, and lay awake for a long time in case she woke again, but she didn't.'

'So – what happened in the morning?'

'She had a raging headache and was white as a sheet. She didn't protest when I said she should stay in bed, which was unheard of in itself. But when I asked if it had been a particularly bad dream the previous night, she insisted she hadn't dreamt at all, and became very upset when I pressed her.'

'She didn't remember crying and everything?' Rona asked incredulously.

'It seemed not,' Gavin said heavily. 'If I believed all that psychobabble, I'd say that either she was in denial, or the trauma had been so severe her mind had blanked it out. On the other hand, she might have crossed the border between nightmare and night terror, which is much more frightening and, unlike a dream, you've no memory of it when you wake up.'

He drank from his glass while Rona tried to think of something to say.

'In any event,' he continued, 'apart from insisting the dreams have stopped, she's refused to talk about it, though every now and again I see an expression on her face that's . . . I don't know, the only way I can describe it is – *frightened*. I've begged her to go and see the doctor, but of course she refuses. God help me, I've been afraid she might try to harm herself.'

'Oh, Gavin!' After a moment Rona moistened her lips. 'And . . . now?'

He shrugged. 'She's still withdrawn, and, as I said, refusing to talk about either the dreams or the false memories. It's though she's completely wiped them from her mind. Otherwise, I suppose things have more or less teetered back to normal.'

Their lunch arrived, Rona's omelette and Gavin's Cornish pasty, and they began to eat in silence, both thinking over what he'd said. Eventually Gavin looked up with an awkward smile.

'Sorry about landing you with all that,' he said. 'I wouldn't – couldn't – have told anyone else – it would have seemed a betrayal somehow – but you've been in on it from the beginning, and you know Magda better than most.'

'I just wish there was something I could do.'

'Tell you what: she was saying a while back that we must

have you and Max over for a meal. Suppose I get her to arrange this, and you can see what you think? Apart from anything else, it would do her good to have something other than work on her mind.'

'Far be it from me to turn down a dinner invitation!'

'Fine, I'll organize it.' He hesitated. 'How much does Max know about all this?'

'Most of it.'

He nodded. 'Fair enough. Right, now let's talk about something more cheerful. Are you still bedded down in your bio?'

'I should be, but I've allowed myself to be distracted this last week or so.' And she went on to tell him about the photograph and the lines she was following in an attempt to solve the mystery. 'The people involved live just along the road from you – the Stirlings. Do you know them?'

'Only to say good morning to. It all sounds very interesting; you can give me an update when you come to dinner!'

'I might even have the answer by then!' Rona said.

There was a message on her answerphone when she returned from lunch, Beryl Temple thanking her profusely for the photographs of the school that she'd received in the morning's post.

'It fills in quite a few gaps for us,' she said. 'I'll drop a line to Mrs Grayson, of course, but I'm so grateful to you for reminding her about them.'

One satisfied customer, at least, Rona thought.

Lindsey sat in her office, staring moodily at her computer screen. What was *wrong* with her? she thought dejectedly. Other women could function perfectly adequately without a man in their lives; why couldn't she? Why did her current relationship, whoever it happened to be with, colour her whole existence, make it worth getting up for in the morning, lie comfortingly at the back of her mind all day?

'William's not my only option,' she'd said cockily to Rona; 'Hugh would come running if I snapped my fingers and probably Jonathan too'. The words came back to haunt her. Well, pride went before a fall; William had turned out to be a non-starter, and – worse – so had Hugh, her erstwhile prop. Which left only

Jonathan, and he'd been openly hostile since she'd switched from him to Dominic last summer – an attitude that had not gone unnoticed in the firm of which they were both partners. If she *did* revert to him, Rona would probably refuse to speak to her; she'd always been critical of the fact that Jonathan was married, more particularly since meeting his wife at a Christmas party. But damn it, if a woman couldn't hold on to her man, it was hardly Lindsey's fault, was it?

She jumped as a ping informed her she had received an email, and, thankfully abandoning her reflections, she returned to work.

'Jenny? It's Catherine.'

There was a momentary pause, then her daughter-in-law's voice. 'Catherine, hello. How are you?'

'Well, thank you. Did you enjoy your visit to your parents?'

'To be honest, I was getting bored,' Jenny said frankly. 'I'm no longer a country girl, if I ever was, and I missed Daniel.'

Was that final phrase intended to soften her? 'I'm sure,' Catherine answered smoothly. 'Well, it's over a month since I've seen you and Alice; I was wondering if you could all come over for the day on Saturday? Or have you other plans?'

'No, I'm sure we haven't – we'd love to come. Alice has produced two new teeth since we saw you! They're at the back, so you can't see them, but they caused a bit of trouble coming through, poor pet.'

'It does seem hard, doesn't it? Will you need to check with Daniel about Saturday?'

'No, there's nothing in the diary, and I'm sure he'd love to see you.'

'Fine; leave as early as you can, so we can have a nice, long day together.'

'I've invited my family over for the day on Saturday,' Catherine said to Tom that evening. 'I've not seen Alice for over a month, and apparently she has two new teeth!'

'That'll be good,' Tom said easily. 'Well, you won't want me at the reunion, so I'll take the chance of a game of golf.'

'Tom, I didn't mean—'

He kissed her. 'It's all right, sweetie, I quite understand. After all the worry over Daniel and Jenny, this will be your first chance to see them together. You need to be just a family, without any hangers-on.'

Catherine smiled. 'You could never be a hanger-on!'

'All the same, it will be better that way.'

She reached for his hand. 'Another example of why I love you, Tom Parish!' she said.

ELEVEN

Rona set out for Somerset early on Thursday morning, and was glad to find the motorways reasonably quiet. It was still the school holidays, and a lot of people would be away. As directed, she turned off the M5 at Wellington and followed winding country roads to the village where the one-time Little sisters now lived.

It was clear from the first that Bridget intended to be present at the interview, though Maureen did all she could to dissuade her. 'Rona wants to talk about that last term,' she pointed out, 'and you weren't even *there.*'

'All the same, I'm sure I have a better idea of what really happened. You were too close to it, and accepted what you were told.'

Maureen subsided with a tut of annoyance, and as the sisters fussed about seating arrangements, Rona was free to study them. Bridget, the elder, was small and stout, and her elaborate coiffure spoke of a weekly visit to the hairdresser. By contrast, Maureen's short hair was cut in a no-nonsense fringe. She was thinner than her sister, but her face was more lined and, though she tried, Rona found it hard to reconcile the woman before her with the girl in Heather Grayson's photograph. Unlike Heather herself, her contemporaries would have been hard put to recognize her.

'So – where's this photo, then?' Maureen asked as Bridget, claiming hostess duties, brought in the coffee.

Rona produced it and Maureen took it eagerly, then, almost immediately, frowned. 'Who did you say this belonged to?'

'A member of staff; Trish Cowley.'

Maureen nodded. 'I thought as much.'

'Why?' Rona asked quickly, hopes rising.

'Because she's the most likely to have blacked out Miss Baines.'

'Blacked out?' Bridget echoed, and forsook the coffee pot to peer over her sister's shoulder. 'Great heavens, is that who it is?'

'You're sure it's Miss Baines under that ink blot?' Rona pressed.

'Positive. That's me in the back row, and as you can see, she's sitting directly in front of me. I even remember it being taken, because she'd been giggling with Mr Crichton next to her, which had annoyed me.'

'Why was Miss Cowley most likely to have blotted her out?'

'Well, she wasn't even in Brontë; the only reason she'd have had it is because Bainesy was on it. Up to then, they'd been thick as thieves.'

'And then what happened?'

Maureen shrugged. 'No one ever knew. It was clear there was an atmosphere between them, and Lizzie Barclay came across the Cow crying in one of the locker rooms.' She glanced at Rona in embarrassed apology. 'That's what we called her; it wasn't meant to be offensive, just a play on her name. Then one morning Bainesy was gone and never seen again. The consensus among us girls was that she was pregnant, and that was shocking enough, believe me, in 1951, but the sixth form maintained they'd had a lesbian affair and been caught out.' She smiled. 'I didn't let on, but I'd no idea what that meant; we were very innocent by today's standards.'

'I think pregnancy's the more likely,' Rona said. 'Miss Baines had a boyfriend.'

'Well, there you are, then.'

'But why would Trish Cowley black her out? Why not simply get rid of the photo?'

'I've no idea.' She looked down at the print. 'The surface seems scratched, as though a lot of force was used. It was probably done in a fit of temper, and she might have regretted it later.' She peered more closely, as though trying to penetrate the blob. 'Has anyone tried to wash it off?'

'Glenda did – Trish's daughter – but the ink had seeped in and sponging was doing more harm than good.'

'I knew Miss Baines,' Bridget said, determinedly entering the conversation, 'though not Miss Cowley – she must have come after I'd left.'

'What was she like, Susie Baines?' Rona asked, tactfully directing the question to Bridget. 'I'm never likely to see a photo of her, and I've been trying to picture her.'

'She was a pretty little thing,' Bridget said reflectively. 'Fair, curly hair and a lovely smile. She wasn't a pushover, though, far from it. She could be quite strict if she thought you were trying anything on.'

'She'd a mind of her own,' Maureen agreed. 'Once she'd decided on something, it was no use trying to get her to change it.'

Rona thought for a moment. 'I suppose no one knew whether she'd left voluntarily, or been sacked?'

Both sisters shook their heads.

'Could whatever it was have been the reason for the school suddenly closing?'

They answered together, Bridget agreeing the possibility, Maureen emphatically denying it.

'Oh come on, Mo!' Bridget exclaimed. 'There was already the scandal of alcohol on the premises and parents threatening to remove their daughters. This business with Bainsey must have been the last straw.'

'Absolute nonsense!' Maureen declared. 'The Head had a heart attack, poor man, and that was the sole reason for the closure. I suppose it could have been brought on by whatever happened, but that's the only possible connection.'

It was clear there'd be no agreement between the sisters, and Rona was left to make what she could of their observations. They continued to talk about the school, memories having been revived by the discussion, but there was nothing that had any relevance to what interested her. As Maureen had warned, it was a long way to have come for confirmation of Susie Baines's identity, of which she'd already been almost sure.

It was only as she was leaving after lunch that a casual comment made the whole trip worthwhile. She'd already started down the path when Maureen, standing at the door, called after her, 'I've just thought: the headmaster had a daughter. She was a lot younger than we were, but if anyone knew the truth of what happened, it'd be her.'

Rona turned back, her face lighting up. 'That's fantastic! Do you know how I could contact her?'

'I've no idea; to be honest, I'd forgotten her very existence. Now I think of it, though, I remember hearing years ago that she'd gone into teaching. You might be able to trace her that way.'

'You don't happen to remember her first name?'

'Not offhand, but I think it was something biblical.'

'Well, thank you very much. That gives me a new lead.'

Something biblical. Salome? Rona thought facetiously as she drove off. Delilah? Jezebel? They didn't sound quite right for a school teacher. It was as well she had the surname Lytton to work on; it was fairly unusual, which should aid her search.

So – she'd completed the first part of her task: Susie Baines had been positively identified as the face beneath the ink. Now, she must try to discover why Trish Cowley had so ferociously scrubbed out her likeness, and why, over fifty years later, she'd almost passed out on seeing the photograph.

Rona hadn't been home long when Avril phoned.

'I've been speaking to Kitty,' she said, 'and we've arranged to meet for lunch. It'll be lovely to see her again, after all this time. She told me you were going to visit Maureen. How did you get on?'

'I'm just back, actually, and pretty shattered after all that driving. It was quite busy coming home.'

'But did you learn anything?'

'I found out the headmaster had a daughter. My next task is to find her.'

'You know her married name?'

'Oh God, I never thought of that! If she married, I haven't a hope in hell of finding her. She went into teaching, that's all I know. I'll go on line in the morning and see if I can track her down.'

'Well, that's only one of the reasons I'm phoning. The other is to invite you and Max to Sunday lunch. It's a long time since we were all together. Lindsey's coming too; it seems the ever-present Dominic isn't as ever-present nowadays.'

'He never was,' Rona pointed out.

'Well, he was always wheeled out as an excuse when she didn't want to come here.'

Rona bit her lip; that was a touch of the old, sour Avril she'd hoped had gone for good.

'We'd love to come, Mum; thanks.'

But would she really enjoy it? she wondered as she rang off. Sunday lunch at Belmont inevitably brought her father to mind; it would be hard to see Guy Lacey in his place at the head of the table.

'Linz?'

'Hi there.'

'Just reporting back. I've been to see Maureen Little-that-was, and she confirms the anonymous person on the photo is Susie Baines. So at least that's one thing cleared up. She doesn't know why she left so suddenly, though her sister had some lurid theories. The only hopeful thing to come out of it is that they said the Head of Springfield had a daughter, and if we can track her down, we might get somewhere. I'm going to have a go in the morning.'

'Good; keep me posted. No doubt you've been invited to Sunday lunch?'

'Yes, Mum's just been on.'

'She asked very pointedly if I'd be spending the weekend with Dominic.'

'And I presume you're not?'

'You presume correctly.'

'OK; well, I've just got in and I'm starving, so I'm going in search of food. See you on Sunday.'

Jonathan Hurst put his head round Lindsey's office door.

'I hate to intrude, but your nemesis has surfaced again.'

Lindsey looked at him crossly. 'I've no idea what you're talking about.'

'Old man Steinbeck, our wealthiest client whom you stood up to go off sailing with your boyfriend.'

Lindsey flushed, both at the memory of their previous altercation and of that weekend with Dominic. 'Surely he's all yours now,' she answered. 'He'll have written me off after last time.'

'It seems not. He's still convinced we need to work together to protect his best interests.'

Lindsey sighed. 'What does he want this time?'

'You know how the super-rich enjoy rewriting their wills. It keeps their relatives on their toes. Well, number two son whom he struck off in October has apparently now redeemed himself and is to be written back in.'

'That seems simple enough; it doesn't need two of us.'

'Agreed, but Steinbeck likes to play the "Big I Am", and while he pays us megabucks, who are we to argue? I managed to dig you out of the hole last time, but I'm damned if I'll do it again. As always, we'll be treated to dinner at the Clarendon afterwards, which helps to sweeten the pill. Or are you flying off to Mozambique with lover-boy?'

Lindsey bit her lip. 'Don't be absurd, Jonathan.'

'Ah! Touched a raw nerve, have I? Don't tell me the bed of roses has sprouted thorns?'

'I'm not telling you anything!' Lindsey said heatedly. 'But if we must humour the old tyrant, so be it. You arrange it, but this time keep me in the loop.'

She'd expected him to nod and leave the room, but when he didn't immediately move, she looked up to find him surveying her with narrowed eyes.

'Well?' she challenged, and he smiled his lopsided smile.

'I've missed you,' he said. And before she could think of a suitable retort, he was gone.

Lindsey pressed her hands to her hot cheeks, conscious of a quickened heartbeat. It seemed that in one respect at least, her boast to Rona had not been empty; too bad it was her least favourite option. He'd told her he was getting divorced, she remembered. How could she have fallen for that old cliché? Or perhaps, she thought with searing honesty, she never had.

It had certainly had its excitements, their time together, not least because of its forbidden pleasures: the secret meetings at her flat when she was working from home, and the time her mother nearly caught them; the occasion when his wife arrived unannounced in his office as they were on the point of embracing. Sexy, self-indulgent Jonathan, with his overlong fair hair, his deep-set grey eyes, his mobile mouth. A shudder ran through her. Oh God, she thought, here we go again.

To her relieved surprise, Rona struck gold almost at once. After the expected links to Lytton Strachey and Bulwer-Lytton, she came across one Esther Lytton with a choice of sites to her name.

Until recently, Rona learned, moving from one to the other, she'd been principal of an eminent girls' school, and was on a number of committees and associations connected with education. She had also been an external examiner and school governor, and had taught for a while at an international school in France.

Rona clicked hopefully on 'Biography', but was rewarded only with her professional appointments; no mention of her own education or background.

But despite the listed information, when she phoned the named schools to ask for a message to be forwarded her luck ran out and she repeatedly came up against a brick wall. 'I'm sorry, we have no means of reaching Miss Lytton,' was the standard reply. Nor did she do any better with the BT on-line phone book, that had stood her in good stead in the past. No entry appeared for Esther Lytton; ex-directory, it seemed.

Rona sat back in frustration. So near and yet so far. Well, all she could do was write to her at the last school mentioned with the request that it be redirected; and she'd mark it 'Private and Confidential' for good measure. It was less than a year since Esther Lytton had retired, and Rona couldn't believe she'd not left a forwarding address, with the post office if not the school.

Later, she phoned Glenda Stirling.

'Rona, hello! Have you some news for us?'

'Nothing very exciting, I'm afraid. I've seen both the lady who stayed at the hotel and the friends of my mother, and have at least confirmed the person behind the blob was Susie Baines. But no one has been able to suggest why. She and your mother were close friends, as you know, but for some reason their friendship ended acrimoniously.'

'Oh, dear.' Glenda sounded despondent.

'My last hope is the headmaster's daughter,' Rona continued. 'She's recently retired from teaching and I've been trying to trace her, so far without success. However, I'm going to write to her at her last school, in the hope they'll pass the letter on.'

'Well, thank you. It's so good of you to give up your time like this.'

'I enjoy a challenge!' Rona said. 'I'll be in touch when, or if, I have any further news.'

*   *   *

Catherine was slightly apprehensive as she awaited the family's arrival that Saturday. Would Jenny feel awkward with her? If so, would Daniel notice? She resolved to be as natural as possible, and hoped her daughter-in-law would respond accordingly.

In the event, it turned out that their big news, held back as a surprise, was that Alice was now walking, and in the excitement any lingering embarrassment painlessly dissolved.

'She took her first unaided steps on Easter Sunday,' Jenny told her, as the baby tottered unsteadily across the room and sat down suddenly on her well-padded behind. 'I'm so glad it was when Daniel was there.'

Later, when Daniel had volunteered to change his daughter's nappy and Catherine and Jenny were temporarily alone, Jenny said quietly, 'I'm so sorry about what happened. Thank you for being so understanding.'

'I'm not sure that I was,' Catherine admitted.

'Well, at least you didn't shop me. It was just a silly thing, with Daniel being away so much and feeling tired and depressed. The shock of you finding out brought me to my senses; I just needed time away to get my head together.'

'And did it work?'

'Oh yes. I realized how much I loved him and how stupid I'd been. I can promise you it won't happen again.'

'Then it's all forgotten,' Catherine said, and Jenny bent to kiss her.

It was a happy family day, and Catherine reflected contentedly on how lucky she was. After all her years alone she now had a new love, whom she'd be marrying in a few months' time, and her beloved son was himself happily married with an enchanting baby daughter. She had a great deal to be thankful for.

'Who's this?' Jenny's voice broke into her thoughts and Catherine, glancing across, saw she'd picked up the copy of last week's *Gazette*, which Catherine had kept in order to check the crossword. Its front page bore a photograph of Kevin Coombes under the headline 'STILL ON THE RUN'.

'That's the husband of the woman who was murdered,' she said. 'In Belmont, of all places – where Tom used to live.'

Jenny frowned, still looking at the photograph. 'I don't remember hearing about it.'

'It was while you were away,' Daniel told her. 'But it's been in the papers and on TV.'

She shrugged. 'When I'm at the parents' I never seem to see a paper or hear the news – or if I do, it washes over me. He does look faintly familiar, though, so I might have seen something without registering it. What did he do, exactly?'

'Well, he was originally suspected of the killing, but they've now arrested someone else, a chap who called round when the husband was out. The theory seems to be that he tried it on with the wife and was given short shrift. Whereupon he lost his temper, lashed out and killed her, and left in a hurry as seen by a neighbour. All the same, the husband hardly behaved rationally, disappearing like that with their two little boys. The kids are OK,' he added quickly, seeing her eyes fly to Alice. 'He dumped them on their grandparents' doorstep a few days later.'

'But it says here he's still on the run?'

'That's last week's paper, I'm afraid,' Catherine put in, 'printed before the arrest. I suppose it's not technically correct now, but the police still want to see him, and though there've been reported sightings of him all over the place – Scotland, Devon, even the Continent – they've not been able to find him.'

'He must still be in the country, though,' Daniel maintained. 'They'd have put an immediate watch on ports and airports, so once the body was found it would have been hard to get out. And we know for a fact he was still around four days later, when he returned the children.'

'But if he didn't do it, why doesn't he come back?' Jenny asked.

'Good question – he still might have. Although this other chap's been arrested, he's still maintaining his innocence and hasn't been charged yet. The police have asked for an extension of time to question him.'

'So you think the husband could still be guilty?'

'Let's just say if he's nothing to hide why doesn't he come forward?'

Jenny shivered. 'Well, wherever he is, I hope they find him soon,' she said.

*   *   *

It was Saturday evening, and Max was engrossed in a sports programme on TV. Rona had cleared away their supper, switched on the dishwasher and laid the table for breakfast. And all the while, her mind had been turning over the mystery of Susie Baines and her defaced photograph. Oh, *why* was Esther Lytton, who offered the only remaining hope of solution, proving so inaccessible? She'd posted the letter, but it was like sending it into the blue, unsure of where or even if it would land. Was there really nothing else she could do?

She came to a sudden halt in the middle of the kitchen. *'Catherine!'* she said aloud, causing Gus to look up enquiringly from his basket. Of course! Why hadn't she thought of it before? Catherine too was a retired head teacher, albeit of a primary rather than an exclusive public school. But she and Esther must be roughly the same age, and could have moved in similar circles. It was certainly worth a try.

She glanced at the kitchen clock. Nine thirty. Not too late to phone, surely?

'Hello?'

'Catherine, it's Rona. I hope I'm not disturbing you?'

'Not at all, dear; I'm just relaxing after a lovely if somewhat hectic day with the family.'

'How are they?' Though Catherine didn't know it, Rona's query wasn't mere politeness; since her father had told her of their problems, she'd thought several times of Daniel and Jenny, hoping things were working out for them.

'Oh, they're fine. And Alice is walking! They hadn't told me in advance and the first I knew of it was when they set her down in the hall and she came toddling towards me.'

'That's lovely!' Rona said warmly.

'Still, I doubt if you phoned for a report on my family. What can I do for you?'

Rona crossed her fingers. 'I was wondering if by any chance you'd come across someone called Esther Lytton?'

'Esther? My goodness, that's a name from the past!'

'You *know* her?' Rona's voice rang out excitedly.

'Well, I used to. We did our teacher training together.'

'But are you still in touch?'

'Not really, though I saw her relatively recently at a reunion and we had a brief chat.'

'But would you be able to contact her? I mean, do you know her address?'

'Goodness, Rona, what is this?'

Rona took a deep breath. 'Sorry. I'll explain, but just tell me this: did she ever talk about her father or her childhood?'

'Now you really *are* making me curious! But to answer your question, I don't remember any in-depth conversations with her, and I'm sure we didn't discuss our backgrounds. Why, is it important?'

'It could have been.' Rona went on to explain the reasons behind her questioning. 'I've exhausted all other possibilities,' she ended, 'so you see I really am anxious to get in touch with her if at all possible.'

'How very interesting! This is definitely the first I've heard about her father being a headmaster, let alone about possible goings-on at the school. Let's see, now; I've probably got her address somewhere; we both belong to an association that sends out annual lists of everyone's whereabouts. As you know, I retired early to look after my mother, but Esther only stepped down at the end of the last school year. There was a write-up about her in the magazine. I can look it up for you, provided I still have it.'

'I'd be most grateful,' Rona said inadequately.

'It might take me a while to lay my hands on it but I'll have a look tomorrow, if that's all right?'

'It's perfect, Catherine, thanks. We're going to Maple Drive for lunch, so we'll be out between twelve and about four, but any time before or after would be fine.'

'Very well. I'll speak to you then.'

Rona switched off and drew a deep sigh of relief. Perhaps, after all, she was nearing the end of the trail.

TWELVE

Catherine hadn't phoned by the time they left for Maple Drive. Perhaps, Rona thought anxiously, she'd thrown out the relevant magazine. Was she after all back to square one?

'It'll be odd, going to Sunday lunch without Tom,' Max commented.

Rona nodded. 'Every time I go there the house seems somehow – depleted without him. I expect his coat to be on the hall stand.'

Max glanced at her with a half-laugh. 'No need to sound so tragic, love – he's not *dead*!'

'I know, and I also know that both he and Mum are happier now than they've been for years. I suppose it's tied up with childhood memories, but I really love that house; it's part of the family, and it doesn't feel right without him.'

'Well it won't be part of the family much longer,' Max reminded her.

'I know. I'll have to start bracing myself for that. The thought of it being dismantled . . .' She shuddered.

'Come on, don't make a drama of it. Most people move house several times, without inviting death and disaster.'

'But that's the whole point. We *never* moved, so Maple Drive has been "home" all my life. Even this morning, when I first woke, I thought, "What's on today? Oh yes, we're going home for lunch."'

'Well, thanks,' he said drily.

'Oh Max, you know what I mean! I adore our house, you know I do, it's just—'

'Only teasing,' he said.

'Tell me about your visit to Maureen,' Avril instructed, when they were sitting with drinks before lunch. 'I only remember her very vaguely as one of Kitty's "big sisters" who told us off if we made too much noise.'

'Well, for one thing she's not at all like her school photo,' Rona said.

'Who is?' Guy interposed. 'I'd hate to see mine!'

'She's tall and thin and Bridget's short and stout. They kept bickering, which was a bit embarrassing, but they both had vivid memories of the school.'

'And they knew who'd been inked out?'

'Yes; as it happened Maureen was standing directly behind her. It seems this teacher left suddenly in the middle of that last term and no one knew why. Or at least none of the girls did. So we're not much further on that.'

'When you rang you mentioned the headmaster's daughter?'

'Yes.' Rona paused. 'Actually, it turns out Catherine knew her; she's going to look up her address for me.'

Avril's lips pursed, but she said evenly, 'That should be useful.' Then, with a barely discernible change of direction, 'Did you know Kitty was with me at the tennis club the night I met your father? She was my bridesmaid, and a year later I was hers. We kept in regular touch for a while, then they moved to Stokely, we both had children, and our lives moved in different directions. Gradually it dwindled to Christmas cards and holiday postcards. It'll be good to see her again, and catch up.'

Guy refilled their glasses.

'How's Sarah?' Lindsey asked him.

'Not too good after this morning's news. Did you hear they've released that chap without charge?'

'No?'

'A school friend of Lucy's had phoned her about nine o'clock that evening before she went on holiday. Lucy told her she'd just had an unwelcome visitor, and she wasn't looking forward to telling Kevin, because he was jealous of the man. The poor girl arrived back to news of the murder, and was able to establish that Lucy had been alive a good hour after Crane was seen leaving. Which, of course, means Coombes is back in the frame.

'Meanwhile the school's still in shock. Lucy was on the PTA and frequently helped out, accompanying them on outings, hearing the children read and so on.' He shook his head sadly. 'Sarah's still having nightmares.'

The word 'nightmares' brought Magda to mind, and Rona

resolved to make another attempt to speak to her. After her talk with Gavin she was convinced something was still very wrong. He'd said they'd invite Max and herself for a meal; had Magda vetoed the idea?

'Well, we've got a bit of news for you,' Avril was saying brightly. 'We've found a house that we like very much, and since it's on the market we've decided not to wait till we're married but to go ahead and buy it.'

Both her daughters stared at her, identical expressions on their faces, but neither spoke.

'After all,' Avril hurried on, 'it would be stupid to let it go just for the sake of a few months when it's exactly what we want.'

'You're moving out of here *now*?' Rona asked into the lengthening silence. Max, sitting next to her on the sofa, patted her hand.

Lindsey said in a low voice, 'I've been hoping you'd change your minds and stay on.'

Avril glared at them in exasperation. 'Oh, *twins*!' she exclaimed, and the phrase, together with the tone in which it was uttered, was so familiar from childhood that they involuntarily smiled and the tension eased.

'Actually,' Rona said, 'I think it's a good idea. I mean, you'll be together somewhere new that hasn't any memories, that'll be *yours*.'

'Exactly,' Avril said with satisfaction.

'So where is this new house?' Max asked.

'In Brindley Grove,' Guy answered. 'It's halfway between here and Marsborough, off Belmont Road. You know whereabouts I mean?'

Rona's hand clenched. 'Oh, I know where it is,' she said.

Both Avril and Guy were looking at her. 'Is something wrong?'

Lindsey said lightly, 'No doubt it's connected with one of her gruesome discoveries, but you'd be hard pressed to find anywhere that isn't.'

Guy said, 'Rona? Is it going to be a problem?'

Rona shook herself. 'Of course not. But . . . it's not the house at the end, is it?'

Avril frowned. 'The Tarltons'? Why . . .? Oh God!' She clapped a hand to her mouth. 'I'd forgotten all about that! Oh, darling, I'm sorry! Are you sure it'll be all right?'

'Of course it will,' Rona said firmly. 'It's an attractive road; it'll be good for it to have pleasant associations for a change.'

In truth, the upsetting discovery at the Lodge was only one of several unhappy memories the road conjured up for her. It had not been a good time in her life; she and Max were going through a difficult patch which had culminated in his unwarranted arrest. All in all, a more positive outlook was well overdue.

'It's a cul-de-sac, of course,' Avril was continuing, 'and our house is on the right as you go in, about halfway down.'

'And what's it like?' Lindsey asked.

'It's one of the smaller ones, but detached, with a lovely garden. Guy, have you got the details?'

He produced a folder with the estate agent's description and photograph and they crowded round to look.

'It seems ideal, Mum,' Rona said, guilty at her momentary lapse. 'So your offer's been accepted?'

'Yes, on Friday. The present owners aren't in any hurry, so it will give us time to put this on the market.' She gave a little laugh. 'Only a few weeks ago we were going round Guy's house, marking who wanted what. We never thought we'd be doing it again so soon. Needless to say, if either of you would like anything specific, you only have to say. We already have what we kept of Guy's furniture, so we'll have to be fairly selective. Now –' she stood up – 'enough chat. I'll go and put the finishing touches to lunch. I hope you're all hungry.'

'Well, that was a turn-up for the book,' Max commented on their way home. 'Particularly in view of our conversation earlier.' He gave a short laugh. 'You should have seen your and Lindsey's faces! Talk about a lead balloon!'

'Well, it was a shock for both of us, even though we knew it'd come eventually. But I meant what I said; I actually think it will be easier all round. I can go there thinking of it as Mum and Guy's house, with no ghostly Pops lurking in the background.'

'And in due course there'll be a Tom and Catherine's house, too. The old order changeth, my love, and we have to change with it.'

*   *   *

Catherine phoned an hour after they got back.

'I've found it!' she said. 'Just as I was giving up hope, I came across it at the back of a drawer.'

'Oh, Catherine, that's wonderful! Does she live locally?'

'In Buckford, actually. Have you a pen handy?'

'Yes?'

Catherine read out the address and phone number. 'A word of warning,' she added. 'If there were nefarious goings-on at the school she mightn't be best pleased to be asked about them.'

'I'd thought of that. Can I mention your name as a softener?'

'By all means, for all the good it might do you.'

'It would at least show I wasn't calling completely "cold".'

'Well, go easy. She's a successful woman with a formidable reputation; she's unlikely to want to rake up scandals from the past.'

'I'll be discretion itself,' Rona promised. 'And thanks so much, Catherine. I'll let you know how I get on.'

The voice that immediately answered Rona's call was crisp and firm, simply stating the phone number.

'Miss Lytton?'

A slight hesitation, then, 'Who's calling?'

'My name is Rona Parish, and—'

'Can you tell me how you obtained this number? It's unlisted.'

'I know; I'm sorry. I was speaking to Catherine Bishop, and she—'

'Mrs Bishop gave it to you? Might I ask why?'

It was obvious she'd no time to be circumspect. In for a penny, Rona thought. 'I was hoping to have a word with you about Springfield Lodge.'

Total silence.

'I believe your father was headmaster there?'

'Are you the press?' The tone was coldly accusing.

'No; that is, I do occasionally—'

'I'm sorry; I don't give interviews to the media.' And the connection was cut.

'Well,' Max observed, 'that went well.'

'Damn and blast!' Rona exclaimed. 'She didn't even let me get a word in.'

'Obviously a past master – or mistress – at dealing with unwelcome callers.'

'But if she'd just let me explain—'

'It would have made things even worse.'

Rona sank her head in her hands. 'Oh Max, what am I going to do? Having got this close to her, I can't give up now!'

'I doubt if you've any choice,' he said.

Catherine phoned the next morning.

'I've just had a very irate Esther on the line.'

'Oh Catherine, I'm so sorry! She didn't give me a chance to be tactful! What did she say?'

'Slated me for handing out her private number and demanded to know who you were and why I'd given it to you. I explained you were a much-respected biographer who occasionally wrote articles for the prestigious magazine *Chiltern Life*, and that you would shortly be my stepdaughter.'

Rona gave a choked laugh. 'That should have given her food for thought!'

'It certainly calmed her down a little. I might add that I professed total ignorance about what you wanted to discuss, though I imagine, if it was as traumatic as you say, she'd have a pretty good idea.'

'Frankly, I'm beginning to wonder if it was all a storm in a teacup,' Rona said flatly. 'OK, so a member of staff left suddenly in the middle of term. So what? It must happen all the time – family emergency, illness, a hundred reasons. If it hadn't been for Trish Cowley's reaction on seeing the photo, I'd never have taken this on.'

'Well, I suppose you win some, lose some. Sorry it didn't work out.'

Feeling somewhat deflated, Rona returned to Elspeth Wilding and her diaries, but their content did little to lighten her mood. Despite Elspeth's renown there'd been a lot of sadness in her life and even more in her death. It was possible to trace in their pages the progress of her long friendship with fellow artist Chloë Pyne and its tragic end, and the malign influence of Nathan Tate, whom she'd met herself with such disastrous consequences. Hindsight, she thought, could be a curse as well as a blessing to a biographer, particularly one who had known her subject personally.

She was roused from her melancholy by a phone call from Magda.

'Rona, Gavin and I have been looking for a date when we can have you and Max over. I know Max prefers weekends because of his evening classes, but we're tied up for the next few. Could he make an exception, do you think, and come to us on Wednesday, following his afternoon class? Otherwise we're into next month, which is ridiculous.'

'I'm sure he could,' Rona told her, vowing to twist his arm if necessary. 'We might have to make it a little later, though, if that's all right? His last class doesn't finish till six thirty; then he has to tidy up, come home, shower and change, and drive to you.'

'No problem at all. Shall we say this Wednesday, then, between eight and eight thirty?'

'Thanks, Magda. We'll look forward to it.'

Rona replaced the phone thoughtfully. Magda had sounded brisk and businesslike, but then she must have been phoning from one of the boutiques and wouldn't have time to chat. And if they were seeing each other in a couple of days, they could catch up then. She hoped desperately that her friend would prove to be her old self again.

Lindsey had dressed with care, choosing an outfit that wasn't too dressy for a day in the office, but would carry her successfully into dinner at the Clarendon. Jewellery, she would add at the end of the working day.

'Very delectable!' Jonathan murmured as she passed him in the outer office, and she felt herself flush. She really must school herself not to react to everything he said – it would only encourage him.

Jacob Steinbeck arrived promptly for his appointment at five thirty – a concession, as appointments were normally scheduled no later than five. He was short and plump and habitually wore pinstriped trousers and a bow tie. His sparse black hair was combed carefully over a shining pate, and he addressed Lindsey as 'dearie', a habit that set her teeth on edge but, as Jonathan had pointed out more than once, she'd no choice but to accept it. Another concession that had been neither requested nor granted was that he smoked a fat cheroot throughout the meeting, blandly ignoring the office no-smoking rule and filling the room with a pungent haze that unfailingly brought on a headache.

'Well, now, dearie,' he greeted her, advancing with outstretched hand, 'I'm delighted to see you; you were indisposed in the autumn, I believe?'

Lindsey, who'd told Jonathan to explain her absence by saying she had yellow fever, could only hope he'd not taken her literally. She took the proffered hand, which was as small and smooth as a woman's. 'I was so sorry to miss the appointment, Mr Steinbeck,' she lied.

'The disappointment was mutual; I always say a pretty woman helps to oil the wheels.' He rubbed his hands together. 'Right; if you're ready let's get down to work.'

For all his idiosyncrasies, Jacob Steinbeck was a hard-wired businessman. Having started as a London barrow boy at the age of fifteen, he had worked his way up to become one of the foremost entrepreneurs in the country, renowned for knowing the names of all the staff throughout his empire and most of their salaries. For the next hour or so his will was gone through yet again in painstaking detail, and as well as reinstating his son he took the opportunity to alter several other bequests, enlarging some and reducing others. It was almost seven by the time the business was concluded to his satisfaction.

'I'll have it drawn up for you tomorrow, Mr Steinbeck,' Jonathan said. 'Will you be able to call in to sign it, or would you like it sent to your home address?'

Steinbeck waved a cheroot-holding hand, sending clouds of smoke towards Lindsey, who had difficulty holding down a cough. 'Put it in the post, dear boy; I'm leaving for Spain first thing. Now –' he consulted the Rolex on his wrist – 'time, I think, to stroll across the road. The table's booked for seven fifteen, which allows for a visit to the bar beforehand.'

On the first of these occasions – dinner always followed an appointment with Jacob Steinbeck – Lindsey had expected it to be a tedious affair, with the onerous task of finding enough topics to keep the conversation going throughout the meal. However, not for the first time, their host had surprised her, proving himself to be a witty conversationalist with a wealth of amusing anecdotes of his experiences around the world, and contrary to expectations she had thoroughly enjoyed herself.

This evening they had had their customary – and obligatory – champagne cocktails in the bar, but Lindsey was now limiting herself to mineral water, aware of the fifteen-minute drive home.

It was while their host was discussing with the wine waiter which vintage to choose that Jonathan leant over and murmured in Lindsey's ear, 'A certain gentleman across the room seems disconcerted to see you here.'

Glancing in the direction indicated, she was startled to find herself meeting Dominic's steady gaze. As their eyes made contact he gave a slight nod before turning back to his companions, two men whom she guessed to be business colleagues.

Fortunately Mr Steinbeck's attention was still engaged. 'You might have warned me!' she whispered furiously, aware of Jonathan's perverse delight in the situation. He and Dominic Frayne had crossed swords before and the last time Dominic had emerged as the victor.

The wine waiter moved away with a bow, putting an end to their private conversation. Lindsey's heart was pounding; she'd not seen Dominic since storming out of his flat, nor had he tried to contact her. If he now assumed she was back with Jonathan, so be it. In the meantime, she could only hope Steinbeck wouldn't notice her heightened colour.

For the rest of the meal she studiously avoided glancing in that direction, but as they were having coffee Jonathan's murmured 'Uh-oh!' gave her a second's warning before, to her horror, she found Dominic standing beside her. His gaze, however, was directed at Steinbeck.

'Good evening, sir,' he said.

Steinbeck looked up, his face creasing into a beam. 'Frayne! My dear chap! I'd no idea you were here! May I introduce my guests?'

'We've already met,' Dominic said evenly. 'Lindsey. Jonathan.' He nodded at each in turn.

'Splendid, splendid. On your way out, are you? Will you join us for a liqueur?'

Lindsey held her breath but Dominic gestured towards the two men awaiting him in the doorway. 'Regretfully, no. I must rejoin my colleagues.'

'Another time, then. We must eat together.'

'I look forward to it.' And with another nod at each of them, Dominic rejoined his companions and left the room. Lindsey let out her held breath in a long sigh.

'So we have a mutual friend?' Jacob Steinbeck remarked. 'Excellent chap. Handles a lot of work for me.'

Fortunately he did not seem to expect a reply and the conversation veered back to its previous topic – a visit to Calgary at the time of the Stampede. But Lindsey took in hardly a word of it, her mind racing with possibilities as to whether or not Dominic would use this chance meeting to make contact again. And what if he did? She didn't know the answer.

Half an hour later they were on the pavement outside the Clarendon, watching their host climb into his chauffeur-driven Rolls.

'Now what?' Jonathan asked, as the car drove off.

'Home,' Lindsey said shortly.

'If you say so.' He took her arm as they crossed the road and made their way to the car park behind their office. Theirs were the only cars remaining.

Jonathan took her keys and unlocked the door for her. Then, as she held out her hand for their return, he pulled her towards him and kissed her thoroughly. He tasted of wine and coffee, she noted incoherently, unable to prevent herself responding. For a long moment they clung together, then, summoning her willpower, she pushed him away.

'Oh Lindsey, Lindsey!' he said unevenly. 'I didn't realize things really had turned sour between you and Frayne. But he doesn't deserve you, you know.'

'And you do?'

'Possibly not, but at least I still want you.'

Lindsey shook her head blindly and climbed into the car. 'Goodnight, Jonathan,' she said.

Alice was still teething and hadn't settled all evening. In despair, Jenny lifted her out of her cot and carried her downstairs to the living room, where Daniel was watching *Crimewatch*.

'I know, I know,' she forestalled him. 'We said we wouldn't bring her down, but it's cold up there. Be a love and get me the Calpol, will you? It's on the kitchen dresser.' She lifted the baby to her shoulder, patting her back and murmuring comfort as she idly watched the television. Suddenly she straightened, her attention focusing, and as Daniel returned with bottle and spoon, she said sharply, 'Who's that?'

He glanced at the screen. 'The man we were talking about at Ma's. He's number one suspect again, which doesn't surprise me.' Noting her tenseness, he added curiously, 'Why?'

'I've seen him somewhere,' she said.

'Yes, in the *Gazette*.'

She shook her head, supporting the baby while he spooned medicine into her mouth. 'No, I mean in the flesh.' The programme was showing a home video of the man, referred to as Kevin Coombes, at a friend's party with his wife.

Jenny shook her head, unable to pin the memory, and, holding the baby against her, resumed her rhythmic patting. Alice's head lolled into her shoulder and her breathing steadied. Another couple of minutes and she could go back in her cot. Meanwhile the story on screen had switched to a getaway car, and the presenter was calling for witnesses. And a switch clicked in Jenny's memory.

'I know where it was!' she exclaimed, breaking into a comment of Daniel's. 'It was when I was up with Mum and Dad. I was stationary at some traffic lights, and as they were changing this man ran across right in front of my car and I had to jam on the brakes. He turned and lifted his hand in apology before disappearing.' She paused and frowned. 'On second thoughts, though, it can't have been him; the man I saw was fair.'

'There you are then,' said Daniel.

THIRTEEN

'By the way,' Max said on his bedtime call that evening, 'I've decided to pay a flying visit to Tynecastle next week, if that's OK.'

'Of course. Nothing's wrong, is there? With your father?'

'No, but apart from a brief visit at New Year, I've not really seen him since we were there last summer. It's too long to leave it, especially at his age. Cynthia's always nagging at me to make more regular visits; this time I thought I'd forestall her.'

Max's sister lived near their father and made daily contact with him, a fact which every now and again smote him with guilt.

'So when are you thinking of going?'

'Up Monday, back Wednesday? Several students can't make next week for one reason or another; so it seemed a good chance. I'll let the others know, and tell them I'll make up the lesson at the end of term.'

'Fine; do you want me to come with you?'

'Not this time, love, if you don't mind; if you're there I won't get a look in, and I think some father–son time is called for.'

'Fair enough. Have you let him know?'

'No, I wanted to clear it with you first. I'll phone both him and Cynthia tomorrow. With luck she can put me up, but I suppose it depends on whether the boys are home. It would avoid adding to Doris's chores; she has enough on her plate as it is.' Doris Pemberton had been Roland's devoted housekeeper since time immemorial.

'Give them all my love when you phone,' Rona said. 'And don't forget we're going to the Ridgeways' tomorrow, so get home as soon as you can.'

'Will do. Sleep well, my love.'

'You too,' she said.

The phone rang just as Rona was thinking of turning off the computer and going down for lunch. It hadn't been a profitable morning's work; her mind was on Magda rather than Elspeth, wondering anxiously if, during the evening ahead, she'd be able to discover what was wrong. After the lunch break, she promised herself, she'd knuckle down to work. As it happened, though, the phone signalled a break of a different kind.

'Ms Parish?'

Rona tried and failed to place the voice. 'Speaking?'

'This is Esther Lytton.'

Ah! Expectation flared. 'Good morning, Miss Lytton. Or rather, good afternoon.'

'I'm afraid I was rather short with you the other evening; I made it a rule some years ago never to accept unsolicited calls from strangers.'

'I quite understand,' Rona murmured. 'You must—'

'However, I have since spoken to Catherine Bishop and learned you are not what I'd assumed, so I must apologize for having cut you off so peremptorily. What exactly was it you wanted to discuss with me?'

Rona hesitated. She didn't want to burn her boats just as there seemed a glimmer of hope. On the other hand, she knew Esther Lytton required an honest answer.

'Springfield Lodge,' she said. 'And particularly its final term.'

There was a pause. Then Miss Lytton said quietly, 'Incredible, after all this time! I must say I'd be most interested to learn how and why you came to hear of it, when I've spent most of my life trying to put it behind me.' Rona heard her sigh. 'Perhaps it's time it came into the open; it might almost be a relief. I doubt there's anyone left to be hurt by it, and from Catherine's comments, you might be just the person to deal with it.'

So there really *was* something behind Trish's reaction! Rona held her breath, waiting while Miss Lytton considered her options.

'Would you care to visit me?' she said then. 'I live in Buckford – quite a drive for you, I'm afraid.'

'That's no problem,' Rona assured her, 'I go there quite often. When . . . would be convenient for you?'

'Friday would suit me best, if you could manage it?' Esther was her brisk self again.

'Friday would be fine,' Rona confirmed.

'How well do you know Buckford?'

'Fairly well.'

'I live on the west side of town, just past the college. You know where that is?'

'I do, yes.'

'Good. Mine is the first turning on the right past the college grounds – Blandford Drive. There's a fairly new apartment block, and I'm on the third floor – number six, Eton House. I'll expect you about eleven.' And she rang off.

Rona gave a low whistle. For a moment she considered phoning Lindsey and Glenda but decided against it. Better to wait till after her visit when, with luck, she would have something interesting to report.

Gavin greeted them at the door.

'Come in, come in! Good to see you both!'

'Sorry we're on the late side,' Max apologized. 'A student came up with a query at the end of class, which delayed things.'

Magda emerged from the kitchen, and the bottle of wine and cyclamen plant were handed over and received with thanks. As they took their seats in the sitting room and Gavin poured the drinks, Rona surreptitiously studied her friend. Though Magda was determinedly smiling, she looked pale and there were lines round her eyes that she hadn't noticed before. Not out of the woods yet, Rona thought worriedly.

On the surface, the evening followed the long-established tradition of their visits to the Ridgeways. Over drinks, Magda informed Rona what colours would be 'in' next season and they discussed the ongoing biography, while the men talked about the painting Max was working on and a course Gavin would be attending the following week. When the time came to eat, the meal, Italianate as always, was delicious, the wine flowed, as did the conversation, and Rona wondered if she were the only one aware of underlying tension. The elephant in the room, she thought helplessly.

As usual, they returned to the sitting room for coffee and amaretti, and it was then that Gavin said, 'I meant to ask you, Rona: did you get any further with solving the puzzle about the school photo?'

He turned to Magda. 'Did you hear about this? It involves our neighbours down the road.'

Briefly, Rona outlined her investigations. 'It's still not over,' she ended, 'because although we've confirmed the identity of the woman behind the blot, we still don't know what happened to her.'

'Odd, isn't it?' Magda said, her voice strained. 'We've both been trying to establish an identity, you the woman in the photograph, I the person whose dreams I was having.'

They all tensed, not knowing what to say, and her eyes, unfathomable, moved from one of them to another, awaiting their reaction. It was Gavin who found his voice.

'Well,' he said, in an unconvincingly light tone, 'Rona now has a name at least, so I suppose—'

'So have I,' Magda said ringingly.

'So have you what, sweetheart?'

'The name of my fellow dreamer. I've known it for a week or two.'

There was a moment's stunned silence. Then Gavin said, 'So – are you going to put us out of our suspense?'

Magda straightened her shoulders, bracing herself. 'It was the man who murdered his wife,' she said. 'Kevin Coombes.'

Everyone was staring at her, their faces mirroring their shock. Gavin cleared his throat. 'And how, might I ask, did you arrive at that conclusion?'

'I recognized the photos of his wife and children; they were the ones I'd been dreaming about.' She looked round their incredulous faces. 'No, I'm not out of my mind, though I *have* been sharing it for a while; and for that you can blame that bloody hypnotist.'

After a minute Gavin said weakly, 'Now you really have lost me.'

Magda leant forward, dark eyes burning. 'Didn't you recognize him, when you saw his photograph? He was the one sitting next to me on stage.'

Rona said, 'Magda . . .'

'Oh, I *know* it seems far-fetched and impossible, but remember the *power* that man had, making us fall asleep when we were safely back in our seats and thought it was over? All I can think

is that when he did finally give us back our minds, there was a
hiccup and Kevin's and mine somehow fused.'

She looked round at their sceptical faces, but no one spoke.
'It affected us differently; I simply tuned in to his dreams and
memories, but the effect on him was altogether more serious.
I've been going over and over it, and I think I see what must
have happened.'

She waited for some comment or question, but none was
forthcoming and after a moment she went on. 'From what you
told me, Bauer, or whatever his name was, made us indulge in
some aggressive role play. Well, I believe Kevin never completely
snapped out of it. From that evening on his aggression escalated;
I could *feel* it, permeating his dreams.'

'I'm sorry, Magda,' Max interrupted, 'I just can't go along
with this. The whole idea is preposterous.'

She ignored him. 'As Gavin knows, the dreams started almost
at once and from the first there was something unsettling about
them, even when they were just about children playing or washing
the car. And it struck me as odd that they were all of the same
people, whom I didn't know. Later, there were flashes of "memories" that seemed incredibly real, but that I couldn't possibly
have. And some of them were . . . violent.'

A shudder ran through her. 'Then there was the last dream,
which was so beyond bearing that I totally lost it and Gavin
could do nothing with me.' She took a deep breath. 'And that
was about him strangling his wife.'

Her hands twisted in her lap and she stared down at them, as
though she wasn't sure they belonged to her. 'When news of the
murder broke and I saw the photos of Lucy and the boys – and
recognized them – I was convinced I was going mad. The only
way I could cope was by totally blocking the dream, refusing to
admit its existence, though God knows it's haunted me ever since.
But at least there haven't been any more.'

There was a long silence as they all fought with varying degrees
of disbelief.

Magda drew a deep breath. 'I still had no idea how I'd become
mixed up in all this, because although Lucy and the boys had
featured in my dreams, Kevin never appeared – he was always
the "I" figure, the spectator. It was only when I saw *his* photo a

day or two later and realized who he was – that we'd actually met on stage – that it all finally made sense.'

'Why in God's name didn't you tell me?' Gavin demanded hoarsely. 'Why go through all that on your own?'

She reached for his hands with both hers. 'Because talking about it would have made it real! I was terrified, don't you see? I still am! Gavin, I have psychic links with a *murderer*! Have you any idea how that feels? Believe me, it's quite literally mind-blowing! I was convinced you'd all think I was mad – you probably do now – so I forced it out of my head, made myself go on as usual.'

She paused, then continued more quietly, 'But in the last few days I've had to accept that it's not over. Yes, the dreams have stopped, thank God, but memory flashes still come during the day, and I realize now it won't finally end till we meet face-to-face.'

'Like that's going to happen!' Gavin said explosively.

Rona leant forward. 'Look, Magda, this could all be some huge misunderstanding. It's weeks since you saw the hypnotist; your memory of the man next to you is sure to have blurred a bit, and it would be easy to mistake him—'

'He was called Kevin,' Magda interrupted, 'the man next to me. We all had to give our names, didn't we? Surely you remember him now?'

Max said firmly, 'Speaking personally, I'd be hard pressed to recognize *anyone* who went up on that stage, apart from you. Don't forget we were several rows back; we never saw any of the contestants up close.'

Magda lifted her shoulders. 'Well, I was up close, all right.'

'We don't even know *for a fact* that Kevin Coombes went to the show that night,' Rona said a little desperately. 'It could still have been another Kevin sitting next to you.'

Magda wearily shook her head. 'I knew I'd never convince you,' she said.

They were no sooner in their car than Max said forcefully, 'Well, now I've heard it all! Gavin will have to do something, take her to see someone. She's away with the fairies.'

Rona shivered. 'I'm frightened for her, Max. Why, in the name

of heaven, did we ever go to that show? Paola was worried, you
know, when she heard Magda had taken part. Said she was
"susceptible" and as a child had had difficulty distinguishing
what was real.'

'So, no doubt, do most children. The difference is most of
them grow out of it.' He glanced at her. 'I don't like it, Rona,
this identifying with a murderer. Of course it's arrant nonsense,
but for the moment I'd rather you kept your distance. If she's
really set on meeting this man – to "break the thread", or whatever it is she imagines is between them – then it could become
really dangerous.'

'But she's my *friend*, Max! I can't just abandon her!'

'Well, don't say I didn't warn you. Believe me, the best way
you can help her is by persuading her to see a psychiatrist.'

The rest of the drive home passed in silence.

'Sarah? It's Rona.'

'Hi, Rona! This is a surprise!'

It would be, Rona thought; the two of them had met only a
few times, and then in the company of their parents. 'I hope I'm
not interrupting anything. This is your lunch break?'

'Yes, the bell's just gone, but I'm on playground duty. I'm
making my way there now. What can I do for you?'

'This might seem a long shot, but I was wondering if Lucy
Coombes ever mentioned going to see a hypnotist?'

'*What?*'

'I know it sounds mad; I'll explain later, when you've more
time, but it could be important.'

'Well, she certainly didn't in my hearing.'

'Could you possibly ask around? See if she said anything to
anyone else?'

'Look, Rona, Lucy's still a touchy subject here. Everyone's
very uptight over her death, and—'

'I appreciate that, but this isn't idle curiosity. It might even
lead to her husband being caught.'

There was a pause, and Rona could hear children's voices in
the background. Sarah had reached the playground. Then Sarah
said, 'I must say, I can't see how.'

'Trust me. Please.'

'It's really that important?'

'It could be, yes.'

'Well, there's one person you could try asking, and that's her next-door neighbour. They were fairly close, I think.'

'That's great! You know her?'

'I wouldn't say "know", but she was with us when we . . . found the body.'

'Oh Sarah, I'm so sorry! I didn't—'

'It's all right. Look, I must go – someone's just fallen over. Her name's Frances Drew – she'll be in the phone book – but go carefully with her. And if I get the chance, I'll ask around here. Yes, Sammy, I'm coming!' And she rang off.

Frances Drew was indeed in the phone book and Rona sat staring at her name, undecided how best to approach her. Normally, she'd simply have phoned, but two things made her hesitate. The first was that it was a difficult subject to bring up over the phone, particularly if the women had been close friends, and the second was her experience with Esther Lytton, who, not wishing to speak to her, had simply hung up. There was no help for it; she'd have to go round in person.

Rona had decided six o'clock was the best time for her visit. If Frances Drew had a job she'd be home by then, and hopefully it would be too early to interrupt a meal. That her husband might also be there was a risk she had to take; she could only hope he wouldn't be too protective and forbid her entry.

It was odd to be driving into Belmont and not turning in the direction of Maple Drive. Her mother, she knew, would be avidly awaiting the outcome of this visit; Rona had had to explain why she wanted Sarah's mobile number, and Avril made her promise to call in before going home. Not that she'd any intention of revealing the real reason for her visit; it would only lay her open to ridicule.

Finding the road she was looking for, she turned into it and began checking the house numbers, drawing in to the kerb just short of the one she wanted. The house she'd stopped by had a neglected air, she noted as she got out of the car; the plants in the garden were straggly, the grass overlong, and on this warm

May evening all the windows were closed. Perhaps the owners were away. Then, as realization hit her, Rona stopped dead. Oh God – of course! This was the Coombeses' house! Kevin would never mow that grass again, nor Lucy tend the plants.

Quickening her footsteps, she hurried past and turned in the Drews' gateway.

It was indeed Frances's husband who answered the bell. By the look of him, he'd just arrived home; his tie was loosened and his jacket still over his arm. Behind him was a wide-eyed little girl of about seven.

Rona began her prepared opening. 'I'm so sorry to disturb you, Mr Drew; my name is Rona Parish, and I'm a friend of Sarah Lacey.' She paused, unwilling to go into the ramifications of their relationship, and was relieved when the name appeared to be familiar, if not particularly welcome.

Drew was frowning. 'Yes?'

'I wonder if I could have a word with your wife?'

'Why?'

Rona glanced past him at the little girl, now standing on one leg and staring at her curiously. 'It's about your neighbours.'

His face hardened. 'Press?'

'No.' She wouldn't risk qualifying that, as she had with Esther. 'It's . . . important, and it'll only take a minute.'

A woman appeared in the hall behind him. 'Who is it, Greg?'

'Someone wanting to speak to you. A friend of Sarah Lacey.'

'Please!' Rona cut in quickly, before she could refuse. 'I really do need your help. It won't take long.'

'I don't see how I can help, and I really can't face having to—'

'I promise it's not about . . . that evening.'

Frances hesitated, and Rona saw the resistance go out of her. 'All right, then, come in. Rosie, go back to the television, there's a good girl.'

Reluctantly the little girl obeyed, and Rona was shown into the dining room. The table, she saw, wasn't laid; either it was too early, or, perhaps more likely, they'd be eating in the kitchen. As she'd expected, Greg Drew accompanied them, closing the door behind him.

Rona turned to Frances. 'I just have one question for you. It probably won't make any sense to you, but all I can do is assure you it is important – perhaps vital — and might lead to Kevin being found.'

Greg put his arm round his wife. 'Go ahead.'

'A few weeks ago, a hypnotist was appearing at the Darcy Hall. Do you by any chance know if Lucy and Kevin went to see him?'

The Drews were both staring at her in total bewilderment.

Greg said, 'You've come here to ask *that*?'

'I know it seems ridiculous, but yes.' She looked at Frances, waiting with held breath for her answer.

Frances said, 'I can't imagine why it matters, but yes, they did. I babysat for them.'

Rona's hands clenched at her sides. 'Can you remember which day of the week it was?'

'It must have been the Friday, because Rosie goes to Brownies and it was a bit of a rush getting next door on time.'

Rona's mind reeled. So the first part of Magda's theory held; Kevin Coombes *had* been at the theatre that night.

'So?' Greg Drew prompted.

Rona was wondering how to phrase her next question when Frances unwittingly answered it.

'They told me about it when they got back,' she added. 'Kevin went up on stage and was hypnotized.'

'Thank you,' Rona managed. 'That's all I need to know.'

'That they saw a *hypnotist*?' Greg said unbelievingly. 'Look, you can't leave it there! At least tell us why this is so important?'

'I can't explain now, but it might lead to finding Kevin. That's honestly all I can say.'

They weren't satisfied, either of them, and Rona couldn't blame them. But if she launched into an explanation they'd probably phone for the men in white coats. Somehow or other, fending off their questions as she went, she managed to extricate herself from the house and didn't really draw breath until, finally, she heard the front door close behind her.

She had just switched on the engine when her phone rang. Max.

'Where are you?' he demanded. 'I've just tried the home number.'

'I'm in Belmont,' Rona said, steeling herself for his disapprobation. 'And before you say anything, Kevin and Lucy Coombes were at the theatre the same night we were, and Kevin went up on stage.'

There was a heavy silence. Then Max said, 'And how did you glean that little gem?'

'By speaking to their next-door neighbour, who babysat for them. So at least Magda was right that far; she did actually meet the murderer.'

'Are you going to tell her she's been vindicated?'

'There's no point. She was adamant about it anyway.'

'So, despite what I asked, you're determined to fight her cause?'

'There was an off-chance of corroborating that part and I took it, that's all. Luckily, it paid off.'

'Have you any other strategies up your sleeve?'

'No, I seem to have reached a dead end.'

'I'd rather you rephrased that! Damn, there's the doorbell – I'll have to go. I'll speak to you later. Love you.'

'Love you,' she repeated, and started the car.

Avril was harder to satisfy even than the Drews, and considerably less inhibited in her indignation at being 'fobbed off', as she put it.

'Look, Mum, all I can say is that Kevin and Lucy Coombes went to see the hypnotist the same night as us, and both Kevin and Magda were hypnotized. Telepathy was involved – Max had his fingers burned when he challenged it earlier – and this might possibly help to trace Kevin.'

'I don't believe that for a minute!' Avril declared. 'It's a load of nonsense, all that thought transference thing.'

'"More things in heaven and earth . . ."?' Rona suggested mildly.

'I can't believe you're being so *gullible*!'

'Let's just say I'm withholding judgement. Now, I really must be on my way.'

'Can't you stay till Guy gets home? See what he makes of all this?'

As if his opinion would make any difference, Rona thought. But all she said was, 'Sorry, I have to go. You can fill him in, and give him my love.'

Wherever she went, she was leaving disgruntled people in her wake, she thought gloomily as she drove home: the Drews, Max, her mother. Well, she'd done all she could for Magda in the meantime. Now, she must turn her attention to her meeting with Esther Lytton the next day.

FOURTEEN

Friday morning, and still no word from Dominic. Over the last few days Lindsey had managed, by a process of wishful thinking, to convince herself that he'd phone. Surely, she reasoned, after seeing her with Jonathan he'd make some attempt to contact her, apologize, try to repair the damage? But he had failed to do so, and the fact that Jonathan was making it only too obvious he was ready to resume their relationship was of little or no comfort.

Fine! she thought viciously. He could console himself with bloody Carla! And was furious when the papers in front of her blurred suddenly through a veil of tears.

Rona had dropped Gus off with Max before setting out for Buckford. Animals were likely to be frowned on in an apartment building, and a total of five hours in the car was a lot to ask of him. Max would in any case be home that evening; he could exercise him if Rona was delayed.

So, she thought, driving along the familiar roads, was this really the end of the rainbow regarding the mysterious photograph? And was there a pot of gold awaiting her? Whatever the outcome, she had firmly resolved to put the whole thing behind her; she'd wasted enough time already on what was probably a wild goose chase, and that, together with Magda and her traumas, had distracted her from her work long enough.

The college clock was striking eleven as Rona drove past and turned in to Blandford Drive. Perhaps, she thought fancifully, by the time it struck again, she'd have an answer to the mystery of Susie Baines.

Eton House was an elegant building in rose-coloured brick, its woodwork picked out in white. She parked in a space reserved for visitors and made her way between neat flowerbeds to the front entrance, where she was greeted by a concierge in peaked cap. Having checked that she was expected, he accompanied her to a bank of lifts and pressed the button for the third floor.

'Apartment six,' he intoned solemnly, and she sailed upwards, trying to avoid her reflection that greeted her on all sides. Why, she wondered irrelevantly, should anyone in a lift require a mirror, let alone three of them? Or were the multiple images designed to ward off claustrophobia?

The doors glided open and she stepped out to find herself in a square, carpeted hall. Immediately opposite was a picture window, in front of which stood a pedestal bearing an elaborate flower arrangement, and to either side was a polished mahogany door. Two apartments to each floor, seemingly, and number six was to her right.

Forewarned of her arrival, Miss Lytton opened her door as Rona approached, and came forward to shake her hand. 'Miss Parish, how do you do? Do please come in.'

Rona followed her through a spacious hallway to a large and elegant room whose windows gave out on the college grounds, and, as she seated herself, she looked about her with interest. The cream walls were for the most part bare, boasting only a small set of prints, and the cane-backed suite, upholstered in pale blue, looked like an antique. So, more obviously, were a glass-fronted cabinet, a bureau and several spindly-legged chairs. Over by the window a Regency rosewood table was laid for two, which Rona hoped was indicative of lunch.

Esther Lytton herself was tall and slim, her dark hair was streaked with silver, and, though she was now smiling, her pale blue eyes were gimlet-sharp. It was clear she'd have had no difficulty holding sway over a large number of girls, and Rona was amused to find herself conscious of her own deportment.

'How was the journey?' Miss Lytton was asking, as she busied herself with a cafetière.

'Plain sailing, once I was through the Marsborough rush hour,' Rona replied, gratefully accepting a cup of what proved to be excellent coffee. 'It took two hours and forty minutes, which is about average.'

'I hope you'll feel it was worthwhile. Catherine tells me you're a writer,' she went on quickly, before Rona could follow up the point. 'Do tell me about your work.'

Diffidently, Rona did so, suspecting that her hostess was deliberately delaying the discussion that was the reason for her visit.
Her biographies were discussed, including the one she was
working on, and the nature of the articles she wrote for *Chiltern
Life*.

'I hadn't connected you with those,' Esther Lytton confessed,
'but I must say I enjoyed the ones you did for Buckford's octocentenary.' There was a brief pause while she refilled their coffee cups,
and then she sat back, folding her hands. 'Now, *revenons à nos
moutons*, as they say: firstly, I must admit to being curious to learn
how you heard of Springfield Lodge and, as you put it, its final
term. I'm surprised anyone even remembers it, after all this time.'

Rona braced herself. 'Before I begin, would you have any
objection if I recorded our conversation? I'm acting on behalf
of someone else, and should like her to have as full a record of
it as possible.'

'Might I ask who that is?'

'I promise I'll explain in just a minute.'

'Very well, then I have no objection.'

'Thank you.' Rona took her recorder out of her bag and set it
up on the table between them. Then she reached in again and
produced the much-travelled photocopy, which she handed over.

Esther Lytton drew in her breath sharply. 'My goodness! Where
did you find this?'

'It belonged to the mother of a friend, who used to teach there.
Trish Cowley?'

'Trish! Is . . . she still alive?'

'No, she died a few months ago. Her daughter found this
among her things – she's the one who asked me to look into it.
All we had to go on was the note on the back.'

Esther flipped it over. 'Springfield Lodge, July 1951,' she read
slowly.

'Her daughter, Glenda, was curious to know who had been so
thoroughly eliminated.'

'And . . . did you find out?'

'Yes; a lady my mother knew was at the school at the time. She
identified her as a teacher, Susie Baines. She also said she left in
the middle of the last term, but Glenda's still anxious to know
why her photo was obliterated, presumably by her mother.' She

paused. Esther was still staring down at the photograph in her hand. 'We were hoping you might be able to tell us,' she ended.

'As you'll appreciate, I was a young child at the time,' Esther said at last. 'It was years later that I heard the story from my mother.'

'So there *was* a story?'

Esther sighed. 'Oh yes, there was a story, all right, though they managed to keep it quiet. The school's connection, that is.'

She was silent for so long that Rona tried a prompt. 'Glenda found some diaries Trish had written at the time. She and Susie seemed to be very friendly at first, but then there were entries about Trish being worried, having long talks with her and Susie refusing to listen. We wondered if perhaps she was pregnant, though even in the fifties it seemed an extreme reaction.'

'That was what the girls assumed,' Esther agreed, 'and my parents did nothing to deny it. Wrongly, perhaps, but I remember my mother saying bitterly, "It's not as though she had a reputation to protect, and at least it diverted attention from what would have been a far greater and very public scandal."' She laid the photograph on the table, straightened her shoulders, and met Rona's eye. 'Tell me – what do you know of 1951?'

Rona hesitated, thinking back to Trish's diary. 'There was the Festival of Britain, wasn't there? To commemorate the Great Exhibition of 1851?'

Esther nodded. 'That's right, there was; but there was also a darker side to that summer. Tell me, do the names Burgess and Maclean mean anything to you?'

Rona frowned. 'I'm . . . not sure.'

'They were part of what came to be known as the Cambridge Spy Ring – a group of young men who had been recruited by a Soviet agent while at university. They were the first to come under suspicion, and defected to Russia in May '51, after years of passing on sensitive information. But it was always known that several others were involved.'

Esther met Rona's eyes. 'One of whom turned out to be Andrew Daultrey, who worked at the Foreign Office.' She paused, and, seeing no reaction, added, 'And who also happened to be the boyfriend of one Susie Baines.'

Rona gasped. 'Susie was a *spy*?'

Esther shrugged. 'No doubt she would have been, if she'd had anything to divulge. As it was, she was completely in thrall to Daultrey, and when he was about to be rumbled and fled to Moscow, she went with him. Of course his defection made front-page news, but thankfully the connection with Springfield was never made public.'

Rona was staring at her incredulously. 'I'd no idea this had worldwide implications. Did anyone at school know the real reason she left?'

'Well, obviously Trish Cowley did. My mother found her in the staff cloakroom, in a terrible state. It took her a while to discover what was wrong, but eventually the whole story came out.

'That term, Susie had started preaching communism among the staff, but no one took her seriously except Trish, who was her closest friend. Trish knew it emanated from Daultrey, and became more and more concerned about his influence over her, but Susie refused to hear a word against him. To give her her due, she didn't actually know he was a spy until he was about to flee, but by the time he told her she was in too deep and had no hesitation in going with him. It destroyed her parents, Mother said. They never got over it – and they weren't alone. The strain of it all brought on my father's heart attack, and Trish suffered what was then called a nervous breakdown. Both her parents were dead, she'd no other family, and my mother felt responsible for her. She actually lived with us for several months after the school closed and we moved to Farnbridge.'

Rona digested all that in silence. Then she asked, 'Did the authorities know about Susie?'

'Oh, yes. As soon as my parents found out they contacted the police. Someone from MI5 came up to interview Trish and Susie's parents. But it was abundantly clear she'd been no threat in herself and was simply an infatuated young woman who'd allowed herself to be brainwashed by her glamorous lover. And since she wasn't directly culpable and the school was in the clear, it was agreed not to implicate it.'

'But if the scandal didn't touch Springfield, why did it have to close?'

'There were other underlying reasons – chiefly my father's health. He'd been ill the previous year and they'd discussed his retiring then, but, despite Mother's wishes, he decided to carry on. Then all this blew up, and although it was being contained, he felt the staff had a right to know the truth of it. So he told them, in the strictest confidence, and they backed him to the hilt. They were wonderful – none of them ever breathed a word. But despite managing to avoid the crisis, the stress of it all proved too much, resulting in a full-blown heart attack. He fought hard to find a replacement, as much for the sake of the staff as the girls, but the time frame was too short. No one came forward, and in the end he'd no choice but to close down.'

She shook her head sadly, remembering. 'And the most tragic part of it all was that once in Moscow, Daultrey lost interest in Susie. She became desperately homesick, but the Soviet authorities wouldn't allow her to leave, and eventually, after a year or so, she . . . committed suicide.'

Rona's hand went to her mouth. 'Oh, *no!*'

Esther glanced down at the photograph. 'So you see this encapsulates a moment of history. It was taken two months after the defection of Burgess and Maclean, and three months before that of Daultrey.'

'Trish almost collapsed when Glenda came across it a few years ago,' Rona said reflectively, 'but she refused point-blank to explain. In fact, Glenda didn't even know she'd taught at Springfield. It must have affected her whole life.'

Esther nodded. 'She suffered from depression for years. Basically, she blamed herself for not having done more to stop Susie – specially after we learned of her suicide, via the British Embassy in Moscow. Mother kept in touch for some time and did what she could, but after Trish married they lost touch.'

Rona said diffidently, 'Your father recovered, didn't he? Did he return to teaching?'

Esther shook her head. 'He recovered to a certain degree, yes, but he was advised to avoid stress of any kind, and told categorically that any attempt to run a school again could prove fatal. So he contented himself with marking exam papers and giving the odd lecture. It gave him a toe in educational matters and he felt he was doing something useful. He was delighted when I chose to go in for teaching myself.'

There was a little click as the tape came to an end.

'Perfect timing!' Esther said with a smile.

'Thank you for allowing me to record it.'

'And now you're going to ask if you may write an article for your glossy!'

Rona smiled sheepishly. 'If you'd rather I didn't—'

But Esther made a dismissive gesture. 'Go ahead if you'd like to. It makes a good story with plenty of local interest, and it can't hurt the reputation of either my parents or the school. Added to which it is, after all, a small piece of history.'

She stood up, brushing the palms of her hands against each other, perhaps symbolically washing them. 'Now, I think we've delved into the past quite enough. Would you care for a sherry before lunch? I feel we've both earned one!'

Rona, though not overfond of sherry and with the long drive home ahead of her, felt it only politic to accept. 'Just a small one, please – I'm driving!'

By mutual though unspoken consent, Springfield Lodge wasn't mentioned during the meal – cold salmon and salad, followed by a selection of cheeses. Instead, Esther turned to Catherine, asking about her later career and her activities since her retirement. 'I understand she and your father will be marrying shortly?'

'That's right, yes.'

'How did you all meet?'

'My father was her bank manager, but coincidentally I'd been given her name when I was researching education for the octocentenary article. She was head of St Stephen's Primary here until relatively recently, and was able to give me a lot of information about it and, of course, the college.' Rona glanced through the window at the building in its lovely grounds.

'I've not seen her for quite a while,' Esther commented. 'We must arrange to meet.'

It was only as Rona was leaving that the reason for her visit was referred to again.

'It's strange, thinking back to those times,' Esther Lytton remarked. 'It was the height of the Cold War, and Russian spies seemed to be everywhere – the "Reds Under the Beds" syndrome. No doubt spying continues even now, but we hardly ever hear of it.'

'I hope I've not revived too many unwelcome memories,' Rona apologized.

'Not really, though I'm sorry I didn't have the chance to see Trish before she died. For a short while, she was almost part of the family.'

Remembering Trish's reaction to the photograph and her refusal to visit Marsborough, Rona doubted she'd have wanted to renew the acquaintance. Her memories had been considerably more traumatic than Esther's, and she'd spent the rest of her life trying to escape them.

'So how did it go?' Max asked, as she flopped into a kitchen chair and succumbed to Gus's enthusiastic welcome.

'You wouldn't believe it!'

'Try me.' He handed her a glass of her favourite vodka. 'Mystery solved?'

'And then some.' She took a sip of her drink. 'In a nutshell, Susie Baines did a flit to Moscow with her boyfriend, who was one of the Cambridge spies.'

Max stared at her. 'You're not serious?'

'Oh, but I am. Result: years of depression for Trish, heart attack for the headmaster, and closure of the school. And the crowning tragedy was that Susie committed suicide a year later.'

'Ye gods!'

'And before you ask,' Rona said, with the ghost of a smile, 'I have Esther's permission to write an article on it.'

'A scoop indeed! Barnie will be delighted.' He retrieved his laptop from where he'd dumped it on his return from Farthings, and, placing it on the kitchen table, sat down next to her. 'What was the chap's name?'

'Andrew Daultrey.'

Max Googled it, and a list of options appeared. He clicked one at random, and they found themselves looking at the photograph of a good-looking man, probably in his late thirties.

'He seems quite a bit older than Susie,' Rona commented. 'I wonder how she met him.'

'Do you *know* how old she was?' Max asked.

'Come to think of it, no, I don't, and I never saw a photo of her. I'd assumed she was the same age as Trish, but of course she mightn't have been. Trish was twenty-two, Glenda said, so Springfield must have her first school, but Susie was already there. Bridget remembered her, and she left before Trish came.'

'So she could have been knocking thirty herself.'

'I suppose she could.'

Max scrolled down, and together they read the potted biography of Andrew James Daultrey, including date and place of birth (14th May 1913 in Shaftesbury, Dorset), parents' names (Sir Edward and Lady Daultrey, née Elizabeth Pennington), and education (Winchester College and Trinity College Cambridge).

They also learned that he joined the Communist Party while at Cambridge and was recruited into Soviet intelligence by Anthony Blunt. His position at the Foreign Office gave him access to information very useful to the Soviets, but having come under suspicion of spying, he fled to Moscow in October 1951. He married Svetlana Bagnova in February 1952 ('while Susie was still alive,' Rona noted), and they'd had two sons and a daughter. He died in Leningrad in January 1982.

'No mention of Susie,' Rona commented, sitting back in her chair.

'All to the good,' Max replied. 'So – what's your next move?'

'To tell Lindsey and the Stirlings, I suppose, but not this evening. For now, I've had more than enough of Russia and all things Russian.'

'Too bad it's beef Stroganoff for supper!' Max said with a grin.

'You've solved it?' Lindsey sounded excited. 'Go on, then – spill the beans!'

'It's a long story, Linz, and I'd rather not go through it twice. Would you like to phone the Stirlings – you know them better than I do – and perhaps arrange a time we can meet?'

'Yes, yes, but at least give me a hint!'

'Sorry – you'll have to wait!'

'You really can be most aggravating,' Lindsey complained. 'OK, I'll phone William and come back to you.'

'William', Rona noted, not Glenda, who was far more involved.

She rang back ten minutes later. 'Monday evening at eight, and I've invited them to the flat. Come early for supper, and why not stay the night? Max won't be home anyway.'

'He won't even be at Farthings,' Rona said. 'He's flying up to Tynecastle for a few days, to see his father.'

'How is the old boy? Still painting?'

Roland Allerdyce was a member of the Royal Academy and known to his irreverent grandsons as R.A., R.A., or Rahrah.

'Yes, Max says he's working on some huge canvas at the moment.'

'Must be well in his eighties,' Lindsey marvelled. 'An example to us all!'

'Well, we've a way to go yet, and in the meantime, thanks, I'd love to stay over.'

'Fine. Bring Gus's basket and he can sleep in the kitchen. I'll try to leave work early, so come any time after six thirty. And this story had better be good!'

'Oh, it is,' Rona said drily.

On Monday morning, having seen Max off to the airport, Rona settled at her desk to go through Trish's diary one last time, concentrating on the summer term. She'd be handing it back to Glenda that evening, and wanted to check for any mention of the Burgess and Maclean affair. On her first reading, she'd been searching only for items relating to Susie and the school.

She found just one brief reference: 'The papers are full of a story about two British spies who have fled to Moscow. It seems they've been passing secret information to the Russians for years.'

This was, of course, before her friendship with Susie began to cool, and though the arguments had started later that term, it had been only in the autumn that Susie became more extreme in her politics. At the time of the Burgess and Maclean defection, neither she nor Trish could have had any idea of the personal parallel that lay ahead.

Resignedly, Rona closed the diary and put it and the recorder in her bag, ready to take with her that evening. After which, perhaps, she could give her undivided attention to Elspeth Wilding.

Lindsey had, as usual, prepared a lovely meal, and as they ate she tried to pump Rona about the forthcoming revelations. Rona, however, remained adamant.

'You'll hear soon enough,' she said.

The Stirlings arrived within minutes of eight o'clock, Glenda full of enthusiasm for Lindsey's new colour scheme – coffee-coloured upholstery, duck-egg blue walls, and floor-to-ceiling curtains an amalgam of both colours against a white background.

'It makes our sitting room seem really drab!' she said. 'We must think of redecorating, my love!' She turned to Rona. 'When we spoke on the phone, you were going to see the headmaster's daughter. Did she hold the answer?'

'She did indeed,' Rona replied, 'and I recorded our conversation. I think the best thing would be for me to play it straight through, so that you hear it exactly as I did. It starts where I've just handed Miss Lytton the photograph.'

There were murmurs of anticipation as they settled themselves on the sofa and Lindsey came in with a tray of coffee. Once everyone had a cup, she nodded to Rona, who leant forward and switched on the recorder.

The first sound they heard was a gasp, followed by Esther Lytton's voice: 'My goodness! Where did you find this?'

The tape wound slowly on, and Rona couldn't have wished for a more attentive audience. They sat in enthralled silence, broken only by a general murmur of incredulity at the first mention of the spies. As Esther went on to describe Trish's distress, Glenda reached for her husband's hand and held it tightly until the tape came to an end.

There was a moment's complete silence, then she turned to Rona, her eyes full of tears. 'I can't thank you enough for this. It explains all kinds of things I didn't understand about Mum; not only why she'd never come to Marsborough, but how she sometimes reacted – things she wouldn't talk about, books she refused to read, like the le Carré novels. I could never fathom out why.'

She glanced at Rona's photocopy, somewhat creased now from all its handling. 'She must have scrawled Susie out as soon as she left, full of rage for her betraying her country. But even then she couldn't bring herself to throw it out, and when she heard of her suicide it must have been almost unbearable. Then I had to drag it up again, all those years later.'

Her voice broke, and William said quickly, 'Don't blame yourself, sweetheart; there's no way you could have known.'

Glenda dried her eyes and turned back to Rona. 'You talked of writing an article.'

'Would you mind?'

She thought for a moment. 'I don't think so. It's no reflection on Mum, after all.'

'I needn't mention her, if you'd rather not.'

'Oh, I think I'd like her to have her due; after all, she did her best to talk Susie out of it, at the expense of their friendship. She deserves some credit for that.'

They continued to discuss the matter, going over and over it, probing and conjecturing, and when the Stirlings finally left, it was with renewed thanks.

'In a week or two, when this has all mellowed a little, you must both come to dinner,' Glenda said. 'As an expression of our thanks.'

'I didn't do much,' Lindsey protested.

'You brought Rona in!' Glenda pointed out. 'If you'd not done that, we'd never have learned what happened.'

When they had gone, Rona helped Lindsey carry things back to the kitchen and load the dishwasher. It was almost ten thirty, but their minds were still turning over the events of the evening, and neither of them was tired.

'Let's change into our dressing gowns like we used to, and sit talking over some more coffee,' Lindsey suggested.

'OK. I'll give Gus his biscuits and settle him for the night.'

When she returned to the sitting room in her night clothes, Lindsey had turned off the main lights and the corners of the room had sunk into shadow. She was on the sofa with her feet tucked under her, holding her mug in both hands.

Rona curled up in a capacious chair. 'This is nice!' she said. 'When did we last do this?'

'God knows,' Lindsey replied. She took a sip of her coffee. 'Who else do you have to tell about this business?'

'Well, Mum will be all agog, that's for sure.'

'Anyone else?'

Rona considered, sipping her own drink. 'There's really only Heather Grayson and Maureen – oh, and perhaps Mrs Temple at the hotel. They didn't ask to be kept informed, but I'm sure they'd be interested. I can probably get round it by sending them each a copy of *Chiltern Life* containing the article.'

Lindsey nodded. 'What a mess that woman made of so many lives,' she mused. 'At least I only make a mess of my own!'

'Oh, Linz!'

'I have, though; you can't deny it. One disastrous relationship after another.'

'At least you haven't counted a Russian spy among them!' Rona said, hoping to lighten her mood. But Lindsey smiled only fleetingly.

'Missing Dominic?' Rona asked softly, and her sister nodded. 'And too proud to make the first approach?'

That stung her, and her head came up. 'He was the one in the wrong, sleeping with bloody Carla.'

Rona smiled. 'You always call her that, and you've got me doing it! I think of her now as Bloody Carla! Didn't you once say she claimed to be his comfort blanket?'

'He'd no need of one when he was going out with me,' Lindsey retorted sharply. 'I saw him, Ro,' she added more softly. 'At the Clarendon, last week.'

'Did you?' Rona stared at her in surprise. 'You never said.'

'I was at a business dinner and so was he. He stopped at our table on his way out, but to speak to our host, not me. All I got was a cool nod. I fooled myself into thinking he might phone after seeing me, but he didn't.'

Rona eyed her consideringly. 'Who were you with at this business dinner?'

Lindsey flushed. 'One of our clients, Mr Steinbeck.'

'And?'

'Jonathan.'

Rona leant back. 'And you wonder why Dominic hasn't contacted you? No doubt he thinks you've gone back to him.' Her voice sharpened. 'You haven't, have you, Linz?'

'Not exactly.'

'And what does that mean?'

'It means that we kissed after the dinner, and he wants us to start again.'

'Oh Lindsey, will you never learn?'

'It's all very well for you, with your handsome, faithful husband always on hand! I've told you before, I *need* a man in my life; why won't you believe me?'

'What about Hugh?' Rona asked, suddenly suspicious.

Lindsey was silent.

'Linz?'

'He's not interested,' she said in a low voice.

'How do you know?'

'Because I . . . persuaded him to take me out on Easter Sunday. It's always worked before, but this time nothing came of it. This new girlfriend must really be something.'

Rona looked at her twin in despair, but before she could think of anything to say, Lindsey leant forward and put her coffee mug on the table.

'I'm getting maudlin,' she announced. 'It's probably bedtime after all. Things will look brighter in the morning – they always do.'

Rona, uncurling from her chair, could only hope she was right.

FIFTEEN

They were up early the next morning, Lindsey needing to get into the office and Rona to return to her own work. The Springfield distraction having been satisfactorily solved, she intended to postpone writing the article till she'd made considerably more progress on the biography.

Neither of them had referred to their late-night discussion though it was still on both their minds, Lindsey half-regretting having shown her vulnerability, Rona wondering with helpless impatience why her sister couldn't meet the right man and settle down once and for all.

'Are you likely to be seeing Pops in the near future?' Lindsey asked, as they stood at the breakfast bar, cereal bowls in hand.

'I hadn't particularly planned to. Why?'

'Just that he lent me some jump leads a while ago when I was having problems with my car and I've still not returned them.'

'I could drop them off on my way home, if you like?' Rona offered.

'Could you, Ro? I'd be very grateful. I keep worrying *his* car might play up, and he'd have nothing to fall back on.'

'Consider it done.'

'Give him my love,' Lindsey said.

Having extracted the admission that she'd had only a bowl of cereal that morning, Tom insisted, despite Rona's protestations, on providing her with a mug of coffee and a slice of toast.

'I really only meant to drop these off; Gus is asleep on the back seat.'

'He'll be fine, and you can't start work on an empty stomach! So Max is away, you said?'

'Just till tomorrow, and since we never see each other from breakfast on Monday till Wednesday evening, I've hardly missed him. He phoned before I left for Lindsey's and says his father's in great form, which is a considerable relief; we were quite worried about him a year or so ago. He's tackling an enormous canvas at the moment – something allegorical, Max said.'

'All power to his paintbrush! Any other family news?'

'Well, we all went to Mum's for lunch the Sunday before last. It was . . . odd, you not being there.'

Tom smiled. 'I reckon she's better off with Guy. He seems a nice chap.'

'Yes, he is; I like him more each time I meet him.'

'No more on that murder his daughter stumbled on, I suppose? There's been nothing in the papers since they had to let that chap go.'

Magda's startling declaration reverberated in Rona's head, but she swiftly dismissed it. 'Not that I've heard.' A sudden thought struck her. 'Oh, Pops – remember when we had lunch, I said Mum and Guy were going to sell Maple Drive?'

'Um?' He laid a second slice of toast on her plate, and she absent-mindedly buttered it.

'Well, they've found somewhere they want to buy, so it's going on the market straight away. Did she tell you?'

'No, she didn't, but there's no reason why she should. Where are they moving to?'

'Brindley Grove,' Rona said expressionlessly.

'Oh, sweetie! Will that present problems?'

She shook her head. 'As I said to Mum, from now on it'll have pleasant associations.'

'It's a desirable address, certainly.'

'Have you and Catherine thought where you'd like to live?'

'Not really, but if something comes along no doubt we'll also go for it. You have to move fast on the property front.'

'And all's well with Daniel and Jenny?'

'Yes, thank God. They spent a weekend with Catherine and she and Jenny had a heart-to-heart. I don't know exactly what was said, but Catherine told me she'd come to her senses and they were back to normal.'

'That's good news.' Rona put down her mug. 'Now, before you slip another slice of toast on my plate, I really must go. You must both come to supper soon. When Max gets back, we'll consult our diaries and be in touch.'

'That would be lovely. And thanks for the jump leads. To be honest, I'd forgotten all about them.'

Rona had just settled at her desk when there was a prolonged ring on the doorbell, followed instantaneously by repeated knocking and Gus's excited barking from the hall.

'Oh, for God's sake!' Rona muttered irritably. The postman had been – she'd picked up the letters on her return – and she could think of no one else who might be calling, certainly no one who'd be demanding such instant attention. Even as she pushed back her chair the bell rang again, almost continuously this time, as though a finger were holding it down.

'All *right*!' she shouted, starting down the stairs. 'Be *quiet*, Gus! I *know* someone's there!'

'The house isn't on fire, you know!' she said crossly as she pulled the door open. And found herself staring at Magda's white face.

'Mags!' she exclaimed. 'Whatever's the matter?'

'I know where he is!' Magda said.

'What? Where who is?'

'Kevin. I know where he is, Rona!'

Rona caught her arm and pulled her inside, holding on to Gus's collar with her other hand and pushing the door shut with her foot. 'What are you talking about? *How* do you know?'

'It just came to me suddenly, when I was about to set out for Stokely.'

Rona searched her face for signs of hysteria, disorientation – *anything* – but she was preternaturally calm. She moistened her lips. 'So where is he?'

'In Cheshire.'

Rona looked at her blankly. 'Where in Cheshire?'

'I don't know exactly, but I could find my way there.'

Rona led her into the sitting room. 'I thought you weren't having any more dreams,' she said accusingly. This, she could do without!

'I'm not, this was a memory flash. I told you I still have those. He's staying in an ordinary-looking semi. The path to the front door is lined with pebbles.'

Rona looked at her helplessly. 'You're quite sure?'

'Positive. God, Rona, what should we do?'

This was madness! Rona thought. How *could* she know? Yet there was something unnervingly convincing about Magda's certainty. 'You'll have to . . . tell the police,' she said uncertainly.

Magda made an impatient movement. 'Tell them what? That their murderer is somewhere in Cheshire, but I can't be more specific? And that the reason I know is because we're linked telepathically? They'd laugh me out of court.'

'Well, at least you could tell them the general area.'

'And you think they'd believe me?'

'They have to follow everything up; Archie told me that once. In case, against all the odds, it turns out to be right.' Archie Duncan, a former pupil of Max's, was a detective sergeant and had come to Rona's assistance on more than one occasion.

'Come to think of it, he'd be our best bet. I'll see if I can get hold of him.'

Magda raised a hand as though to stop her, then let it fall as Rona hurried into the hall to retrieve the phone book. A minute later she was back, the phone in her hand and the open directory under her arm. She perched on the arm of a chair and Magda watched in silence.

But she was out of luck. Archie, it transpired, was on annual leave, and, after a moment's thought, Rona asked to be put through to someone dealing with the Coombes inquiry. Magda waited impassively as she gave both their names and addresses and went on to give as plausible an account as she could of Magda's *im*plausible intuition. Coming to an uncertain end, she was smoothly assured her information would be looked into, and the police would contact Magda when someone was available to travel up to Cheshire.

'They'll look into it when they've someone free,' Rona reported. 'Sorry, that's the best I can do.'

'They think I'm round the bend,' Magda said jerkily, 'and I really can't blame them. They must get a lot of crank calls; how can they be expected to know when one's genuine? Anyway – ' she shuddered – 'on reflection it's better this way.'

A chill inched its way down Rona's spine. 'What do you mean?'

'Well, even if they *did* agree to drive me up there and I directed them to the house, they'd never let me within a hundred yards, would they? At best, I'd be stuck in the car while they rounded him up. And that wouldn't do at all.'

Rona moistened suddenly dry lips. 'I'm not sure I understand.'

'I told you, Rona,' Magda said patiently, 'it's essential we meet face-to-face, or the link will never be broken. Even if he's convicted and sent to prison, we'd *still* be joined unless we'd managed to untangle ourselves.'

'But there's nothing more we can do,' Rona pointed out, not without relief.

'Yes, there is; we'll have to go up by ourselves.'

Rona shook her head disbelievingly. 'Tell me you're not suggesting we drive to God knows where, beard a murderer in his den, and say, "Hi, I'm the one who's been having your dreams and I know you killed your wife!"'

'That's the gist of it, yes.'

'Magda, are you *mad*?'

She smiled, a mere twist of her lips. '*Et tu, Brute?*'

'You know what I mean!' Rona said impatiently. 'Look, phone Gavin, for God's sake, and let him talk some sense into you!'

'He's away on a course.'

Rona's heart sank. 'Max isn't here either,' she said numbly.

'So we're on our own.'

Rona repressed a shiver. 'Magda, I tell you categorically there's no way I'm going to jump in a car and drive up to Cheshire to meet a murderer!'

Magda sighed and rose to her feet. 'Fair enough. I'll go by myself. It's my problem, after all.'

'You know I can't let you do that.'

'I don't see how you can stop me.'

They stood for a moment facing each other, and Gus, on the rug between them, wagged his tail uncertainly, uneasy at the sudden tension.

'Look,' Rona burst out, 'let me try the police again. If they realize how—'

Magda was shaking her head. 'It has to be this way. We'll need them once we've found him, though; we'll phone when we get to Cheshire and can give them definite directions.'

'You do realize he might kill us too?'

Magda gave a wan smile. 'Safety in numbers.'

Rona gazed at her helplessly, her heart thumping. In her head, Max's voice said, *If she's really set on meeting this man, it could become really dangerous.* Oh Max, why aren't you here? 'You're really determined to go, with or without me?'

'I've no choice, Rona. This is my last chance to break free of him.'

But what would it take to break free? Rona wondered fearfully.

For a moment longer they held each other's eyes, Magda's fierce with determination. Then Rona sighed. 'All right. Since I can't let you go alone, I suppose I'll have to go with you. At least one of us will have our feet on the ground, but I shall most definitely phone for help once we know where he is.'

'Bless you. I knew I could count on you.'

Perhaps, Rona thought desperately, Magda's nerve would fail her when they were actually on their way. 'So – we just set off?'

'It's pretty straightforward – I checked on the road map. Motorway virtually all the way – M1, then M6. It shouldn't take more than three hours.'

Rona's eyes went to the clock on the mantelpiece. Ten thirty. 'We'll have to stop somewhere for lunch.'

Magda gave a choking laugh. 'Trust you to think of that!'

'We'll need a break anyway, on a three-hour journey. And are you proposing to come home this evening?'

For the first time Magda hesitated.

'It's the heck of a lot of driving in one day, and heaven knows what we'll have to face in-between. We'd better take an overnight bag, and we can book in somewhere on spec.'

'OK,' Magda agreed. 'We'll go in my car; it's just outside, and I'm the one who knows the way. Go and pack your night things and we can stop briefly for me to collect mine.'

'If we're to be away overnight we'll have to take Gus,' Rona said. 'Come to that, it won't do any harm to have a large dog with us.'

Magda nodded without replying and Rona sensed her impatience to get going.

'Right,' she said, 'I'll get my things.'

As she hurriedly collected nightdress and sponge bag she wondered briefly if she should phone Max. But whatever he might say, there was no stopping Magda. Little point, then, in worrying him, and possibly Roland too, and by the time he phoned this evening, it should all be safely over. *Safely.* She bit her lip.

When she reached the hall, Magda was already at the front door, car keys in hand.

'Hang on a minute, while I get a couple of tins of dog food.' Rona ran down the basement stairs, returning almost at once, tins in hand. She slipped them into her bag, took her jacket off the peg and unhooked Gus's lead. 'His blanket's in my car, I'm afraid. Have you . . .?'

'There's an old coat in the back that he can lie on. Ready?'

Rona cast a quick look about her, aware of extreme reluctance to leave the house. But there was nothing else she could do. 'Ready,' she said.

Rona and Gus waited in the car while Magda hurried into her house to collect her things. Having given his new surroundings a thorough sniffing, the dog had settled happily enough on the coat laid out for him. She was the one who hadn't settled; she felt decidedly twitchy, wishing she were anywhere but here, about to set out on this crazy mission. She could only hope that when it all came to nothing – as, logically, it must – Magda would abandon the whole ridiculous idea and they could come home.

On the way here they'd driven past the Stirlings' house and Rona reflected ruefully how, only the day before, she'd thought herself free now of distractions. But Magda had been a ticking bomb ever since they'd visited the hypnotist, and in her heart of hearts she'd known her traumas were not over. And now Magda herself was coming back down the path, case in hand.

Having tossed it in the boot, she slid into the driver's seat beside Rona. 'OK,' she said, '*on y va.*'

SIXTEEN

They made good time in the first hour, and shortly afterwards stopped at a service station for a snack lunch. Neither of them had much appetite, and Rona thought back to the buttered toast at her father's. Little had she dreamt, then, where her next meal would be. Outside the entrance a bowl of water was provided for dogs, and when they'd eaten she let Gus out to stretch his legs and have a drink.

Then they were on the road again, but within minutes came upon a line of almost stationary traffic. Magda swore softly. 'We shouldn't have stopped,' she said.

'Magda, it's roadworks. No matter what time we'd got here, there'd still have been a build-up.'

'It stretches as far as I can see.'

'Then we'll just have to be patient.' Personally, Rona would have been grateful for an indefinite delay. She nodded at the radio. 'Let's have some soothing music.'

Magda located Classic FM and sat drumming her fingers on the steering wheel. 'I'm worried that if we delay too long I'll forget the way,' she admitted anxiously.

Rona, who'd been trying to close her mind to the purpose of their journey, looked at her curiously. 'How will you know it?' she asked.

Magda lifted her hands from the wheel and let them fall again. 'It's hard to explain. I can visualize the route in my head, though I don't know the names of the town or any of the roads. I suppose it's . . . the way he remembers driving.'

Weird, Rona thought. And what would happen if, when they got closer, the route wasn't as Magda envisaged it? Would she accept defeat?

'He hit her,' Magda said suddenly, breaking into her thoughts.

'What?'

'Kevin. He hit Lucy.'

'That's . . . awful, but how can you possibly know?'

Magda shrugged. 'It's in his consciousness. I think it's a new thing, though, a legacy of his hypnotism.'

'That doesn't exactly fill me with confidence,' Rona said after a moment.

'All bullies are cowards at heart – he wouldn't take on two of us. All the same, there'll have to be some kind of physical contact, because that's what will end it.'

Rona turned to stare at her. '*Physical contact?* You said meeting face-to-face would do it!'

'That's what I thought, yes, but on reflection it must have started with us touching in some way. Otherwise, why would our two minds blend, rather than with any of the others on stage? There must have already been contact between us.'

'*Did* you touch him?'

'I was hoping you could tell me – I was in a trance, remember. Was there a time when we came close? Please, Rona, try to think.'

Rona closed her eyes, willing herself back into the Darcy Hall, the lurch in her stomach when Magda, along with the other contestants, fell helplessly asleep, the acts they were instructed to perform, the role playing . . .

'We told you about the play-acting, when you were divided into pairs and told you were quarrelling, that you'd let each other down. If it was Kevin who was your partner, I think I remember you catching hold of his arm.'

Magda let out her breath in a sigh. 'Thank you,' she said.

They lapsed back into silence, letting the strains of the music drift over them. The need for physical contact had increased Rona's tension, sounding altogether too dangerous. Somehow, she'd have to dissuade her from that. Oh God, she thought, I wish I was safely at home!

It was a good half-hour before they were able to pick up speed again, but it proved to be only the first of several hold-ups. Two more sets of roadworks and an accident accounted for another hour, and by the time they turned off the M6 at the exit for Chester it was four thirty.

'Are we going to Chester itself?' Rona asked.

'I don't know, I'm just following my instinct. Please don't talk to me now, Rona; I need to concentrate.'

Behind them Gus stood up, shook himself, and after turning round a couple of times lay back down again. He'd need to be let out soon, Rona thought anxiously. Surely they couldn't be far from their destination? What with the lunch break and the hold-ups, the journey had already taken almost twice as long as they'd calculated.

After twenty minutes or so, Magda veered left into a road signposted 'Nestbourne 3 miles'. Rona glanced at her quickly but her face was taut and she didn't dare question her. Now, away from the heavy traffic, they were entering a residential district, rows of houses, a parade of shops, a school.

Suddenly, Magda drew in to the kerb and stopped the car.

'Are we here?' Rona asked, looking quickly about her, her heart in her throat.

Magda shook her head. 'We're only a couple of roads away, but I've just realized I've not considered what happens next. For instance, who's likely to open the door?'

'You're asking *me*?'

Magda swivelled to face her. 'God, Rona, all I've been thinking about is finding my way here, but *what happens next*?'

'The first thing that happens,' Rona said firmly, 'is that I'm going to let Gus out for a pee. He must have been crossing his legs for some time now.' She suited her action to her words and the dog jumped gratefully from the car. Rona attached his lead and he made for the nearest tree while she looked up and down the road. There were cars in several driveways and ahead of her some children were circling on their bikes, calling to each other. It was all so *normal*, Rona thought, so everyday. How would these families react if they heard a murderer lived just round the corner? If, of course, it was remotely possible that he did.

She let Gus snuffle his way along the gutter for a couple more minutes, then returned to the car, opened the passenger door and leant inside. 'Come to any decision?'

Magda shook her head. She looked panic-stricken.

'Then I suggest we drive slowly past the house and size it up. It might give us a clue how to proceed.'

'Good idea,' Magda said with relief. 'Get in, then.'

They cruised forward, passing two roads leading off to the right before turning into a third, which a metal sign identified as

Elliott Close. Magda crawled slowly along, her eyes switching feverishly from side to side.

'There!' she exclaimed suddenly, and Rona, her head swinging to the left, saw a small, unpretentious semi, its front path bordered by pebbles. Her breath caught in her throat. God, they really had found it, and Kevin Coombes might indeed be behind that front door! It was only as they passed it that she spied a notice in a downstairs window. 'BED AND BREAKFAST. VACANCIES.'

'Did you see that?' she demanded excitedly. 'It's a B and B!'

Magda was slowing and came to a halt four houses down. She switched off the engine, and in the sudden silence Rona added, 'It's the solution to all our problems! All we have to do is go in and ask for a room!'

To her surprise, Magda was shaking her head. 'No, that wouldn't work. Don't you see – it would put us on entirely the wrong footing. We'd have to go in to high tea or whatever and sit down at a table next to him. How, in that context, could I possibly confront him?'

Rona, deflated, sat back, and after a minute Magda struck the steering wheel with her hand. 'I know! I'll pretend I'm looking for my husband, then play it by ear. At least that way we should find out who's staying there; for all we know there might be several lodgers.'

'The house doesn't look that big,' Rona said doubtfully 'I'd say two rooms at the most would be let out.' Impulsively she turned to her. 'Magda, are you sure you want to go through with this? It's not too late to back out. We've found the house – let the police handle it now.'

'But he mightn't be in. We have to know he's actually there.' She drew a deep breath. 'So – are you ready?'

'As ready as I'll ever be. Thank God we've got Gus.'

They climbed out of the car. A boy was coming along the pavement distributing free newspapers. In a garden down the road a baby started to cry. Rona realized she was shaking. Oh God, she thought, holding tightly to the dog's lead, if only Max was here! Hearts pounding, they walked back to the house with the pebble-lined path, and, after briefly squeezing each other's hands, Magda pressed the bell.

*   *   *

Lindsey sat at her desk, gazing unseeingly into the distance. There was a mound of work awaiting her attention, but she was totally incapable of tackling it. She had just returned from lunch with Jonathan, and her mind was a maelstrom.

He must have followed her, because they'd not arranged to meet. She had set off for the Bacchus – five minutes' walk from the office – with a new paperback in her bag, looking forward to an hour's peace from the pressures of work; but no sooner had she seated herself in one of the little booths than he had slid into the seat opposite her.

Her request that he move to another table, on the grounds that other members of the firm came here, had been summarily dismissed.

'If they do, they'll see us having a business lunch, as colleagues often do.'

It was obvious from the first that he was in a mood she didn't recognize, more serious and reflective than his usual laid-back manner. They'd ordered their tapas and, to her surprise, he'd added a bottle of house red. Alcohol at lunchtime was avoided during the working week – a rule he invariably kept. Then he'd started talking in a low voice, and she'd been startled into silence.

'Lindsey, this past week I've not been able to get you out of my head. That evening at the Clarendon changed everything, and I just have to know: am I in with a chance?'

Her eyes fell before his intent gaze. 'A chance of what?'

'Of our getting back together, on a more serious basis.'

'*Serious?*'

He gave a wry smile. 'I won't insult you with the old line of being about to leave my wife, because of course I've no intention of doing so. I'm a selfish bastard, and I want to have my cake and eat it. I'm lucky enough to have a comfortable home, an attractive wife – who's also a social asset – two bright kids, membership of the right clubs and a good career. If we went public all that would vanish in the twinkling of an eye, added to which we'd be slung out of Chase Mortimer on our ears. That is not the way partners of the firm are expected to behave.'

Lindsey cleared her throat. 'So let's get this straight. Are you quaintly proposing to set me up somewhere discreet as your mistress? Because I have to tell you, Jonathan, those days are long gone, added to which I have a home and a life of my own already, thank you very much.'

He leant forward urgently. 'No, no, that's just the point. We'd carry on as we are, but with regular times slotted in when we could be together. No one would be any the wiser.'

'"Carry on" being the operative words. It sounds to me like same old, same old.'

He shook his head. 'There's one big difference, and that's what's churning me up. Last time – and I'm being honest here – I fancied you like hell but I wasn't in love with you. This time, I think I am.'

A new line, certainly. 'And you maintain that makes a difference?'

'It sure does to me.'

She stared at him. 'Have you any idea how grossly selfish you're being?'

'Yes I have, but I don't see any way round it. I won't have Carol hurt.'

'What the eye doesn't see?'

He grimaced ruefully. 'You could say that. But first we need to clarify one point: I am right, aren't I, in thinking you've completely finished with Frayne? Everything hangs on that.'

Her anger flared. 'So although your comfortable life will continue unchanged – loving wife and children etc. – I'm not allowed to look elsewhere?'

He flushed. 'Perhaps I'm not putting it too well. But you haven't answered my question.'

'Nor am I going to. It's none of your damned business.'

They sat in silence while their food was served and the wine poured, though Lindsey put a hand over her own glass. When they were alone again, he wiped a hand across his face.

'I've made a right pig's ear of this, haven't I?'

'You most certainly have.'

'If it weren't for Carol and the kids, I really would ask you to marry me.'

'Well, thanks. But don't lose any sleep over it, because I'd say no.'

He was silent, picking listlessly at the selection of tapas, and she watched him through her eyelashes. She'd never seen suave,

self-assured Jonathan at such a loss. Could it really be true, about
his loving her? For her part, there was no denying she was
strongly attracted to him, despite his inherent self-centredness.
With his studied nonchalance and that slow, falsely self-depre-
cating smile, he was as different from Dominic as it was possible
to be, yet he pushed much the same buttons for her. And, God
help her, though she'd never fooled herself that she loved him,
she very much wanted to sleep with him.

But there was a side of his character which must also be
borne in mind; when she'd dropped him in favour of Dominic
he'd been both bitter and malicious, causing trouble for her
wherever he could. She was under no illusion that he'd not do
the same again, love or no love. Yet overriding all this – what
it all came down to – was that she was undeniably still in love
with Dominic.

Jonathan looked up wretchedly, intercepting her scrutiny. 'Have
I been speaking completely out of turn? I thought, when we
kissed, that you felt at least something for me. I apologize if I
was mistaken.'

Her anger evaporated as quickly as it had arisen. 'No, Jonathan,'
she said tiredly, 'you weren't mistaken. But –' she went on
quickly, as his face brightened – 'that's not to say that I'm going
to fall in with your proposition. If we do come to some arrangement, it will be on my terms.'

And that, basically, was how they'd left it. Now back in her
office, conflicting emotions continued to buffet her and she swung
from one decision to another. When her phone suddenly rang, it
was with a feeling of relief that she reached for it.

Rona was just wondering, with a spasm of anxiety, if Kevin
himself would answer the door when it opened to reveal a
pleasant-looking woman in her fifties.

'Can I help you?' she asked with a smile.

Magda said rapidly, 'Good afternoon. I'm sorry to trouble you,
but I'm looking for my husband. I see you take in lodgers, and
I wondered if he could possibly be staying with you?' As further
explanation seemed called for, she hastily improvised. 'He's lost
his memory, you see. I'm very concerned about him, and I heard
he's been seen in this area.'

'Well, I'm sorry to hear that, but I don't think I can help you. We've only one gentleman with us at the moment, and—'

'How long has he been here?'

'Just coming up to three weeks,' the woman said slowly, a frown forming.

'Dark and thickset, with a groove between his eyes?'

She looked startled. 'Well, apart from being dark, that would fit Mr Cooper – certainly the groove bit – but he has fair hair.' Dyed, thought Rona; an attempt at disguise. 'Though come to think of it, I did see him early one morning and was surprised how dark his stubble was.'

'Is he in?' Magda asked quickly.

'No, he's still at work but he's due back any minute.'

Magda swallowed. 'Could we possibly come in and wait, so I could make sure it's him? Please, Mrs . . .?'

'Frodsham.' She hesitated. 'How is he likely to react when he sees you? Do you think he'll recognize you?'

That, Rona thought, was the burning question.

'I'm not sure,' Magda said truthfully, 'but it might be all that's needed to . . . bring back his memory.'

'Well, I don't suppose it could hurt. He shouldn't be long.' She stood to one side.

'Could we bring the dog in?' Rona asked. 'He's very well behaved and I think he'd be grateful for a drink. We've come quite a long way.'

'Of course.' Mrs Frodsham bent to pat Gus, who responded by licking her hand. 'Come through to the kitchen, then.'

They followed her down a tiled passage to a door on the left, where she gestured to them to seat themselves and filled a bowl with water, which Gus lapped up greedily.

'And perhaps you're thirsty yourselves; would you like a cup of tea while you're waiting?'

'That's very kind.' Rona hesitated. 'Could I possibly use your loo?'

'Of course. It's just inside the front door.'

Having locked herself in, Rona took out her mobile and with shaking fingers punched out 999.

'Emergency. Which service?' enquired an impersonal voice in her ear.

'Police. Please listen,' she went on, speaking rapidly and softly, 'I've only a minute, but I'm speaking from number fifteen Elliott Close, Nestbourne. Kevin Coombes, whom the police want to interview about a murder in Buckfordshire, is due back any minute and we urgently need help. There are three women in the house.'

The operator started to speak, but Rona cut her off, fearful Kevin would return before she could regain the kitchen. 'Sorry, I must go. I'll leave the line open so you can hear what's going on, but please don't talk to me – it could be dangerous. Fifteen Elliott Close.'

She slipped her phone into her bag, being careful not to close it. Then she flushed the lavatory and almost ran back down the passage. Had she phoned too soon? she wondered anxiously. How long would it take the police to get here? Suppose they arrived before Kevin? He'd see their cars and disappear again.

'Come to think of it,' Mrs Frodsham was saying, as she poured boiling water into a teapot, 'him losing his memory makes a lot of sense. He seems at a bit of a loss somehow, and keeps very much to himself.'

'You say he's at work?' Magda asked.

'Yes; he told us he'd been made redundant, and when he couldn't find any work in London he came up here. There was a part-time job going at the corner shop, so he took that to tide him over while he looks round.'

The ideal solution, Rona thought; it was probably family-run, perhaps with no questions asked when extra staff were required. And he'd need to work because he wouldn't dare use his credit or debit cards as they'd give away his whereabouts. He must have reckoned it a risk worth taking, specially since it seemed he'd changed both his name and his appearance.

The sound reached them of the front door opening and closing, and Rona and Magda tensed.

'Mr Cooper?' Mrs Frodsham called. 'Could you come to the kitchen for a moment? There's someone to see you.'

There was a short silence, followed by cautiously approaching footsteps. Magda stood up, her fists clenched at her sides. And suddenly he was there, framed in the doorway, his eyes widening as he took in Magda.

'*You!*' he said in a strangled voice.

'He seems to recognize you,' Mrs Frodsham murmured incongruously.

If he turns and runs, Rona thought, we've had it. Why did that never occur to us?

But Kevin Coombes showed no sign of running. His feet seemed rooted to the spot as he stared unbelievingly at Magda, his fingers tugging to loosen his tie, and those few seconds gave Rona the chance to study him.

She'd wondered how anyone could fail to recognize him when his face had been in the papers and on TV throughout the country, though admittedly context would be a key factor; people simply wouldn't expect someone going about his business among them to be a hunted killer. Now, though, she acknowledged that she wouldn't have known him herself. The blond hair, brushed forward in a different style, changed his appearance to a surprising degree. It was only the groove between his eyes that he couldn't disguise, and that was a common enough feature.

Magda was about to speak when, abruptly emerging from his trance, Kevin stepped quickly into the room, pushed the door shut and looked wildly about him. On one of the counters was a chopping board, the remains of a cooked chicken, and a small sharp knife – Mrs Frodsham's interrupted preparations for supper. He darted forward, caught up the knife and spun to face her.

'Lock the back door,' he instructed, 'and give me the key.' And as she stared at him, transfixed, he snapped, 'Do it!'

Fumblingly she obeyed, holding out the key at arm's length, and he snatched it from her and slipped it in his pocket. There was a look in his eyes that made the hairs rise on the back of Rona's neck. God, what were they *doing* here?

Gus growled softly. She slipped her hand inside his collar and pulled him close, conscious of her bag lying open at her feet. Were the police getting this?

'There's no need for the knife,' she said clearly. 'Please put it down.'

Kevin ignored her and turned to Magda. 'I don't know who the devil you are, but you must be from Marsborough.'

'It's your wife, Mr Cooper,' Mrs Frodsham ventured timidly, hoping to calm troubled waters.

Kevin swung round and she shrank back against the sink. 'My *wife*? Did you say *my wife*?'

'She doesn't know anything!' Magda said quickly, her voice shaking. 'I'm the one you need to speak to. You recognize me, don't you?'

Kevin's eyes flickered, but he didn't reply.

'*Why* do you recognize me, Kevin?' Magda persisted. 'Where have you seen me before?' Rona could see a pulse beating in her throat and hoped the tactic she was employing was the right one.

He gave a violent shake of his head. 'In my dreams, goddammit! How corny is that? Except they were nightmares!'

'And you were in mine, but as you were the dreamer I never saw your face. How did you see mine?'

He pushed a hand through his hair. 'Just shut up, will you, and tell me how the hell you found me?'

'*How did you see my face?*'

He stared at her, nonplussed, then, with a what-the-hell gesture, answered truculently, 'Because in one dream I looked in a mirror, didn't I? And it was your face staring back at me!' He rubbed the back of his free hand across his mouth as though to negate the words.

'Ah!' Briefly, Magda closed her eyes.

'So how did you find me?' he repeated. 'Are you a goddamn witch or something?'

'Our minds are linked,' Magda said.

He gave a snort of derision, but she went on quickly, 'It was the hypnotist, Kevin. You were sitting next to me on stage, and when he released us our memories must have merged.'

'Women's bloody fashions,' he said slowly. 'Was that down to you? Luce thought it was hilarious.' A spasm crossed his face and he looked about him blankly. 'Lucy – is she with you? She is – all right?'

Magda said, almost steadily, 'I've come to break that connection, to free us.'

He gave his head a shake and his eyes refocused. 'You don't seriously expect me to believe that rubbish? OK, so we met on stage, but as for *minds merging* – give me a break!'

Before she could reply the doorbell clarioned into the room, making them all jump, and was immediately followed by a knock on the front door. All four of them froze and Gus started to bark.

Rona, who was facing the window, caught a brief movement, as though someone were pressed against the wall just out of sight, but her relief was short-lived.

'Nobody move!' Kevin rasped, raising the knife menacingly.

The four of them remained motionless, staring at each other, and Gus continued to bark. Mrs Frodsham cleared her throat. 'It could be my husband,' she whispered. 'He's due home about now.'

'Since when did he ring the bell?' Kevin demanded.

As though in answer, it rang again. There was a clatter as the letterbox was pushed up and a voice called, 'Mr Coombes? This is the police. We know you're inside. Could we have a word, please?'

'Police!' Kevin spat. 'All that nonsense about merged minds! You were filling in time till they got here!'

'No, it's true!' Magda choked, 'but now we've—'

'Shut up!' he snarled. 'Instead of wasting time listening to you, I should have got the hell out while I still had the chance.'

'Mr Coombes?' the voice came again. 'Kevin? We only want to talk. If you let the ladies go, it will make things easier.'

'I bet it would!' said Kevin between his teeth, then, his voice rising, 'Can't you shut that bloody dog up? How can I think, with that infernal racket going on?'

'He always barks at doorbells,' Rona said helplessly, scratching Gus's neck in an attempt to calm him.

'Well if he doesn't stop, I'll take this knife to him!'

Knowing it to be no idle threat, she jerked the dog on to his hind legs and clutched his warm, vibrating body against her. '*Hush*, Gus!' she whispered frantically, burying her fingers in his fur, and, seeming to sense her urgency, he subsided with a final yap. At which moment the telephone on the wall suddenly shrilled, and her hand closed quickly over his muzzle, stifling a resumption of barking.

'That really *will* be Jim!' Mrs Frodsham maintained shakily, moving towards the phone.

'*Don't answer it!*'

Terrified, she came to a halt. The phone went on ringing and

Rona could feel Gus's jaw muscles straining to remove her hand.

'All *right*!' Kevin exclaimed after another couple of minutes. 'Anything to stop that din!' He nodded at his landlady. 'Bring it over, but don't try to say anything or it will be the last thing you do!'

Tremblingly she lifted the phone and held it out to him, but he made no attempt to take it. A disembodied voice reached them in the sudden silence of the room.

'Kevin? Please speak to me.'

Pause.

'Look, we're not going to try any tricks. We just want to have a chat, lower the tension in there.' Another pause. 'Tell me about your boys. You must be missing them.'

Kevin shut his eyes involuntarily, raw pain on his face.

'We know why you took them,' the speaker continued. 'It wasn't abduction, was it? It was to spare them walking in and finding their mother in the morning.' A longer pause. 'Their grandparents say they've been asking for you.'

'Shut up!' Kevin shouted. 'Just bloody shut up about my kids!'

'Look, suppose we discuss this face-to-face? I'm going to come round the back of the house. I won't wear a jacket, so you can see I'm not armed. You don't even have to open the door, we can—'

'No!' Kevin shouted, his face contorted. 'I warn you, if anyone appears I'll use this knife!'

And in one movement he swept the phone out of Mrs Frodsham's hand so that it skittered on to the floor and, reaching forward, grabbed hold of Magda and pulled her roughly towards him, spinning her round and pinioning her against his body, the point of the knife at her throat. And as their bodies made contact a simultaneous shudder shook them and both gave an audible gasp. Mission accomplished, Rona thought sickly, but at what cost?

'Kevin, listen to me!' Magda gasped. 'You're not responsible for all this – none of it is your fault! It was the hypnotist – that quarrelling he made us do. Something went wrong – he didn't free you from it, so your aggression kept on growing.'

He continued to hold her, though he lowered the knife and his expression had changed, become frightened and unsure.

'But we've broken the connection now,' Magda continued desperately. 'You felt it, didn't you, when we touched? You're free now, and so am I!'

'Lucy?' His voice was strangled. 'I never meant to hurt her, but when I saw the papers Roger'd brought round, and realized they'd been alone in the house . . . I *knew* she'd never . . . oh God, *Lucy*!'

Tears were coursing down his face, and all the time the disembodied voice, calm and measured, trickled into the room from the phone on the floor. Then everything happened at once. Kevin gave a great cry of grief, despair and frustration and kicked out at it, sending it skidding across the tiles; Magda, taking advantage of his distraction, tried to free herself from his grip, and Gus, barking wildly, launched himself across the kitchen and leapt up at Kevin, his front paws landing forcefully on his chest. Totally disorientated, Kevin stumbled and fell, cracking his head on the sharp edge of the cooker as he went down.

Anxious faces appeared at the window and the doorknob rattled ineffectively, and while Rona and Magda ran to hug each other convulsively, it was Brenda Frodsham who, steeling herself, slid her hand into Kevin's pocket, retrieved the back-door key, and stumbled across to open it.

It was two hours later, and Rona, with Gus beside her, was sitting in the foyer of the local police station, waiting for Magda to finish giving her statement. Kevin, even more dazed after the bump on his head, had been taken under police escort to have it checked at A&E. With luck, she thought, his temporarily diminished responsibility at the time of the murder would make for a more lenient sentence. His children would need him.

She leant her head back against the wall, feeling thoroughly drained. It had been a traumatic day – the long, anxious drive, the confrontation with Kevin, and Magda held at knifepoint. All she wanted now was a hot bath followed by bed, but they had yet to find somewhere to spend the night.

She was startled out of her reverie by her mobile, its low battery warning flashing. Max! She glanced round, but no one was paying her any attention.

'Hello?'

'Hi, there, sweetheart! What have you been up to today?'

She fought down hysterical laughter. What should she tell him? That she and Magda had driven a hundred and fifty miles to confront a murderer, and been held at knifepoint in a locked room? That . . .?

She drew a steadying breath. 'Sorry, darling,' she said, 'my battery's about to give out. I'll tell you all about it tomorrow.'